THE
SLIME PIT

THE SLIME PIT

*A murder mystery story of corruption,
drug dealing, bribery, honesty and love.*

BRIAN EVANS

The Slime Pit

Spiderwize
Remus House
Coltsfoot Drive
Woodston
Peterborough
PE2 9BF

www.spiderwize.com

A CIP catalogue record for this book is available from the British
Library.

The views expressed in this work are solely those of the author
and do not necessarily reflect the views of the publisher, and the
publisher hereby disclaims any responsibility for them.

ISBN: 978-1-911596-13-4

This is dedicated to Hedda Valbruch who died a painful death from cancer. She lived in Casa Crao in Gorjoe's Portugal and finally passed away in her home city of Hamburg Germany.

Author's notes

- The time line of this saga is set between 1975 and 1978 when Portugal was still using the Escudo, so the financial matters are quoted in that currency. As the narrative predates decimalisation, the distances are in miles, the temperatures in degrees Fahrenheit and the measurements are quoted in feet and inches.

- The story flits backwards and forwards through the months and years with no apparent logic until all the chapters merge together in the final conclusion.

- The forensic methods used during the period were not as sophisticated as they are now in 2017. Although DNA was discovered in 1869 by a Swiss chemist Friedrich Miescher, it was not used to solve crimes until 1986. Therefore most of the forensic procedures described in the Oporto path lab were pretty basic.

- Some of the items found in and around the Slime Pit and on the body are factual.

- Many of the characters and situations described are taken from real life but some of the names have been changed to protect individual's privacy. Others are all fictional. Place names, towns and villages are real and can be found on any Portuguese map.

- The references to homosexuality are written in the vernacular of the time. These would not be acceptable in modern day.

- The challenge for the reader is to try and spot the difference between the truth and the fiction.

A MURDER MOST OBSCENE IN THE WORST OF CIRCUMSTANCES IS ONLY A SMALL PART OF THIS SAGA.

In this saga there are myriad components and tentacles which come into play backwards and forwards over various parts of the Middle East, the Mediterranean Sea and the Iberian Peninsula. This is a story of intrigue, bribery, drug dealing, violence, stupidity, romance and people missing in unsolved situations, where the strands rarely seem to coalesce or make any sense until the complicated plots unfold.

There is a heart breaking personal tragedy for Shak, who has lost the love of his life; and for his daughter who finally after many years finds the man of her dreams, her life will become complete. His other daughter, estranged to him by ending up in Australia through unusual circumstances, finally cracks the code of the tentacles through her jet setting husband. At the risk of his own life, who with her starts to unravel the complex elements which weave collectively, holding this yarn together.

Powerful people, corrupt police, scumbags, lovely individuals, politicians, Romany's and innocent folk are drawn into a web of intrigue and danger as the conspiracies unravel and morph together to reveal the guilty and the innocent.

Contents

1

Murder Most Dire

Contrary to most people's perceptions of the Iberian Peninsula, Portugal's weather is generally thought to be idyllic, warm and sunny in the summer. But this 1975 winter was bitterly cold and wet with the driving rain pouring down in a westerly gale on a dark moonless night in the disused mine near Oporto.

The shadowy figure puffed and panted as he dragged the body from the dilapidated old grey antique Renault van which he had stolen from a public car park. The old crock had barely made the journey to the mining area which he understood had been worked out many years ago. The body was extremely heavy, as in life the man was large in stature and well overweight. The acrid smell and vapours from the pit pervaded the whole area with the fumes infiltrating his nose and throat and causing him to cough violently. The felon felt totally safe and away from prying eyes as his bitterly cold hands pushed the severely mutilated body into the Pit. Then it slipped slowly into the foul smelling acrid and acid slimy depths, descending to the mud filled bottom some two hundred and seventy feet below.

The powerfully built frame of the killer was hardly recognisable, due to his dark waterproof clothing. His head was covered by an enormous hood and he chuckled to himself as he pocketed the plastic bag full of the fingertips and teeth he had cut and torn from the luckless body. He would keep them as souvenirs of his crime. He had not severed the toes as he knew toe prints were not kept on police files. In any case he knew that the corpse would never be found due to the two heavy lead divers weight belts wrapped around the body's waist.

As a second thought he fired the engine of the old crock and drove it sliding all over the mud to the edge of the Pit, jumping out of the driver's door just in time as the van gurgled its way to the bottom of the Pit. Hopefully it would lay on top of the body as additional weight to hold it down.

He slithered away from the Pit through the deep mud which was clogging his boots and setting like concrete, whilst scratching his stomach, he knew this was the perfect unsolvable murder. Or was it! He was convinced that with the meticulously detailed plans that he had laid down for the future, this dastardly evil deed would set him up in millions of escudos and luxury for the rest of his life.

He had considered burying the remains of the naked body in the mine shaft but after long consideration felt that it may be discovered by inquisitive visitors. Alternatively by those who mistakenly thought there may be some money to be made if there were some copper or aggregates left un-mined that they could retrieve and sell. He thought the Slime Pit was a much better option for hiding his kill.

The mine was constructed many years ago by Roving Global Zink, a multinational company with similar interests all over the globe. Once they had extracted all the copper and minerals from the mine, they abandoned the area leaving much of the old equipment to rust and rot where it was left. The entrance to the excavation was still open and workings ran down to several hundred feet, a real danger and hazard to anyone who entered. The worst aspect of the site was the deep and dangerous Slime Pit. The Oporto Camera (council) had tried in vain to force RGZ to make the site safe but to no avail. The directors were too busy making more money in their new mine in Spain. So the Pit was just right for secreting a mutilated body.

2

Oxford University

Oxford University has been home to many brilliant students who have gone on to become famous people in society and have made fortunes or have reached the dizzy heights of the glitterati. But it rarely had students who achieved double firsts in their degrees and to obtain three double firsts is unusual and is almost unheard of but Caroline Fisher-Hatch achieved them all. She was one of the most intelligent, quick witted and far seeing graduates with an off the wall whacky sense of humour that Oxford had ever seen pass through their hallowed halls.

Pathology was her passion and wanted to continue with her doctorate. However that required a Masters in which she intended to qualify but needed to live close to her father who was in bad health and living in Oporto Portugal. So with much reluctance she studied her masters in Braga University Do Minho, also receiving the qualifications with distinction. She crammed for her doctorate and passed whilst undertaking her new career with the Oporto police department as a senior pathologist leading a team of Portuguese interns. The Portuguese language is one of the most difficult to learn but with her razor sharp intelligence mastered it in six months. Even the Portuguese people still struggle with the tortuous grammar.

She always called her father 'Dad' as he was in fact her step-father who had taken her on at age one, after her paternal father had died from an abdominal disease so she had never known her real father. Her mother had remarried some five years before his death to a rock musician who never made the big time but earned a meagre living until his health deteriorated due to chronic arthritis. This meant he could no longer play the guitar because of his crooked fingers. Although he was her step dad they were very emotionally close as he brought her up on his own after her mother disappeared, so he reared her as he would his own children. She always said. 'Any man can become a father but it takes a lot of love, hard work and cherishing to become a Dad.'

So it was that when her dad became incapacitated, she wanted to be near him and to care for him as he had cared for her all of her life. As it happened she loved Oporto and the Portuguese people, having visited there on many holidays, so it was no hardship to move to her new home.

Caroline was an unusual girl, six feet tall and slender as a reed. She could have been a top model due to her curvy figure and striking good looks, together with her long dark raven black hair, she glided rather than walked. Her skin tones were a bit darker than most and she suspected that in past generations there had been a touch of mixed gypsy blood or some tinkers in the background but she was an absolute beauty and was admired by most men who met her.

However she was not generally interested in the opposite sex, although she did have a long term relationship with a student whilst at Oxford, but this fizzled out due to his selfish nature. She resolved to be a bachelor girl for the foreseeable future and was definitely not interested in having children after seeing a film of a baby being born when she was eleven years old. She said. 'I will never have that happen to my body!'

Always secretive about her age and when asked she replies 'I am old enough to vote and younger than the Monarch.'

4

The Portuguese police department was not as we would expect the administration structures and procedures to be in England. In the UK we know that our police force is the envy of the world, with its strict disciplines and high moral standards. If an innocent or guilty person was apprehended in England, we would trust that the case would be fairly investigated, as the court procedures had been well established over many years and honed almost to perfection.

Caroline was quite shocked to find that this was not the case in Portugal. It was not so long ago that Salazar the dictator for some thirty years had only recently been deposed by a bloodless coup organised and carried out by the Army. After that, a form of democracy was put in place but some of the old guard from the Salazar regime were still in quite high positions and the deep-rooted bureaucratic practices, corruption and bribery was still rife. Quite a lot of this had spilled over into the police force. Added to this the GNR (Guardia National Republica) a branch of the army, still carried out and duplicated some of the police duties, which left many conflicts and aggravations between both organisations.

Caroline found these encounters very difficult to deal with and on many occasions found she was caught in the middle of some tricky and difficult political situations. But in most cases she was savvy enough to work her way through them without becoming too embroiled.

Despite all these setbacks she was the best pathologist the force had ever employed and was deeply respected for her qualifications, knowledge and expertise in solving some incredibly complex murders.

3

The Hill

The 'Hill' was very similar in desirability to the Victoria Peak in Hong Kong, only the rich and famous, (or corrupt?) would be able to afford the real estate prices in this fashionable and expensive area of the Algarve.

The Chief Inspector of Police for the whole of Portugal, Fernando Martins, last year had bought the 27 million escudos (about two million pounds in today's money) luxury villa called Travessa do Pastor. The name translated means House on the Shepherd's Crossing. The wealthy neighbours wondered how a policeman could afford the best piece of real estate in the area, they were sure that the police salaries were not that generous.

The Villa was a magnificent property built by him to the most exacting standards, architect designed and constructed by a highly reputable English builder to UK specifications. There were five bedrooms, all spacious with on-suite rooms finished in Italian marble floors and wall tiles with the latest plumbing for the baths and showers. The whole building was finished with gigantic plate glass windows with chrome and black detailing.

The views through the lounge windows were stunning. They looked out across a wonderful vista of undulating fields, hills, and with valleys covered in green olive, carob and palm trees; revealing a natural sparkling river and tumbling waterfalls abounding, all running down with distant views of the sandy beaches of the Algarve. The enormous heated swimming pool was kidney shaped with under water lighting, diving boards and a high plastic slide. Next to the pool was a heated Jacuzzi, everything all very Nuevo Riche and extremely tacky. As with all Portuguese properties built after the great Lisbon earthquake of 1750, it had reinforced concrete foundations and walls similar to a concrete bunker, to protect the structure from the possibilities of future tremors.

Built into the hill and underground was the most opulent four car garage with electric up and over doors, housing his issued unmarked police vehicle, his privately owned Porsche two seat sports car and his pride and joy, a Harley Davidson motorcycle. Also in the garage were his other toys, a fast speed boat with a hundred horsepower Sea Horse engine and trailer, complete with deep sea fishing rods, diving equipment and water-skiing gear. Not bad for a copper!

Fernando stretched out nude on his sunbed in the hot Sunday noon sun topping up his tan on an already darkened torso. As the warmth permeated through his skin he thought how lucky he was to have reached the zenith of his career in such a short time, even though he had trampled on many colleagues whilst climbing the greasy pole. To be fair, he did have a history of managing and leading men very effectively, as he had been a Captain in the army of a different country, a fact he kept well hidden from his superiors, the management and his team. When pressed on the point he always wriggled out of the question with much waffle and an aggressive attack on the questioner.

Money was not a problem to him as he was extremely well paid for his highly responsible position and he also made quite a bit on the side from some lucrative corrupt side-lines!

He had never been married, although with his handsome good looks and muscular body, he oozed charm and bonhomie which he could turn on with the ladies, so he was never short of female company. He was also too selfish and too much in love with himself to share his life and good fortune with a permanent wife. Something had happened in his murky past that had turned him into something of a split personality. Although on first meeting one would think he was no worse than anyone else in his exalted position. In the right circumstance he could be an absolute charmer but when not, he could be a nasty bastard! Altogether he was not a nice person to know and one to be avoided.

All his domestic chores were attended to by his hard working peasant maid Maria, who lived down the bottom of the Hill in very poor circumstances. But she adored him and attended to his every domestic whim for which he paid her a pittance. She was in her mid-fifties and had worked very hard all her life as a domestic help which had taken a substantial toll on her body. She was well over weight and had an enormous bust which made her look a bit top heavy. So large was she in the Bristol department, Fernando often referred to her as the 'The Granden Busten Housen' but not to her face of course!

She was totally responsible for the care of the villa and its security and kept the keys safe and in a secret place at all times. On one occasion Fernando was looking for a spare set of keys and asked Maria for them. Without a thought and in a heartbeat she fumbled around in her capacious bra and with a flourish pulled out a set of keys. She said. 'Nobody would dare look in there; if they did they would get a shock!'

4

Waterford Marina

Irelands Waterford Marina was an extremely up market berth in which to keep a leisure boat or sailing yacht, the owners mostly being the well-heeled Irish aristocracy or wealthy business people. Multi million pound vessels were the norm. The annual subscription to the Marina Club would have paid most peoples gas bill for ten years, therefore not the place for downmarket sailors or vessels.

So it was very strange to see the twins, Paddy and Mick O Leary's old and hardly seaworthy rust bucket of a sixty foot motor yacht moored next to such affluent hardware. Other owners wondered how they managed to pay the mooring fees and join the Club and after much subversive enquiries by the chairman of the Club the matter was never resolved. They were tolerated rather than accepted when included in any social event. Their social skills were not SA; socially acceptable.

The boys had bought the boat from an Irish Tinker who as he said 'Dabbles in all sorts of trades including horses, cars, caravans, dilapidated buildings and anything that might turn a profit for a poor man.' He assured them that the vessel only had one owner from new and they later found that to be true. It was owned by a shipyard run by a fly-by-night immigrant Iranian who rented it out as a holiday ship to anyone daft enough to pay his exorbitant fees. Most renters did not know anything about sailing or boats and after ten years of neglect with very little maintenance, it was in a very sorry state. The boys had to sell the family home which their parents left them when they died, to raise the purchase price. They decided to live on the boat and make it their home, as the inside was quite comfy with three bedrooms a bathroom and an adequate galley. It was never worth the price but both Paddy and Mick were a bit short of the O levels and not very bright but saw it as an opportunity to see the world and make a living from trading on the boat.

Although not socially acceptable, Mick and Paddy were a jolly pair, harmless in their dealings with most people and situations. They were always ready with a tale to tell and full of mischief, good humour and ready for a laugh, especially when they had too much of the Guinness! Thirty five year old twins they were but not very similar in looks. Mick was dark haired, short and Paddy was ginger and six foot tall.

They never married, spent most of their time in each other's company and rarely tired of talking about the good times they had and those to come, sailing around the world. There were rumours around the boat club that as there were never any women around them that they might be a bit 'Ginger' or 'Precious' but this was never proved.

They were making the final preparations to ensure the old piece of junk was ready to sail prior to setting off for the Mediterranean. There was much to do, not only making the vessel seaworthy but there were provision to buy and minor repairs to make to the engine, although they never resolved the vibration which seemed to come from the drive shaft leading to the single propeller, which had dropped off on a few occasions. But they had always been able to dive over the side and re-fix it without any difficulties but the shuddering always returned. The vibration was so bad that the teacups would rattle in their saucers on the coffee table.

Both qualified PADI and BESAC deep sea divers, they were off to illegally dive for Red Coral, which is an endangered and protected salt water sea animal. They would then sell the Coral for what they believed would be vast profits to the jewellery trade in the flesh spots around the Middle East area. They were never too worried about breaking a few laws on the way as they always had in the past, but they had never been caught.

With high hopes they set off in fair weather. First stop they would berth in Menorca, intending to buy some more dive equipment from the local Police Auction houses, although being run by the police they would keep a very low profile! They had never paid the full price for anything as they had always been short of the readies for most of their lives. After harvesting and selling the Coral they would then sail to the Algarve to relax, have a holiday and spend some of their ill-gotten gains. By this time they may have made enough money to sort out some of the vitally needed mechanical problems with the boat.

5

Katricia Hart

Katricia Hart had spent most of her life as a Potato farmer's wife in Africa. She left England at age twenty one to seek an adventurous life abroad, there she met and married John Hart and never returned to the UK except for the occasional holiday. After thirty five years of really hard graft supporting her husband on the farm, sometimes under great hardship and working in dreadful conditions, they both felt it was time to retire.

A lot of Kat's time was spent looking after the Black workers on the farm and had become a well-trained and trusted nurse, confidant and friend to the workforce. So being a social and caring person she never had a problem meeting new people and serving the community, which she thought would stand her in good stead in a new country. After much searching around for the best place to move to, they chose the Algarve in Portugal as this was the nearest climate to that which they had become accustomed to in Africa.

Sadly after a few years in their new home, John was struck down with an incurable medical problem which left him paralysed from the waist down and confined to a wheelchair for the rest of his life. Although the new care home was a perfect place for John to be looked after, the fees were exorbitant and were a constant worry to Kat and she was very concerned knowing that all their savings were being used to pay for his nursing and there was very little left. What would happen eventually when the funds dried up was a constant worry to her.

It was a bit of a coincidence that their new home was not half a mile from the Hill where the Chief of Police lived in his Gin Palace. Whilst Kat had heard of Fernando Martins, she did not know him personally but the locals had told her of his nefarious dealings and advised her to steer well clear of him. Apparently the area in which she lived was not as opulent as the Hill, so she was able to avoid him it like the plague!

Kat spent most of her free time looking after John, helping with the parish Church of England Mission and attending the local jail as a regular prison visitor. Prisons in Portugal are not the best places to be incarcerated, nor is the legal system the most speedy, fair or impartial in the civilised world. It must be remembered that after the fall of Salazar, his subsequent government in nineteen seventy four and the introduction of Portugal's first communist government; one of the last priorities of the administration was the health and welfare of what they saw was the criminal element in society.

Kat was quite a formidable figure of a woman, tall, slightly built, wiry with a stern face, large twinkling dancing eyes which missed nothing and belied her age. She was tough both mentally and physically; she had to be, as living in Africa for most of her life she was the one who most people depended upon to make life bearable in the society in which she lived. Once on Safari she fell and broke her arm and because they were hundreds of miles from a hospital, she strapped it up with bandages and continued with their journey for another two weeks until it could be set and plastered in a Nairobi hospital. Just the sort of woman one would need in a third world country, which of course Portugal was when she moved there. So she was just the right tough personality to deal with prisoners.

She had just heard from the local Vicar that two new villain's had been apprehended and awaiting trial at the local court and had asked for an English speaking visitor to help with their support and defence. She would soon have wished that she had never started prison visiting!

She had been visiting for the past five years and had seen all types of offenders; most of who tried to tell her that they had done nothing wrong, had been stitched up by the system and should not have been convicted. It is a sad fact that two thirds of all prisoners are illiterate, which is why so many of these poor unfortunates were locked up sometimes for trivial offences.

Kats role was as a sympathetic Samaritan to listen, support and not to judge the merits or de-merits of their situation. Although in her quiet hours at home she would try to sort the truth from the lies and attempt to make some sense of their plight.

6

The Blue Cornflower

'Musical Madness' was the name of the shop that Caroline's dad rented in the Avenida Dos Aliados, in the once bustling expensive and fashionable district of Oporto, with the River Douro at its soul. After finishing with the band called 'Shakin Shak' due to his ill health, he made a living selling and buying all types of instruments. His nickname became Shak as it reflected the name of the band. He lived quite a lonely and reclusive life in a rather tacky and unkempt rented two bed apartment over the shop. The highlight of his week was when Caroline visited and sometimes stayed for a few days.

When a customer opened the door of the shop, a warning jingle would play 'Hey you get off of my cloud' by the Rolling Stones, a source of great amusement to many shoppers. A useful clarion if he was in the back room teaching music to his students.

Caroline breezed through the door, past the recorded sound to find the shop empty, which was unusual as Shak was very careful about security. She called out.

'Hi Dad.' No reply. She called again. 'Hi Pops are you there.'

Then she heard a noise from the back office, concerned she hurried to the rear of the shop to find Shak lying on the floor with his back against the wall weeping profusely.

'Oh dear,' said Caroline with a sigh, 'another Blue Cornflower day dad?'

Between sobs Shak replied. 'Yes, after thirty years I still can't get over your mum disappearing as she did.'

'What brought this on again today?'

Trying to bring himself back to normality Shak said.

'I was sorting though some of the old group records, you know the one, Blue Cornflower which we recorded and it got to number seven in the charts.'

Caroline remembered it well as it was struck to mark the loss of her mum. They both lay there hugging each other for some minutes with tears rolling down Caroline's cheeks.

'Dad you mustn't reproach yourself forever, you did more than most people would have done to find mum, you spent five years searching Europe for her. You sold our family home to finance your search and you must accept the fact that she has gone forever.'

This he could not accede as he had many dreams of finding her eventually and quite often in the past his dreams became reality. He knew that one day he would surrender himself to happiness but not until she turned up unharmed.

Caroline was quiet in contemplation for a few minutes then said.

'Dad I'm under enormous pressure at work at present and I've just been told that we have yet another body in the pathology lab which I must attend to before rigor mortis sets in. I have enough time to stay with you tonight but I must leave first thing in the morning.'

'That's very kind of you Flopsie and under normal circumstances I would say no but yes thank you.'

Her mum and Shaks marriage and their relationship was one of the rare ones made in heaven. They were so much in love and devoted to each other, one could feel it in the air, when they were together the atmosphere almost crackled. When they were living in Berkshire in the UK she went out to the local garden centre to buy some blue cornflower seeds and never returned.

The police were called but they said nothing could be done until she had been missing for twenty four hours, as usually by this time the person comes home. Shak was beside himself, yelling at the police that they don't know his wife as he does and she would never disappear without phoning home to say where she was. But they were adamant and said they would come back in twenty four hours.

In the meantime Shak could not rest or sleep, his imagination ran riot. Had she been murdered, raped and sold into slavery, forced into prostitution, lost her memory, held for ransom, although no demands were made? Had she contemplated suicide? Unthinkable! The horrors were endless in his imagination. He was going crazy with worry. Caroline whilst only eight years old was also distraught and they both tried to console each other.

Sure enough the police returned the next day and a full scale missing person search was undertaken. Not just in the UK but through Interpol as well. Shak came under suspicion, as in many similar cases a family member would often be the culprit. After many intensive interviews with him and Caroline, it was obvious that he was not the offender, as they were both in each other's company for the forty eight hours prior to the disappearance. One of the mysteries was that her Fiat 500 car was never discovered. After two years the operation was scaled down as she was not to be found and the case was passed to the cold case section of the Thames Valley Police.

7

President Nasser

President Gamel Abdul Nasser came to power in 1952 as a result of a military uprising in Egypt which deposed King Farouk, the much despised playboy King who did very little to run the country or help the ordinary Egyptian people to improve their lot. Together with Assad and Mubarak they took over as military leaders with Nasser as President. Nasser changed Egypt forever when he kicked the English out of the Suez Canal in the six day war. He then built the new two and a half mile wide High Dam which tamed the river Nile and irrigated the farms. He also enshrined schooling for all Egyptian children.

Born an Egyptian peasant with a very poor upbringing he was welcomed warmly by the ordinary Egyptians as a normal man and was seen as the saviour of the people. He was a big strong individual with enormous charisma and was welcomed everywhere when he visited along the Nile. He only had one objective in life and that was to improve the lot of all his countrymen without help from other countries. Independence was his objective. Unlike most leaders the power didn't go to his head and he was uncorruptible, dissimilar to many other rulers who feather their own nest at the expense of the populace.

After a few years having achieved these momentous changes he felt there was very little more he could do to improve the country and he had also had enough of power. Assad was assassinated by gunfire and Nasser died of an apparent heart attack but reportedly in very suspicious circumstances where poison was mooted. When his bank account was checked he only had £500.00 to his name. Apparently he was a very honourable man. Mubarak then took over the country as the new dictator.

Prior to Nasser's death he underwent a serious operation to remove a twelve inch cancerous growth in his stomach, the scar of which never healed properly and there was a chance of the cancer coming back. He was a very large and heavy moustachioed man and the pallbearers carrying the coffin at the funeral thought he was unusually heavy to hold on their shoulders. Soon after the cancer operation he decided to plan his disappearance.

8

Portuguese Prime Minister

The Prime Minister of Portugal Sr Rabbit did not get re-elected at the last election as he was a pompous self-important egotist who came to power on a popular vote from the left wing working classes, as they had enough of the communist party. Their party had promised fair deals for all and untold wealth for people who voted for them. In the two years they were in power, they bankrupted the country, ruined the economy and made themselves extremely wealthy in the process.

The Portuguese people, although poor from the Salazar regime, were not to be fooled again by the communist party. So they then backed Sr Rabbit as they believed the propaganda spewed out at his election campaign would change the country and their impoverished lives. Yet again the government of Sr Rabbit and his administration did no more than the communists. So when he was not re-elected, he was pensioned off from politics and retired on a handsome income to live the rest of his life in Paris and Switzerland.

There was some extremely dodgy goings on when the new motorway system was built across the whole of Portugal which linked up with Spain and France. It was built in double quick time and to poor quality standards. There were rumours afoot that there was some enormous back handers given to a number of the individuals involved in agreeing the contracts but nothing could be proved at the time. Following Rabbits demise, a lengthy investigation into his personal life of fraud, embezzlement and corruption, was undertaken. As a result he was extradited from his opulent Paris apartment to Portugal, together with his also corrupt minister for finance Sr Coelho. They were both arrested without trial and remain in prison to this day awaiting court procedures, whilst other co-conspirators are being traced within the local Camera, parliament, police and the GNR. There are currently many Portuguese officials in high places with very worried looks on their faces.

9

The Germans

There was a lovely wealthy German retired couple, Roly and Hedda Valbruch, who lived in a flat in Hamburg on the Winkestrasse and they recently moved onto the Hill just a hundred yards down from Fernando Martins property. They had their Villa; Casa Crao built quite high and close to Fernando's house to get the best of the views over the hills. They were passionate bird watches and Friends of the Earth.

Recently their house was burgled by local druggies, their safe was smashed out of its concrete housing and the thieves took it away with them. As it happened it was empty as they were at home at the time in their flat in Germany and whilst away from the Villa didn't leave any valuables inside. Luckily the only treasures in the house were their pictures and photographs of rare birds which were hanging on the walls and these were not taken.

The police detective sergeant, Feliciano Neves who came to investigate the crime was also a fanatical bird watcher and Roly and Hedda later became very firm friends with him. They were to go on many Twitching excursions together looking for rare birds, the jewel in the crown of which was the Rappels Vulture which had never been seen in Portugal for the last forty years.

He called for the forensic team, all of whom were dressed in disposable white coveralls and blue overshoes and they crawled all over the house taking photographs and fingerprints from the places the villains would have touched. Feliciano was optimistic that the burglars would be caught, although he did say that the clear up rate for this type of crime was not the most successful in the annuls of the Faro police department.

Feliciano was a quiet studious and thoughtful individual with a highly analytical approach to his job. He had started with the police department many years ago as a motorcycle cop and soon realised that chasing naughty drivers and fining them for transgressions of traffic laws was not the career he wanted. He was far too intelligent and ambitious to stay on the road. So he studied forensic science at Faro University (with a part time interest in pathology) where he qualified with a distinction in the subject. It was not long before the police promotion board recognised his talent and entered him on a fast track course as a detective, at which he became brilliant.

Fernando Martins, although in charge of the whole of Portugal, was based in Faro with a roving commission to work all over the country, trouble shooting and helping other departments with their problems. However he always managed to find himself situated in the Faro police headquarters. Perhaps it was because Faro is a lovely place to work and his Villa was only ten minutes from his office! On first meeting with Feliciano he took an instant dislike to him, he was completely opposite in nature to him, his approach to the job and was also jealous of Feliciano's intellect, intelligence and analytical approach to problems. Fernando's management style was to shoot from the hip and then ask questions afterwards. So they were at daggers drawn for most of the time.

Whenever he could find Feliciano attempting the slightest departure with procedure (even if he was correct in what he did to cure the problem) he would call him into his office and give him an almighty rollicking which far exceeded the perceived misdemeanour. He would always finish the tirade with,

'If I catch you doing anything outside your appointed job or procedure again you'll find yourself back on that motorcycle.'

Feliciano knew exactly what the nasty bastard was trying to do, that was to get him to resign. But he was far too wily and bright to fall into that trap. He would just stand there at attention, take the rebuke, would smartly salute and say curtly, 'Yes sir, will that be all sir' to which the reply was always, 'Get out of my sight.' It was almost a farce and the script was always the same. Feliciano would then briskly about turn, leave the room and carry on with whatever he was doing wrong in the first place, as he knew he was fireproof.

What Fernando didn't know was that Feliciano's uncle was the Minister for Justice in the government and the person in charge of appointing all top ranking officials in the police force. After Feliciano discussed the situation with his uncle, he had agreed that if any disciplinary meetings resulted in a demotion, then he would come down on the police chief like a ton of bricks, threaten him with discipline and no more would be heard of the matter. As his uncle often used to say.

'He will wonder what fell on him!'

10

Hans van Glytch

Prior to the Prime Minister Rabbit fraud debacle and whilst he was still in power, a Dutch entrepreneur and mega wealthy personality in the Golden Triangle area of the Algarve, Hans van Glytch, decided that the Rio Formosa nature reserve close to the beach and Faro, needed a new five star hotel which he would fund out of some dirty money which he wanted to launder.

Nobody knew where Van Glytch came from, how long he had been in Portugal or where he lived. The only habitation in which he had been seen was his ocean going 116 foot luxury motor cruiser built by the famous 'Sundowner' boat manufacturer based in Holland. He kept it berthed in a highly expensive mooring in Vilamoura. It was a floating palace, built on four levels with the fourth being the rooftop cabin. There were three on-suite bedrooms, enormous state room with fitted Italian white leather furniture, a gigantic glass and chromium coffee table, capacious galley and sundecks abounding, plus bunked accommodation for the staff. The whole vessel was painted from bow to stern in white livery which probably gave rise to it name, 'White Ecstasy' which could also be related to other connotations. He regularly shuttled back and forth from Portugal and Munderzand Marina in Holland, so one never knew just where to locate him. Probably the reason for his life on the high seas was that he could be registered as a sailor, therefore avoiding any income tax as he had no fixed abode and was labelled a seafarer.

He employed a permanent crew of 'hired muscle.' They consisted of a captain, handy man cum cook, a deck hand and a very skilful engineer. He looked after the two powerful Volvo Penta turbo charged inboard diesel engines running through twin screws. He also kept all the other services efficient and in peak condition. There were very few boats that could out pace this baby. It was just right for drugs running. All four shipmates were built comparable to brick sanitary buildings and also doubled as Van Glytch's minders. They were always present, if unobtrusive when Glytch was in public. Nobody would mess with these brutes.

The hotel took years to build and there was no problem with planning approval, as in this part of the world, money talks and big money talks even louder. The greatest benefit was that the construction of the hotel and complex gave long term employment to hundreds of otherwise unemployed builders, labourers, architects and clerical staff. The structure covered many acres of the Rio Formosa bird reserve which most locals believed was protected land on which building was not permitted. Running from the hotel was a rustic wooden bridge which wound over the mud flats and terminated on one of the best sandy beaches in the world.

Hans van Glytch was a short rotund individual with a typical arrogant Napoleon complex and had an enormous stomach, which hung well over his Gucci belt. What he lacked in stature he made up in ego which was larger than the Albert Hall. But he was much taller when he stood on his wallet! To add to this he had a bloated round face with what seemed to be a dead ferret under his nose. He always called it his personality moustache. He was balding with a ridiculous comb-over which flapped up and down in the wind. Similar to most moneyed people he loved to mix with the rich, famous and influential local dignitaries. One of whom was the Prime Minister together with his team of sycophantic acolytes.

The hotel was a magnificent and colossal structure boasting five hundred bedrooms all on-suite, with every room having views overlooking the sea and sandy beaches. The bedrooms were decorated by the world famous designer George Dors.

Most of the rooms were identical apart from a few speciality suites. The first was painted in black everywhere, even down to the black lighting. Black grotesque masks were hanging from the walls, together with leather whips, manacles, chains and handcuffs and a four poster bed, all of which finished the gloom of the room. The second was a creation of a baby's nursery, with an enormous double bed which resembled a cot, nappies everywhere and life size baby's dummies. The third resembled a horse's stable. There were saddles for chairs with bridles, bits, spurs and horse whips of all shapes and sizes adorning the room. When George questioned Van Glytch about the quirky styles, he responded.

'Some of our clientele do have some unusual fetishes and we prefer to accommodate all tastes!'

There were three top class restaurants, one having a two Michelin stars, a small casino with roulette and black jack tables and a limited number of fruit machines. Three enormous swimming pools all heated and situated in the sun and shade and Jacuzzi hot tubs were in hidden secluded situations. Three gyms with all the latest equipment completed the needs of the seriously keep fit brigade. In addition for those who genuinely wanted to exhaust themselves, outside were four tennis courts and inside, banks of squash courts.

Conference facilities are now big business all over the world and are huge money earners. Glytch being the greedy slob that he was, decided to build two massive conference rooms each accommodating five hundred people. They were complete with the latest audio and visual equipment available. He had already had some interest from an Australian conglomerate, Richmond International Partnership, wishing to hold their yearly international conference in Portugal. So he was well pleased.

There was enormous car parking facilities manned with armed security staff. One wondered why security was so important. Security was so tight that when the tide went out it wasn't allowed back in! The flat roof had two helicopter landing pads with elevators, one to the private suites and the other to reception. Of course Hans van Glytch was going to make jumbo bucks from the extortionate nightly room charges which looked similar to small mortgages. The whole enterprise was designed for the rich beautiful people who believed they were something special, needing to be pampered. The hotel was called 'Hotel Paradise' which is exactly what it was.

Fernando Martins, being the head of the local police was paid an enormous and outrageous consultancy fee to oversee and advise on the security arrangements and anti-burglary systems. That was not his main reason for getting involved in the planning. He was much more concerned about the high level contacts he could suck up to in order to increase his income.

There was to be a grand opening extravaganza to celebrate the completion of the building. All the local celebrities, glitterati, film stars, minor football players, well known racing car drivers and some regular stars that live in the Algarve were invited. Clifford Rickard and his backing group, 'The Followers', Clive Dunsom and Judy Kalm would attend and other also ran's who would come to the opening of an envelope, especially as all hospitality would be free.

All the people employed in the hotel were handpicked by a very exacting team of over-paid managers and the wheat from the chaff was rejected at application form stage. The main criteria were that perfect English was essential, plus qualifications from the local hospitality and catering training college for the waiting staff. The hostesses had to look and behave as Dior Models. Glytch loved to have his photo taken surrounded by these beautiful girls and always ensured that the local papers had the copy splashed over the front pages. There was also to be some lovely young men for clients those of that persuasion. Maître-d's were poached from other less prestigious hotels. Not a stone was left unturned to select the appropriate staff.

11

Egyptian Funeral

As Gamel filled his coffin with sand and rocks to approximately his body weight, he screwed down the lid with anti-release screws and completed the final plans for his disappearance. He shaved off his distinctive moustache, sheared part of his head to appear balding, changed into his original family tribe Berber clothing and left Cairo in the dead of night. For many months now he had been collecting small trinkets, ornate jewellery boxes, filigree silver and brass light sconces, traditional Egyptian art and Bedouin apparel, all of which he could use as part of his disguise as a Berber trader.

He joined the enormous routine Camel Train of some two hundred camels which was leaving on the edge of the Cairo desert. It would start its journey across North Africa terminating in Morocco and he would pose as a poor and out of work individual down on his uppers. This was perfectly normal as many of these luckless souls tried to make a living in this way and nobody would question another camel being added to the train.

One of the biggest downsides of the journey was that he hated camels with a loathing that nobody else could understand. He thought that they were the most dirty, smelly, ugly animals to walk this earth. They spat, often aggressive between males in the breeding season and can fight to the death. Not very useful if yours is the only one you own when on a journey and it does fight to the death. The main benefits of the beasts are that they are incredibly farsighted which allows them to see danger some two to three miles away and are cheap to run!

From Marrakesh he would top up his goods, then would travel to the coast and planned to work his passage on a tramp ship sailing across the Mediterranean Sea to Spain. Using his military background in Egypt and his knowledge of the Iberian Peninsula, he understood in detail the army and police structures in Spain, so he could easily obtain a job somewhere within one of the forces. Then his disappearance and deception would be complete.

The journey across Africa would take many months and is not the most pleasant way to travel especially on an uncomfortable camel. There would be numerous nightly stops, sometimes they would last weeks if there is a chance of selling their produce in a small town. On these stops he would have to beg a space in another trader's tent and buy food from them. As Arabs, they were always on the lookout to make a few bob out of those less fortunate than themselves but when the deal was struck they were the most hospitable of people and warmed to strangers quickly.

Back in Cairo, Nasser's funeral was being held amongst much mourning by the five million people milling around the cortege. As the coffin crossed the Qasr El-Nil Bridge, soldiers were simply overwhelmed by a mass of communal sorrow as men and women, wailing their loss swarmed around the entourage. In a surge of spontaneity, hysterical mourners attempted to bear their beloved leaders coffin themselves.

Soldiers used rifle butts and batons to repel the crowds in the ensuing pandemonium. Many people were killed in the crush. He was evidently a very much loved leader.

12

Feliciano's Past

Thirteen police case files were piled on the left hand side of Feliciano's desk awaiting his attention, with a scribbled note from Fernando insisting that they all be cleared, sorted and filed before he did anything else that day. Just my luck he thought as it was a lovely day outside and he had planned to attempt some more interesting detective work out in the sunshine. It was typical of his boss to get him to do the mundane admin work inside the sweaty office.

He opened the first file and found yet another murder in the southern part of Portugal. This was the fourth this month. Most of them were either gang killings or drug related. He wondered if there were similar occurrences in the north. He knew that Fernando would know the answer but was reluctant to ask as this would probably lead to another bollocking because he would say that he wasn't fully acquainted with all the facts. He made a mental note to contact the Oporto office to see what their records showed.

The second file was more of the same. His mind wandered due to the stuffiness of the room. The single window of the twelve by twelve feet office was opened wide but did nothing to lower the temperature, nor did the ceiling fan which lazily turned and wobbled on its fixing. His thoughts absentmindedly turned to his family background and upbringing. He was one of eight children born to Roman Catholic parents, him being sired in the middle of the tribe. His parents were poor working class peasants with very little money and he could never understand why they had so many children which left them virtually on the breadline. He didn't have much in common with his mother or his father, who wanted him to go into the building trade as an apprentice. His mother on the other hand, wanted him to marry a nice village girl from Gorjoe's where they lived, get a local job and have loads of children, so she could have grandchildren. He thought what low horizons! But Feliciano wanted to make something of his life and have a career, not just a job.

As a teenager, the time when kids start to question their parent's decisions in life, he asked his mother why they decided to have such a large family. She said it was Gods Will and He decides how many children anyone should have. In addition to this ridiculous notion, his parents had to give ten per cent of their income to the church which has more money than they knew what to do with. He didn't have much truck with such nonsense and told her so. She was terribly upset with his attack on their lifestyle and was adamant that this is how their life worked and that was the way they wanted it to be lived. He was increasingly convinced that he wouldn't be conned by the Catholics and the Pope's domination of people's family, in the same way as his parents had been all their lives.

From this point on he decided to research all other religions and how they related to a God which could not be seen, not proven to exist, had so much influence over people's lives and in many cases has led to wars and religious killings. He studied Judaism, Islam, Hinduism, Sikhism, Paganism, Celtic Polytheism and Italo-Roman Neopaganism, none of which suited his needs for a faith on which to anchor his life.

After some years of reflective thought he decided he would pursue the way of life of a Buddhist. There was no God to decide ones fate, with no dogma to pursue but the concept of the four Global Truths and the Eight Paths to Nirvana appealed to him and had worked well for his life from his teenage years until now. He felt that he had become a much more rounded caring person with a better humanitarian view of life than he did as a Catholic.

The phone rang shrilly on his desk and suddenly woke him out of his reverie. It was Martins yelling down the line saying to get to his office ASAP for a meeting with some thirty other officers. He dropped everything and trotted down two flights of stairs to the big bosses cave. The other officers were mostly traffic police together with their immediate superiors. Some were leaning on the walls and others sat at the many desks situated randomly around the oblong office. There was muted murmuring about the reason for the hurriedly called gathering. Martins was about to start the briefing.

'You took your time Neves, what kept you; we are waiting for you so we can start.'

The question didn't need a reply as he started to speak without waiting for an answer.

'I have been contacted by government ministers at the highest level in Lisbon, about the need to increase the revenue of the country, as we need more money from the population. The government can't tax the people any further through income tax, as they are taxed to the limit already. So the only way forward is to raise more cash by fining drivers for breaking the laws of the roads. This is where you traffic officers can make a difference. You will now carry out multiple roadside checks on vehicles and impose heavy penalties for anything you can find wrong.'

There was a stunned silence in the room as Martins left the bombshell to take effect on the team. Boris Nuno was a giant of a policeman and was seen to be the social leader of the group and accepted as the un-appointed shop steward of the traffic section. He stood up and said.

'I don't think we are paid to be unofficial tax collectors for the government and we should not be treated as such.'

Martins went red round the gills and exploded. 'You're not paid to think, you are paid to do as I say; now shut up and listen.'

Nuno whispered to one of his sidekicks, 'I think he's going bonkers!'

'Where you find the slightest things awry with vehicles, especially commercial vans, you'll check for anything wrong. Drivers licence, insurance, identity cards lights, horn, tyres, indictors and then collect cash and give written receipts to the offenders. You are each targeted to fine forty vehicles per week for the next year. I want all the cash and receipts on my desk each month. There are no further questions. Dismissed!'

'Neves you had better take notice of what I have just said as one day you might find yourself back on that motorbike doing the same job as these guys.'

He did enjoy having a jibe at Feliciano. With that he turned and strode back to his office thinking about the twenty five per cent he would cream off the top of the fines for himself.

13

Bay of Biscay

Paddy and Mick sailed miles of calm waters on the first leg of their journey from Ireland and thought what a lovely way to spend a life on the ocean wave. Not having a care in the world, until they came to the Bay of Biscay. They soon changed their minds! The Bay is a gulf off the northeast Atlantic Ocean located south of the Celtic Sea. It lies along the western coast of France from Brest south to the Spanish border and the northern coast of Spain west of Cape Ortegal. It's known for its rough seas and violent storms and much of this is thanks to its exposure to the Atlantic Ocean. Winds blow from America to Europe and the waves grow all the way as they travel from west to east. Swell waves are long sloping waves that are around twenty foot high but high winds can make them bigger and steeper. Gales are most likely in the bay from October through March.

Had the twins had a brain cell between them they would have researched the waters around this part of the world, avoided March and either waited until later in the year or watched the weather forecasts before they set out. Now they found themselves in some of the most dangerous waters in the world in a leaky small motor launch pitching and tossing like a cork on the high seas. Large ferries and many cargo ships have found themselves in trouble and some have foundered or sunk in these oceans. What chance did their tiny craft have of survival in these treacherous waters? Had they heard of the saying 'Calm seas never made a skilful sailor' they might have paid more attention to planning their route.

With no life jackets and a lifeboat which looked a bit flaky, their chances of survival looked slim indeed. Mick shouted to Paddy over the noise of the gale, he was almost tied to the steering gear in order to keep on course.

'Oie don't tink we are going to survive dis Paddy, put de boat on a southerly course and let's get below.'

They battened down all the hatches, windows and portholes and as an additional precaution tied the wheel securely with rope. They then slithered and fell down the steps to the galley below as the boat bucked and wallowed in the mighty swell.

Paddy said. 'Let's just pray to Mary Mother of God and try to sleep tru dis lot.'

They stumbled through to the bedrooms and they were violently sea sick, as they collapsed onto the berths. They heard the bow thump and crash onto a gigantic wave. This was the last noise they heard as they both passed out into blackness.

14

Hotel Paradise Opening

The day came for the grand opening of Hotel Paradise. The month chosen was August to ensure the best of the hot sunny weather that usually arrives in Portugal at that time of year. There was great excitement from all the staff and management who were involved in the organisation in which they had prepared for months and had worked so hard to ensure its success.

Hans van Glytch was chasing around shouting and cajoling every employee to make sure his orders were being completed to the last detail. Never had he looked so harassed and shattered. Bus boys with brass bell shaped luggage trolleys were waiting at the gigantic plate glass entrance doors. Some pretty boys were employed to park client's cars and were eagerly anticipating the limos to arrive, to get as many tips as they could for their parking services. The kitchens were a hotbed of activity as the chefs busied themselves organising the vast varied menus of international food for the incoming guests.

The two dozen hostesses were in the champagne bar and looked sensational, waiting for the prestigious guests to arrive. Their evening dresses were all the colours of the rainbow with most of them reaching down to the floor. Their hair was also rainbow coloured with blondes, redheads, green, blue and black hair with all the colours in between. Most of them were between eighteen and thirty years old, slim and tall. A number of them were not so, looking a tad overweigh but they were all made taller by the four inch high heeled shoes they wore. To most people's taste they were showing a little too much flesh but Van Glytch said that was the way the customers liked them. They had been told most of the duties to which they had to attend and could only guess at those they had not!

Van Glytch had arranged for a string quartet to play in the champagne bar, a disco in the cellar and his piece-de resistance and one of his best coups, Frank Sinatra had been booked with his sixteen piece band to play in the ballroom. Whatever Van Glytch was or was not, did he have style!

The hour had arrived to start the festivities and the guests arrived in their gross limousines. One had never seen so much bare crêpie flesh, diamonds and rubies flashing in the light as they were greeted by a marching brass band dressed in light grey uniforms with brass buttons and chromium helmets. Plus young drum majorettes with them all marching up and down the driveway to the hotel.

One of the last to arrive was the Prime Minister, Sr Rabbit with his entourage. As he walked through the mêlée of attendees, as most people knew an election was imminent and he would definitely be deposed, they turned their backs on him. For the first time in his position he felt totally ignored. Immediately Van Glytch hurried up to him, gave him a man hug, a kiss on each cheek, whispered quickly in his ear and made small talk for a few moments until returning to more moneyed guests.

Finally Fernando Martins made his entrance being the last to arrive. He looked magnificent in his dark blue full dress uniform covered in gold braid with his peaked cap under his arm. He knew that more than most people, hats should not be worn indoors. Most of the hostesses turned and gave him admiring glances with which he was extremely pleased. Others not expecting such a senior policeman to attend an event of this importance fumbled in their pockets in sheer panic and dropped small packages into waste bins. Some people hurried to the now crowded washrooms to pour white powder into the toilets which was immediately flushed away. This must say something about the moral standards of our popular elite!

Fernando circulated well for the first half an hour exchanging pleasantries with those he thought would be useful in the future. Finally he drifted over to the Prime Minister who after being side-lined had found a corner in which to chat with his cronies.

'Bom Dia Mr Prime Minister,' he called in an overfriendly voice with a smile on his face.

'Oh dear have you come to arrest me?' the Minister said with a sneering oily look on his face and trying to force humour.

'No sir we only arrest people who have broken the law, if you have not, then you have nothing to fear.'

'Oh we politicians would never do that.' He said with as much confidence as he could muster. After more social chat Fernando manoeuvred the Prime Minister and the Finance Minister to a quiet corner and sat them down so they were all facing each other. Fernando was stern faced as he asked his first loaded question.

'Now tell me Sr Rabbit about your involvement in the placing of the contracts for the new motorway system.'

'Oh that's nothing to do with me personally, all that detail is handled by my Ministers in the Highway Department.' He said with great confidence.

'OK so how was it that you had a holiday in the Caribbean paid for by the main contractor?'

Fernando had done his research very thoroughly.

'That is what we call in political circles a brokering fee and is perfectly normal,'

he said with not so much confidence. Sn Coelho the Finance Minister was looking decidedly shifty and squirmed uncomfortably in his seat.

'Then tell me how you can sustain a lifestyle three or four times above that of the salary you are paid?'

'I have made some very astute investments over the years which have yielded well.' He said with less confidence.

'Well done sir, so would those investments be anything to do with a Swiss account in the Hottinger & Clie Bank in Zurick?'

His face went pale.

'I have no idea what you are talking about.'

'Well sir would a numbered account 7896532 help you to have some idea?' Said Fernando triumphantly.

Both Rabbit and the Finance Minister went white and their knees trembled. Fernando allowed the silence to settle over them for some minutes. Rabbit was the first to speak.

'Very well what are the options?' He said in a very quiet dry voice.

Fernando said with a soft menacing tone. 'I can arrest you now in front of all these celebrities or I want a substantial slice of the action, the choice is yours.'

Another silence as the two ministers looked at each other.

'Give us five minutes.'

Fernando left them and went to the men's room. Rabbit was livid with his finance man.

'You stupid little ineffective twerp, you assured me that the account was safe as houses, what went wrong?'

'Don't you go on at me, I did all that was possible to keep the money hidden; he must have friends in higher places than we know about!'

When Fernando returned, the die was cast.

'What happens now?' Said the Prime Minister resigned in defeat.

Fernando glowed with satisfaction inside and said with a restrained voice and with great charm.

'I'll let you know the time and place that we will meet to discuss details. You will receive a sealed and private letter from me delivered by courier, giving you the precise details and you both will arrive alone and in disguise. You won't tell anyone about the meeting and you will not wear a wire, if you do I will have a device that will detect anything.'

With that Fernando saluted them, said gently and quietly. 'Carpe Diem gentlemen; Carpe Diem.'

It was the only phrase he knew in Latin but thought it sounded intelligent and appropriate in the circumstances.

He then turned quickly with a broad grin on his face and joined a group of the hostesses who were only too pleased to have his company for the evening. One of who was a buxom and blousy young lady and by reputation was a bit of a slapper who might keep him entertained later.

15

Rappels Vulture

There was great excitement in Casa Crao when the sergeant rang the bell. One of the reasons that Sergeant Neves called was not only to update Roly and Hedda about the progress of the robbery, which was not going well. But to tell them that the rare Rappels Vulture had been seen in the disused copper mine near Oporto and they should all get up there as soon as possible before other Twitchers arrive and obtain the first sightings.

'As far as the robbery is concerned,' said Feliciano, 'The forensic team think they may have further evidence which may rule out the druggie theory, because they have found minute traces of horse dung and hair which might suggest that gypsies could have done the deed. There's been much activity in this area as hundreds of Romany's have been congregating to assemble at the annual Estoi horse fair and 'Thieves Market' as the locals call the Meet. But in any event we will continue with our investigations until we catch the villains. Of course the drug problems in the area may also be related to the gypsies.'

'That's very thrilling news about the crime and the theft.' Said Roly.

'But we have quite a few things to do and bags to pack before we leave so we will need a few hours before we can depart. We need to book a hotel also, as we cannot get there and back in one day as it's a five hour drive; certainly not in our car, a very old Citroen Mehari, it does nought to sixty in two hours!'

'That's not a problem, as I have a roving commission as a detective over all of Portugal and can commandeer an air conditioned police car for us.'

'That's very kind of you but we think at some point that might land you in big trouble, so it would be more prudent if we used ours.'

'Ok as you wish,' replied Feliciano with some frustration in his voice.

In the meantime Roly wanted to discuss with Feliciano a matter that had arisen about their neighbour who lives at the top of the Hill.

'I understand that Sr Martins is the chief of police and your boss Feliciano, is that correct?'

'Unfortunately yes he is and he wouldn't be my first choice as my superior but I have no choice. A right bastard if ever there was one.'

Roly was a bit concerned as to whether he should continue with the conversation as it might compromise Feliciano, however after much deliberation he continued.

'We didn't know that our neighbour was in the police force and as you know we are Fiends of the Earth and are passionate about protecting wild life. We were walking the hill recently and passed Casa Travessa Do Pastor and saw dozens of bird traps laid around outside the main gate. As we stopped to look at them this enormous Rottweiler dog came bounding down the driveway barking and snarling at us. Soon after, your boss came running down the drive and snarled at us.'

'What do you want and why are you annoying my dog.'

We said to him. 'Don't you know that the trapping and killing birds and animals is against the law in Portugal and if you don't stop the practice we will inform the authorities?'

He retorted angrily. 'Do what you like, now shove off or I'll open the gate and let Bruiser here rip you to bits!'

'Well, as you can imagine we were shocked and quite frightened so made haste back to the house and had a large shot of brandy to settle our nerves. Then thought we should wait until we could talk to you to find the best way to deal with the situation. What do you think?' Feliciano reflected for a while and replied.

'If I were you I would forget the whole state of affairs and steer very clear of both him and the dog. Martins really is a nasty dreadful piece of work and best to be avoided, as there is nothing you can do about the traps. I realised as soon as I met him, he is only miserable when he's awake! Someday he will get his cum-uppance, so until then hold your fire.'

Hedda was particularly traumatised by the event, as she had for some time a nasty illness of which she had not told Roly. She had been seeing the local doctor and specialist consultants in Lisbon for some months and she had been diagnosed with breast cancer, which because of the position of it and its aggressive nature had gone too far to treat. She was determined that Roly shouldn't know about it until the time came, as she wanted him to enjoy his retirement, bird watching and singing in his German choir as long as possible. To minimise the effect on her darling husband when she dies, without him realising what was happening, she gradually encouraged him to spend more time in Hamburg singing in his Oratorial Bach Choir; while she will spend more holidays in the Villa writing her life story for her children to read when she was dead.

Roly and Hedda were not the types to do nothing at present about Martins aggressive attack on them, so put the matter on the back burner until a solution came to mind.

They then all returned to the discussion of the rare bird sighting and made plans for the journey.

16

The Body Found

The alarm rang shrilly at seven o clock am in Caroline's bedroom in her dads flat. She was woken from her unbroken deep sleep after the dreadful traumatic session with her dad about the Blue Cornflower. She quickly dressed in her working clothes as there was no time to shower, not that the shower worked very well, as in everything else in the flat, most of it was second hand and or broken.

She hurried down the wooden staircase which once upon a time had some form of carpet but was now threadbare. She scooped up her long hair and twisted it into a topknot on the back of her head and secured it with a large white hairclip. She looked fantastic; most girls would have spent an hour in front of a mirror trying to look this good.

She quietly closed the kitchen door so as not to wake her dad and started to prepare his favourite breakfast. Cooking with the tatty kitchen equipment was almost as bad as having a shower, with all the pots and frying pans needing replacing. Something her dad would never be bothered with, so she made a mental note to replace them next time she called. A full English breakfast with two fried eggs, bacon and all the trimmings was his favourite. When the meal was almost cooked and the coffee was on the boil, she walked noisily up the stairs to dad's room, knocked on the door and said.

'Morning Pa your breakfast is almost ready.'

'Ok Flopsie I will be down as soon as I am dressed.'

They sat at the kitchen table which was laid as if they were dining at Harrods and chatted amiably and comfortably about what the day would bring for both of them, carefully avoiding the Blue Cornflower subject so as not to open old wounds.

'Dad I really am in a rush. I would love to stay longer but the morgue has need of my presence.'

'That's quite all right my love, you get off and I'll clear the kitchen, by which time the shop will have to be opened.'

She kissed him lightly on the cheek and ran down the stairs opening the door with the clarion call ringing in her ears. Her favourite mode of transport in the busy city of Oporto was her old and falling to bits Vespa scooter. Her dad was always moaning at her to get it serviced but she never took heed and would always wait until it broke down before having it maintained. This morning it started first time after she kicked the engine into life. The traffic as usual at this time of the day was almost at gridlock but this was not a problem to her, as most of the time she would ride on the pavements, scattering complaining pedestrians in all directions. With a wave of her arm she would call out, sorreee to each of them, most knowing of her and smiling at her crazy mode of transport and her daily wild Valkyrie ride.

She arrived at the path lab ten minutes early to find that her assistant interns had prepared and covered the latest body ready for her inspection. She was livid at what happened. Firstly, the body had been removed from the site from whence it was found without her permission. Secondly, the intern had washed the poor soul from top to bottom, destroying any evidence that would have helped to determine the cause of death. Most of the path lab staff and the local police knew Caroline as an easy going fun loving girl who would not say boo to a goose. What they could never get to grips with was that she had a management style which was an iron fist in a velvet glove.

She called all the interns into the lab and lined them up alongside the body.

'Right you lot, who removed the body from the site and who washed all the evidence away.'

The smallest and newest young man owned up right away.

'How many times do I have to tell you, all of you, that you shouldn't move any body from the site as I need to examine it exactly as it was found. This is the third time this has happened and I am not a happy pathologist!'

The offender was red in the face and apologised profusely.

'So why did you do it!'

He said with a nervous quavering voice.

'The victim was found naked and covered in a very smelly slimy substance and it was stinking the lab out. Everyone was complaining about the smell and we knew you would be a day late doing the examination, so I washed the smell away but kept a large sample in a bucket.'

By this time Caroline had calmed down a bit and the guy had stopped shaking.

'Well at least you were smart enough to keep a sample. But if this ever happens again you will all wonder what fell on you. Now get back to your tasks and leave me alone to determine the cause of death.'

She gowned up and pulled on the skin tight rubber gloves. At this point she would have had one of the assistants help her but she was too angry to have them around so started the autopsy alone. First she examined the front, back sides and head for any clues but there were none. She had performed the Y shaped incision on the chest of bodies so many times she could almost do it with her eyes closed. So holding the scalpel firmly in her right hand she started to cut.

As the skin began to part, her mind wandered as she thought about her dads Blue Cornflower problem and this in turn led her to reflect on his unusual and eclectic upbringing. He was born in Billy Smarts Circus which was travelling around Europe. His parents were high wire and trapezes artists and had performed some of the most daring and dangerous feats in order to excite the audiences lust for thrills. Then disaster struck, as his father went to catch his mother on the trapeze, he missed his hold of her hand and she went crashing to the circular dust filled ring. As he realised he had lost hold he tried to reach out to her as she fell and also slipped off the timbered swing, falling also to the ground. There was no safety net!

Caroline could only imagine the crowd screaming and horrified at the crumpled sight of the two stars lying unconscious in the circus ring. The ambulances which were always on site and ready to go in an emergency, ferried the two comatose artists to the local hospital and the performance in the circus was cancelled.

The result of the fall left his mother with a broken back and his father with a broken arm which was so badly mangled it had to be amputated. Billy was devastated by the accident and as with his entire troupe when they were injured or became too old to perform, he would find some kind of job for them to do, even if it wasn't quite a crowd puller or was not really required.

So time passed and when his father recovered, Billy taught him to be the world's first and only one armed lion tamer which was a big crowd pleaser. His mother now having a broken back and was unable to walk. After being heavily made up she was exhibited as 'The Bearded Lady' much to her disgust but she needed to make some kind of living and this was better than nothing.

Shak during his lifetime in the circus, became a skilled knife thrower dressed as a Red Indian, threw knives at a bikini clad girl on a revolving target; doubled as Coco the Clown and a Cowboy bareback horse rider. He had learned to play many instruments and performed in the circus band but found he was a wiz at the electric guitar, hence later in life he left the circus and formed his own band, Shakin Shak. It consisted of a keyboard player, the only one in the group that could read music, a drummer, a bass player and Shak as lead singer and rhythm guitarist. As he told Caroline many times, they were no great shakes as musicians but they could always whip up a party atmosphere and the fans loved them for this. He used to say that the groupie girls used to throw their knickers at them but as they grew older, as did the fans, they would throw their incontinence pants! She never tired of hearing his band war stories and he would have her in tears of laughter at some of the more bizarre situations in which they found themselves.

Nobody would have called Shak handsome or good looking but with his tall six foot slim stature and his long blond untidy hair and a twinkle in his eye, he did have an appeal. One of his fans once described him as 'A bit of a rake!'

Her day dreaming came to an abrupt halt as the Y shaped incision opened up and the most revolting smell rose up into her nostrils. She was quite shocked and ashamed to find how long she had been on auto pilot.

Composing herself and getting back into professional mode she removed the stomach, liver, heart and lungs hoping to find the cause of death. Then she realised that the stench that woke her from her reverie was the smell of ingested heroin. The obvious cause of the poor person's demise was an overdose of this ghastly opiate. The interns said that the corpse was found in a pig's slurry pit on a farm which is why the body has stunk so much.

Caroline was always sad at any death to which she had to officiate but the death of such an attractive young girl only in her mid-twenties was a wretched way to meet her maker. She now had to hand the case over to the police to find the culprit who murdered her.

17

The Letter and Instructions

One of the Prime Minister's offices in Lisbon was in the centre of the fashionable Lisbon Baixa area with its café culture, myriad restaurants and home of the soulful Fado music. Although he thought that listening to too much of the artists playing the mandolin and singing was alright in small doses, it left him lusting for something more classical, played by much larger professional orchestras.

The office as one would expect, was large with high ceilings surrounded by deep encrusted coving depicting scenes from Portuguese history. The walls were lined with highly polished oak panels with pictures and photos of the glory days of the adventurous Portuguese sailing Caravels and of him smiling, or grimacing with other world leaders. The deep pile purple fitted carpet had enough depth to hide a cat! His enormous mahogany desk with its green leather top, edged with gold leaf was littered with papers. He had never heard that the most efficient manager would only have one piece of paper on which he was working on the surface. But he always thought that piles of papers made him look busy and important. In the centre of the desk there were three Bakelite telephones, two black and one red for secure secret and important international calls.

Behind the desk was his favourite exceedingly large dark guilt framed photograph taken in 1975 of him shaking hands with Ted Heath the English Prime Minister, when Heath conned the British people to vote to join the Common Market. The electorate had no idea that the

Market would morph into the uncontrollable monster it would become over the next forty years.

Two gigantic brown leather easy chairs dwarfed other furniture in the room, on which he and Sr Coelho were sitting and they were deep in conversation about what they would do in the near future when they were chucked out of office. Both were looking very glum at the prospect of endless days with nothing to do, although there would be some financial compensation.

Suddenly they were interrupted by one of the black phones ringing. It was reception to say that there was a motorcycle courier wanting to leave a package to be signed.

'What are you calling me for,' he barked, 'sign for it yourself, that's what you are there for.'

There was a long delay and the security receptionist replied that the courier had instructions to hand the package personally to the Prime Minister or he would have to return it to the sender.

'Oh very well, send him up,' he growled.

Some minutes later there was a loud knock on the twelve feet high oak double doors. Sr Coelho strolled over and opened them to find, not a normal courier but a heavily built motorcycle policeman holding a sealed envelope.

'This can only be signed for by the Prime Minister himself,' he boomed handing the package to Rabbit.

As soon as Rabbit saw the policeman, his blood ran cold and his heart started to race. This was the communication he had been expecting and dreading from Fernando Martins and he feared its content. He signed the receipt. The policeman saluted smartly, turned and closed the doors with an unnecessarily loud clunk.

Rabbit went whiter than a sheet just returned from a high class laundry. He fell rather than sat into the leather chair, his heart was beating like a steam hammer and the package fell from his trebling hand onto the floor.

'What's up with you, you great wet, you look like you've seen a roomful of ghosts.' Said Coelho.

'It's one thing knowing that the Sword of Damocles is going to fall at some time but it is another thing when it actually happens,' he moaned.

Slowly and reluctantly Rabbit picked up the package from the floor and looked at it for some minutes. It was a brown foolscap size padded envelope, fastened with a red wax seal on the back. On the front the words read, 'To the Portuguese Prime Minister to be opened only by him in private.' He tore open the seal to find two white envelopes inside. The first read 'To be opened first,' the second read 'To be opened second.' Not too much difficulty in understanding that, even for a Minister! With trembling sweaty fingers he opened the first letter. It read.

You and Coelho will meet me at Rosa's café in Querenca which is in the hills between Loul'e and Sao Bras in the district of Faro, on the second Tuesday this September at 11.00. As I said at the hotel, you will come alone, in disguise, you won't tell anyone of the meeting and you will not wear a wire. You will also bring with you a duplicate key to the deposit box which is held in the vault of your Switzerland bank. This will be a permanent copy for me. BE THERE!!

The Prime Minister gulped with a dry throat as he opened the second envelope. What he saw inside almost caused him to have a heart attack. A grainy black and white photograph slipped out and fluttered to the floor. As he picked it up he saw the image of him naked, handcuffed to the four poster bed with a large black chain around his neck in the totally black S&M bedroom in the Hotel Paradise. Standing over him with his legs astride, also naked except for a pair of the tiniest black leather briefs, was one of the pretty young men who were seen with the hostesses at the opening of the hotel. Although he was a Ganymede, he was holding an enormous leather whip. He had an evil smile on his face and seemed to be enjoying every second of the depraved event.

Coelho looked at the photo and he also went weak at the knees.

'How the hell did he manage to take the photo in what you thought was a private session?' He seems to have the ability to know our every move.'

Secretly and without saying a word to Rabbit it sickened him to the core. He knew that the Prime Minister had some pretty kinky tastes but this was too much over the top.

Rabbit looked at Coelho with a terrified expression on his face and said.

'We have been hung, drawn and quartered, stuffed, hung out to dry and doomed to do exactly as he wishes.'

Not only were they to be drummed out of office at the next election, they would have to share their ill gotton gains with that turd Martins. Any thoughts of a life free of worries were now consigned to the past. They both sat in silence as the enormity of their situation dawned on them. Then Rabbit exploded with rage.

'If I can get hold of that stinking bilge rat, I'll kill the bastard.'

He shouted and fumed; his face was bloated, sweaty and turned bright scarlet. Coelho looked in horror at this explosion of venom, never in all the years of working closely with the Prime Minister had he seen him in such a rage.

They both sank into the leather chairs exhausted and totally defeated. Rabbit thinking the darkest thought he had ever had in his life.

18

The Bay of Biscay Calmed

After twenty four hours of mountainous seas in the Bay of Biscay, the boat had found calmer waters as the storm had subsided. The six cylinder diesel Thorneycroft engine had almost given up the ghost and was slowly coughing and spluttering to keep going in the now waterlogged engine room. The navigation wheel was still secured in the same place with the rope that Paddy had tied and fortunately the vessel was moving slowly in a southerly direction.

The blackness that had engulfed Paddy and Mick was slowly lifting from them as they sluggishly woke from their ordeal. The first sensation they felt was their soaking clothes and the bruising they had suffered whilst being tossed around the bedroom in the gale. The next was the chaotic scene they witnessed in and around the bedroom and later in the remainder of the ship. The room was awash with their vomit mixed with sea spray, everywhere was soaked in freezing cold sea water and they were both shivering with the cold. All the crockery in the galley was smashed and the pots and pans were scattered asunder. They realised that the first job they would have to do when reaching dry land would be to re-equip the whole galley.

When going up on deck and with some relief in their heart they saw the Rock of Gibraltar in the distance and knew that they would soon be sailing into their destination, The Mediterranean Sea and Menorca. Mary Mother of God had done a good job in their salvation.

Mick being the more technical of the two, changed into some dry clothes that were in a locker which had escaped the waters. He tottered rather than walked down to the engine room to see if he could breathe some new life into the aged engine. He discovered that the main problem was that sea water had found its way into the diesel pumps, so once he had these dried out; the old thumper regained its normal sweet running condition. Then off they sailed to happier times in Menorca and the Red Coral adventure.

Unlike other gemstones which are of mineral origin, Coral is organic, being formed by living organisms. It grows from the animals branching antler like structures creating coral polyps in tropical and subtropical waters. When the unfortunate animals die the hardened skeleton remains and this material is what is used as a gemstone. Most coral is white, but nature can create coral in several other colours, including the popular orange to red forms. This Red Coral or Precious coral as it is often known by, is the most used and valuable gemstone form of Coral. In fact, the colour known as *coral* is derived from the typical pinkish-orange colour of many Coral gemstones. The darkest and best red is found in the secret deep waters around Italy's Mediterranean coast.

Paddy and Mick did not care a tinker's cuss about how it is formed or how many animals died to make the stones; they just knew that by diving for the skeletons and selling the little beggars, they could make a small fortune.

However before they could embark on this quite dangerous dive they must have the boat cleaned up, replace the broken equipment from the storm and get to the Police Auctions to buy some more diving gear.

They sailed into the Ribera Del Puerto Marina in Menorca around midday and berthed where the harbour master indicated and due to the lousy berth position he said there was no charge, which pleased the twins no end.

They immediately hurried to the first bar to get sossled, hopefully on Guinness but no luck; this isn't stocked on Menorca. They had to be content with local beer, 'San Miguel' which is extremely potent and has twice the kick of Guinness. After a few litres of this intoxicating brew they were more than relaxed and happy, in fact they were Brahms and Liszt! The bruising they had received from the rough seas didn't seem to hurt as much now. Drunk or not, they still had to get the boat ship shape and Bristol Fashion and as there was so much work to do, they would have to get some additional help from the locals.

The first job they had to get done as a priority was to clean up the boat from the damage caused by the storm and this was a much bigger job than they could undertake themselves, so some additional labour had to be found. Talk about the luck of the Irish, as they were discussing how to do it, five burly young Spanish teenagers sauntered into the bar.

'Glory be, tank Mother Mary, here comes our helpers Paddy.'

'Come over here you lovely lads and let's buy you some beer,' shouted Mick.

The boys sat down and drank the beers in double quick time then asked for another which was quickly ordered by Mick.

'Now you lads what are you doing this time of day, shouldn't you be at work?'

No they said we are all unemployed and have been looking for a job for years. Since the revolution when Franco was chucked out, the unemployment rate has rocketed and we are still looking for work.

'Aha, we have just der job for you all. We have recently sailed through a nasty storm and our boat needs to be cleaned from top to bottom and you look just the sort of tough guys to do the job, wadaya tink?' Said Paddy.

The most mature and biggest of the group, clearly the leader said. 'How much do we get paid?'

'Oh you need not worry about der price, we'll pay you a job and finish rate for a one day contract.'

They haggled for a few minutes with them all drinking too much and arguing about the rate and how long it would take to do the job. So the only way they could resolve the matter was to take them over to the boat, do a thorough survey of the damage and after another hour of haggling the deal was struck.

They all shook hands and it was agreed they would start first thing in the morning.

'Great job.' Said Mick.

'Now we can concentrate on the Police Auctions to get some more dive gear.'

19

The Australian Connection

The financial centre in Melbourne Australia was home to a Venture Capitalist and Stock Broking company called Richmond International Partnership. R.I.P was a most unfortunate abbreviation for a financial organisation where fortunes rise and fall, sometimes terminal with the stock market roller coaster! The company was controlled by James and Jenny Richmond, her being a major shareholder and director, assisted by three other partners.

Jenny was the first born daughter of Shak from his first marriage and she was now in her mid-forties. She had a difficult upbringing after her parents separated. She never got on well with her mother as they argued over everything, with neither of them giving way in an argument. So when she reached age seventeen she left home. She also had an uneasy relationship with Shak, as a lot of the time he was on the road playing in the band and was not home very often. In addition she found him a tad aloof and distant with her. But that improved as she got older and came to realise the difficulties of maintaining close relationships after her parents' marriage breakdown and her living half way around the world in Australia.

Her first job was to take a training course as a Norland's Nanny in Hungerford. When she completed the course, her initial job was looking after two children of a multi-millionaire banker and his Australian Model wife living in Cheyne Walk Chelsea. She led a jet setting life for some years with them, looking after their children as they travelled around the world on business in their private Lear Jet. Eventually, with her employers blessing whilst in Melbourne, she met and married James Richmond.

However, having had to cope with difficult parental relationships, living away from home and making her own way in life at an early age, gave her a steely determination to succeed, which came in very useful as a financial business woman.

The Australian Government had recently imposed a seven and a half per cent national insurance deduction from all employees' income, which they would invest in a superannuation fund for an old age pension for all. In addition, employers will contribute the same amount to the pot. This means that there are billions of Au dollars sloshing around the country to be invested to make the pot grow. R.I.P's main area of business was for its directors to travel the world and find investors who would be interested in participating in this growth.

James was the unfortunate guy who undertook this extremely stressful round the world travel plan to drum up business. The only pleasant aspect of the travelling was that he went first class on all airlines and travels, had a limitless expense account and stayed in the best hotels. Such a hard life! His next trip was to see some clients in Spain, so it seemed a good plan to call into Portugal to find a conference centre to hold the next worldwide investors superannuation investment jamboree. This happens every year and different investment organisations take turns in its organisation. This year it was R.I.Ps turn. He had heard of the new Hotel Paradise in the Algarve and his secretary had arranged a meeting with Hans van Glytch.

When Van Glytch heard that some four hundred people might be interested in holding the first meeting in his hotel, his little piggy eyes lit up with the thought of the substantial fees that he could impose. Also the significant marketing opportunity this would provide for the hotel in the financial world. He would ensure that Mr Richmond stayed in the hotel for free and would roll out the red carpet and personally entertain him within an inch of his life!

20

Citroen Mehari

Citroen introduced the first 2CV car or Duex Chevaux as it is called in French, Two Steam Horses or Two Horses, at the 1938 Paris Mondial De I' Automobile Show and manufactured many models and deviants until 1990. The Citroen Mehari that Roly and Hedda owned was one of the last to be built and was modelled to look similar to the last World War American Jeep. All of the outside panels and inside structures were made of plastic, so nothing rusted. The side and rear windows were also plastic and could be rolled up or removed in hot weather. Their model was white and blue and was called the Azure (Sea). The only other colour was yellow and was called the Plage (Beach).

For the technical minded, the specification for the build was; it was essentially designed for French farmers, must be able to cross a ploughed field in comfort, with a basket of eggs in the passenger's seat without them breaking. This required torsion bar suspension on all four wheels. It also had to be easily maintained by anyone. On bends it would roll over at a crazy angle. When asking the salesman if it would topple and crash, the reply was 'impossible' but if it does, bring it back and we will replace it with a new one! With the rear seat removed it must carry two bales of hay, or two sheep. The original engine was 400cc horizontally opposed overhead valve twin cylinder joby. This meant that it was fine on the flat but uphill it almost stopped, as many French motorist fumed when following one up a hill behind a half mile queue of traffic! This was resolved by upgrading the engine to a more powerful 602cc. The engine ran as smooth as a nut, sounded comparable to a well-oiled sewing machine and the iconic 'blatter blatter' sound of the exhaust was familiar and recognisable all over the continent.

Feliciano was helping Roly and Hedda load all their suitcases, cameras and supports, bird hides and picnic baskets into the tiny Mehari, leaving very little room for the three occupants. Feliciano being the tallest at six feet two inches would have to sit in the front with his knees almost up to his chin, with Roly driving and Hedda who was much smaller, in the back with some of the luggage beside her.

They set off for Oporto in high spirits down the Hill but when trying to get up the rise on the other side, Roly thought that the offer of Feliciano's police car might have been a better option but it was too late now to change horses in mid-stream!

All went well until half an hour later they found themselves in Gia on the EN 125 road which runs along the length of the Algarve.

'Dam and blast,' exploded Feliciano. 'In the excitement of packing the car I've left my mobile phone back at your house. Fernando will have my guts for garters if I don't have it, as he insisted that I keep in touch on our travels. We have no alternative but to go back for it.'

'That's no big deal,' said Hedda, 'leave me here to get some shopping in the local Mini Mercado and pick me up when you get back.'

Roly was not as compliant as Hedda and was very irritated but didn't say anything. The conversation returning to the Hill was somewhat stilted as Roly was dismayed that the journey to Oporto would be now be delayed by one and a half hours. This meant that they would miss dinner at the hotel which he had arranged.

When they arrived at Casa Crao, Roly entered the code into the newly installed burglar alarm system and the warning siren sounded until he switched it off. There was not a lot of sense in paying for this new Securitas alarm but the salesman was extremely slick in convincing Roly that it would probably deter further break ins; as it was connected by telephone directly to their office. If the alarm was triggered by an intruder, the security staff would be at the villa within twenty minutes. This is a bit of nonsense as the average time that burglars spend in the premises is four minutes.

The Motorola mobile phone was still plugged into the electric socket and charging to its full capacity of one and a half hours. Transportable phones were just in their infancy and were bulky and heavy. This model, the 4500X, physical size was a cross between a house brick and a car battery and weighed about the same, some seven and a half pounds, everything in a black colour. The handset was situated in top of the battery and clipped to it so acted as the carrying handle. The dial buttons were inset in white on the handset.

They made haste in returning to pick up Hedda and continued west down the EN 125. This single carriageway road had the reputation of being the most dangerous in the whole of Europe. Partly because it was extremely narrow and the drivers using it were the first generation of car owners after the revolution and drove like maniacs, overtaking two at a time on a right hand bend. Fatal accidents were the norm. When Katricia Hart asked her vicar, how she could pray effectively, he replied, 'Go and drive along the EN125!'

Roly had decided to use this road rather than the new motorway, for it wouldn't take any longer as the Mehari would only average fifty miles per hour due to its heavy load. The coast road to Oporto had beautiful sea views and plenty of small beach bars along the way for refreshment stops, which they would need regularly as the car was not the most comfortable vehicle for this long journey.

Feliciano although a keen bird watcher was finding the endless conversation about birds and the possible sighting of the Vulture was becoming somewhat tiresome and repetitive. So he decided to introduce another subject about the history of the Portuguese police force.

21

Gypsies Horse Fair Meet

The Portuguese Gipsies travel around in their gaily painted horse and carts, with many small children in and hanging all over the sides of the cart, usually laughing and playing around. The cart normally has another animal or two in tow to the rear, perhaps an Ass or a Donkey as a spare. The family dogs trot under the cart in its shadow to keep out of the hot sun. They build makeshift camps out of any material that will make a shelter, usually old scraps of canvass, polythene and tarpaulin held together with string, poles and ropes. Their clothes and washing is thrown over bushes and trees to dry in the sun.

The Gipsy women wear traditional black or coloured dresses down to the ankles. It appears that in the Gipsy culture, so folk law goes, anything below the female waist was deemed to be unclean and must be covered. How much of this has been determined by the men, we leave to conjecture. When Gipsy children are born, irrespective of what the child is named, the mother will whisper in the child's ear a secret name in addition to the given public name, only the child and mother will ever know the secret.

Once every year many of the gipsies and Romany people from around Europe and sometimes far beyond, travel to the Algarve for the regular Horse Fair which is held in the village of Estoi which is not far from Faro. This is the biggest event in the gypsy calendar, with thousands of people attending from their regional clans. The overt reason for the fair originally was to buy, sell and trade horses but over the years it has developed into much more of a market and jamboree where all sorts of goods, owned or stolen are traded. Many acres of fields are taken up to house the event and the local non gypsy community avoid the area of the meeting if possible. Not only were horses traded, there was trap racing, contests of strength and tug of war events, traditional guitar music and flamenco dancing, increasingly replaced by loud beat music etc. The roads are always jammed packed with horses and carts, people on foot and barefoot children swarming all over the place. It was a real celebration of joy and rejoicing.

Colloquially the event is known by the locals as the 'Thieves Market,' which is generally an unfair title as the vast majority of the attendees are law abiding folk. However as in most societies there is the criminal element, which is why the police and GNR are in heavy evidence. The Chief of Police for the local area was Jos'e Barros, a long serving policeman who knows the area and the gypsy philosophy very well, as he has attended the Meet for the last twenty years and has made a study of their culture.

Although Jos'e was a conscientious copper and had a good track record of apprehending the scumbags of society, his biggest downfall and weakness was that he was a sucker for the young girls and gypsy girls in particular. He was married with two children and had numerous affairs, some with gipsy girls, none of which lasted for long and he always returned to his wife.

It was just as well that Jos'e understood the gypsy cultures and traditions, as with all societies there is the good the bad and the ugly. There had always been minor problems with street begging, picking pockets, robbery of properties and law breaking of some sort. But he was most concerned that within the Meet every year there was a small band of cutthroats and odious soulless brutes that would stop at nothing if the price was right. Three individuals, one the self-appointed leader of the group, a powerfully built thug from Eastern Europe, Ivor Gonagetim had always been on the radar for torture, extortion and murder. Interpol was permanently on his tail, so was Jos'e but neither could ever find enough evidence to bang him up. The scroat was determined to rub out Barros as he hounded him mercilessly. If he could do the deed he would but only if it was the perfect murder and he would not get caught. He saw it as his mission in life that it would either be him or the inspector in the grave.

22

Rosa's Café

The whitewashed church of Nossa Senhora da Assuncao with its one bell tower, is far too large and grand for a tiny village. It dominates the centre of Querenca on top of a hill. Opposite the church was the pretty cobbled village square with many trees to give shade and seats dotted in the best cool places. Around the square are small villager's whitewashed houses with tiny shuttered windows to keep out the sun and keep the interior cool. There was one restaurant and Rosa's café situated in the square, which was the regular meeting place for the locals to chat and yarn away the hours; especially on Sundays after the Catholic Church service and this was Rosa's busiest day of the week.

This was why Fernando Martins chose Tuesday to meet the Prime Minister, as it was the quietest day of the week with most villagers out working. Rosa only had one regular customer every day, an old lonely widowed lady who called in regularly for a chat and some company. As the lady was quite deaf, and Rosa's hearing was not too good anyway, they shouted at each other rather than conversed, their voices echoing and ringing around the dark painted walls of the café.

'Goodness gracious me.' Rosa shouted to her guest.

'Look at those two old tramps heading towards us across the square; they resemble Don Quixote and Sancho Panza.'

She laughed out loud but was absolutely correct. One was tall, thin and gangly with a peaked cap, the other short and fat wearing a large straw hat, both shambling across to the café. Their faces were grubby and grimy underneath their beards, which looked quite unnaturally spiky and their Algarvian field clothing was tatty and torn in places. By the look of them they have visibly been working in the local forest.

The Prime Minister and Sr Coelho were not happy souls to be so dressed but thought the disguises were quite suitable and effective in the difficult situation they found themselves, as apparently the two women had no idea who they really were.

They sat outside in the hot sun and when Rosa came out for their order, they chose two white coffees and two very fattening sticky buns, the Portuguese favourite snack. While Rosa operated the steaming noisy Gaggia coffee machine, they chatted quietly about their horrendous trafficky journey from Lisbon. Also getting bogged down with the gypsies travelling to their annual bun fight and the extraordinary dreadful situation in which they had been trapped. They talked in hushed tones, as they didn't want anyone to hear their posh Lisbon accents, which were very different to the field Algarvian twang of the locals. Their coffee and snacks arrived and they ate in petulant silence,

The quiet of the village was soon shattered by the noisy 'potato, potato' exhaust throbs of an enormous Harley Davidson Electroglide motorcycle roaring around the square and stopping right outside the café. The bike looked quite menacing, matt black all over with chrome studs, leather trim and saddle bags. The rider was covered in black leather jacket and trousers with a large white motif of skull and crossbones on its back. He leaned the bike over and kicked the side stand to the left to support the machine.

Fernando Martins swaggered over to the two seated coffee drinkers and with an exaggerated bow showing mock deference to them said with a wide smile,

'Good morning gentlemen, so glad you could make it, did you have a good journey?'

They both glowered at the biker and said nothing. He sat down facing the two unfortunates and his face turned hard as steel as he said.

'Right you two slime balls hand over the safe deposit key and it had better be the correct one.'

With a face that showed no emotion, Rabbit put his hand in his inside pocket and left it there a bit too long for Fernando's liking, so he growled,

'It had better be the key your feeling for and not a weapon. Look over to the church.'

They both turned and saw two motorcycle cops hidden by the corner of the buttresses with rifles trained on the two of them, waiting for the signal from Fernando. In the noise of Fernando's motorcycle they had not noticed the two quieter motorbikes stop silently behind the building. Rabbit pulled out the key and reluctantly passed it to his nemesis. With exaggerated politeness Fernando said. 'Thank you.'

'I won't waste my time or yours and will come straight to the point. I want fifty per cent of all the bungs you have received from your corrupt dealings since you came into office. I want all the statements from your Switzerland bank account, not copies, the originals and I want my share transferred to my Swiss bank within twenty four hours from now.'

Rabbit gulped and exclaimed. 'That's impossible it can't be done in that time.'

Although he knew it could, he was playing for time.

'Yes it can,' sneered Fernando. 'But if you can't do it in the time I'll add five per cent per day, the choice is yours.'

The two looked helplessly at each other and Rabbit said weakly. 'Give us ten minutes.'

'Ok I'll go and talk to my friends over there.'

He walked purposefully across the square. Both were sweating cobs under their disguises. Rabbit said.

'I am not having this, lets agree to the terms and I'll find a villain who will take out a contract on him.'

Coelho was terrified but after seeing Rabbits rage in the office, knew that he was not joking. He spurted out,

'But that is murder, we could hang for this.'

'Tough,' said Rabbit, 'it's my call and that's the deal, like it or lump it.'

They called Martins back and said. 'Agreed.'

'So you saw sense then, well done.'

With some relief they thought that was the end of the deal and started to leave the café.

'One moment, I've only just scratched the surface of this little drama.'

Rabbit's heart missed a beat as he thought what the hell is coming now!

23

James Stays in Paradise

The T.A.P. Portuguese pilot was having trouble landing at Faro airport due to a nasty side wind and was struggling to keep the beast in line with the runway. As he cruised over the mudflats on the flight path and lowered the landing gear, he knew he loved flying the elderly Boeing 111, as it was a dream to fly; it is a pilot's plane. Not that the passengers though so as it does tend to buck and yaw a bit in strong winds. He glanced temporarily to the right of the cockpit at the shambolic group of buildings which laughingly called itself an airport and wondered when it would be built to international standards. He mused at the Portuguese slang for T.A.P. as they called it, 'Take Another Plane! He lowered the aircraft to about twenty feet from the runway checked and re checked that the aircraft was angled at three degrees, and then executed a text book three point landing.

James Richmond drew a sigh of relief as the air brakes threw him gently forwards into his seat belt. Although he had to make his living from travelling by air transport he disliked the process intensely. As the aircraft taxied to what James thought would be an air bridge to passport control, he busied himself packing up his mobile office; calculator, client lists, and his latest toy, a large Filofax with a tiny built in Japanese tape recorder which he used for recording his meetings with clients.

James thought air bridges were standard at all airports but never having flown into Faro before, he didn't realise that he would be bussed from the plane to the reception area in an overcrowded coach full of travellers strap hanging as one would on a tube train.

Boredom is the only word that describes the time it takes queuing through passport control and waiting for the bags to appear on the carousel and was so tiresome but because he travelled so much by air he was resigned to the process.

Black taxis with green rooftops were the standard livery for government licenced vehicles in Portugal and James opened the door of the first one in the lengthy queue outside the exit doors. The short dumpy driver loaded the luggage into the boot, slid into the driver's side and asked. 'Where to sir.' 'The Hotel Paradise please.'

'Crikey that's a very pricey place to stay!'

'Yes but luckily my fees are all on the house.' Said James.

'That must be one of the firsts I have heard about that hotel, rumour has it that the owner is as tight a ducks rear end and doesn't give anything away, a tight fisted old git by all accounts. You must be a big VIP.'

'Not really but I will be putting a substantial bit of business his way.'

The rest of the journey was travelled in silence.

Arriving at the opulent entrance of Hotel Paradise, James was surprised to see a uniformed Bellboy in a smart peaked cap and grey matching uniform waiting for him. Beside the Bell trolley was a stunning looking hostess. He tipped the driver and paid for the taxi. As the driver attempted to unload the luggage from the boot, immediately the Bell Boy snatched it from the driver's hands, loaded it onto his trolley and disappeared into reception.

'Hello my name is Dana, I will be your personal hostess for the duration of your stay and I am at your disposal twenty four hours a day. Anytime you need me just call my extension.' She cooed.

He felt uncomfortable and blushed at the twenty four hour statement. He had never seen such a beautiful girl anywhere in his travels. She was around five feet eight inches tall, slightly overweight, with an ample bosom which was only just holding in there due to the tight low cut dress which almost went down to her navel then flowed down to the floor. Her hair was long, straight, hung down to her shoulders, was jet black and her skin had an olive sheen. She might have had some mixed blood in the family tree. She had a classical oval face and almond eyes. She said to follow her as she wiggled and swayed to reception.

James was surprised to see her go behind the desk and started the booking in process. No receptionist in sight thought James; that is odd that a hostess would also double as receptionist.

'I am frightfully sorry Mr Richmond but I must have your passport for a while as we have to keep a copy in case the police need to know who is staying here.'

Without a though James passed it over. As she placed it into the photo copier her foot pressed a bell push on the floor which was connected directly to Van Glytch's office. As he heard the busser sound he knew that James had arrived. He dropped what he was doing and hurried to reception to greet his new visitor.

Hans strode into reception with his right arm extended to shake James by the hand. He could not believe the apparition he beheld. Van Glytch had a black eye; his left arm was bandaged to the elbow and had an enormous cut on his lip which was still weeping.

'What in heaven's name have you been up to?' exclaimed James with a surprised look on his face.

'You should have seen the other guy,' laughed Hans. 'I'll tell all over dinner tonight at eight thirty, not appropriate now.'

As he shook James hand it felt like a wet lettuce leaf, a real limp wrist, not the handshake an Australian macho man would expect. Blimey James thought to himself, he bats for the other side, a Gay, a left footer! But then he thought that is a bit uncharitable, it may be something to do with his injuries, so he thought he should give him the benefit of the doubt.

When all the registration procedures were complete, Hans said that Dana would take him to his room. They both walked to the lift and Dana pressed the button to the third, top floor. As the doors closed James attempted to make small talk, at which he was not very good.

'How long have you been working here Dana?'

'Ever since the hotel opened and I love the work, especially when I have to look after lovely men like you.'

James again got hot under the collar and blushed. He was getting increasingly uncomfortable with this lady.

They exited the lift, walked down the corridor and she unlocked the bedroom door to number three six nine and said quietly.

'Trois Soixante-Neuf,' and smiled a smoky smile as she passed her tongue around her lips. 'I do love Soixante-Neuf, it's my lucky number,' she murmured as she glided into the room.

The last comment was totally lost on James. She said again anything at all that is required, just to call her number. With that she turned, swept slowly out of the room and softly closed the door.

James stripped off all his clothes and wrapped one of the luxurious white towels around his waist then looked in the full length mirror and sighed. Not quite the Adonis that he was when he met Jenny. Now some two stone overweight and looking shattered as a result of the hectic jet setting working lifestyle, full of hotel and expense account living into which he had fallen.

It was difficult for him to show his blushes at Dana's comments as he had two days heavy growth of black beard on his face, which made him appear as Bluto from the Popeye comics. He stared again into the mirror and looked at his five foot ten tall frame. His square face which at one time was quite handsome now was going to seed. Also he looked at his paunchy stomach which seems to grow by the day and did not like what he saw. He sighed, walked to the gigantic bed, threw himself on top and thought about the last few days and knew why he was so exhausted.

He had flown from Melbourne to Heathrow, a twenty four hour flight. Heathrow to Valencia, had two very successful meetings. Then he travelled from Valencia to Madrid for another three fruitful meetings. Then from Madrid to Faro and on to this hotel. Within minutes he had dropped into a deep sleep.

He was awakened by a soft knock on the door which he opened to find Dana framed in the opening. Conscious that he was only wearing a towel around his waist, he closed the door quickly saying that he would get a wrap with which to cover himself. He opened the door again and without being asked she walked into the room and closed the door. She had changed into a dress similar to the one which she wore earlier but black silk all over and clearly for an evening event. She walked slowly towards him and accidently dropped her evening bag. As she bent down to pick it up, the right side of her dress slipped off her shoulder, revealing far too much of her. She didn't attempt to cover up! James disliked the way this was going and thought this was the moment when he was going to be compromised.

24

Antonio's Bar

Antonio's beach bar was situated on a white sandy beach in a small cove half way between Faro and Oporto on the west coast road. The bay was small and the water calm as a mill pond with a dozen or so little fishing boats at anchor after a nights fishing. There were a few ramshackle fishermen's sheds nestling in the dunes just back from the water.

The weather was perfect, with the hot sun baking the sand to a comfortable ninety degrees, just right for sunbathing. Antonio didn't have many customers, so was reclining in a chair propped up on two legs against the wall on the shady stoop in front of the bar. He wore an old straw hat covering the front of his head and shading his eyes.

He heard the 'blatter blatter' of a Citroen 2 CV pulling into his sandy car park and looked out of one eye to see if the customers were stopping, as some motorists just paused for a picnic. The Mehari rolled to a halt, gave a cough and ran on a bit after the engine was switched off. The three occupants almost fell out of the doors all being stiff and sweating.

'I can't wait to get a couple of beers down.' Said Roly, still wishing they had driven in the air conditioned police car. They all sprawled out on the sand and Roly went up to the counter to order.

Feliciano lay on the sand, stripped off his shirt and enjoyed the moment. Hedda was watching him from a distance and was impressed with his young lithe physique, not too muscly, well-tanned but clearly could look after himself in a brawl. His face was well structured with a lantern jaw, aquiline nose, large blue eyes and short dark hair with curls which framed his face. Together with his six feet two height made him look quite a dish. As he wore long trousers, she wondered what the lower half looked like, whatever she thought; he looked a lovely bit of eye candy. She let her gaze wander about him for a while and realised that she shouldn't be thinking those things about him at her age. She was old enough to be his grandmother!

Roly pitched up with three litres of local beer and they downed them all in one gulp. They chatted amiably for a while, then dropped off one by one and dozed for a while as they enjoyed the rest, the sound of the sea lapping onto the sandy shore, the warmth, the beer and the quiet of the beautiful peaceful location. Feliciano was daydreaming about how to introduce the subject of the history of the police force, rather than more discussion about bird watching. As he woke up he decided to take the bull by the horns and just start the conversation without any overture.

'You know the current organisation of the police structures have not always been headed by one man as Fernando Martins does at present.' He started to explain.

The other two had no idea where this subject came from but were interested to listen.

'Oh no, some time ago the country was split into north and south. José Barros was in charge of the south and Martins covered the north. Jos'e interests were in violence, prostitution, gypsy culture, their petty thieving and drug smuggling. The five he found from experience were inextricably linked. Most of the other specialisms he delegated to other officers, he was not so much interested in traffic, burglary, and street crime etc. He was an extremely successful policeman and all his team respected him for his leadership and clean up rate.' Feliciano continued.

'His biggest and only real problem was that he was over sexed and couldn't keep his manhood in his trousers. He always had a keen interest in younger girls and gypsy females in particular; which is probably why he had a keen hobby in mixing with the gypsy fraternity. He had many mucky liaisons and was well known for seducing girls, mostly against their will but he was a smooth operator, he would win them over in the end and when he had his wicked way would drop them like a hot potato. Because of this compulsive pastime, his nickname around the area was Gollum, from the Lord of the Rings trilogy. Gollum was a nasty slippery customer who was only interested in himself and would lie and cheat to get his own way at everyone else's expense.'

'He always kept a keen eye on the annual gipsies Horse Fair which congregated at Estoi and would often be seen either in uniform or disguise, mingling with the crowds. It was at one such annual Meet he met and fell head over heels in love with a stunning girl called Floralegs Pinto, so called because by reputation she 'spreads easily.' This was the nickname she had been called by the clan, which really was unwarranted but she had been maligned by an ex-lover who spread the rumour and the name stuck. One could understand him falling for her. She was a raving beauty, around twenty years old, well filled all over, dusky skinned with a gorgeous face, albeit slightly ratty looking as some of her kinfolk were, and stunning long black hair. They had a torrid sexual relationship which lasted months longer than most of his liaisons and eventually they decided to elope. The rumour was they fled away with the gypsies to God knows where and were never seen again.'

Feliciano sauntered over to Antonio and paid for the beers as the threesome wearily returned to the car to continue the journey to Oporto. Feliciano watched Hedda as she walked to the car and thought what a well preserved lady she was for her age. She was statuesque, medium height, lovely rounded peaceful face with blond, slightly greying hair down to her waist and it was fashioned into two long plats which were looped into a bun and tied on top of her head. He thought what a delightful mum she was and a wonderful wife for Roly.

They all shoehorned themselves into the car and he suggested that Hedda should sit in the front to make her more comfortable but she would have none of it.

'No.' she said. 'Your legs are longer than mine so I will be fine in the back.'

When everyone was comfortably seated and they were on their way and drove off, he decided to finish the conversation about Fernando and the police structures. He continued with some distain about the subject.

'Fernando Martins on the other hand was a very different character to Jos'e. He was much more interested in promoting himself and his image rather than dealing with crime. He was selfish, brutal, and harsh with his team and would stop at nothing to climb to the top of the tree regardless of who got in the way. There were rumours abounding that he was taking bribes and creaming money off the top of any fines paid for misdemeanours and seemed to have some kind of hold over Prime Minister Rabbit. But he was so smart and slick that nothing could be proven against him. Having said that, although he disliked Jos'e with a passion and he was blocking the promotion he so desperately wanted. He worked well him and cooperated in joint operations especially with drugs and roadside fines for motorists and commercial vehicles, which were furiously resisted by the motoring community.'

'Because Jos'e Barros had been missing for over six months, my uncle the Minister for Justice decided that he would probably never be found he would have to replace him. He thought that the whole of Portugal could be administered by one senior inspector instead of two so he promoted Fernando Martins to the post. Much to a lot of people's dismay.'

25

Three More Dead Bodies

Vespa support stands were never the strongest in the world but Caroline heaved the red (she liked red as it didn't show the rust) scooter up onto the flagstones outside the shop, hoping that it would hold and yet again it did. She pushed open the door of Musical Madness, passed the 'Get of my Cloud' jingle and called out.

'Where are you Papa?'

'I'm out the back and coming through.' Shack walked quickly into the shop area with a broad grin on his face, which was nice to see, as he had a mouthful of beautiful even white teeth and at the moment he looked like the Cheshire cat! Caroline thought thank goodness he is feeling better today with no thoughts of the Blue Cornflower.

'What are you looking so pleased about Pops?' Said Caroline lightly.

'Yesterday I sold two Yamaha Keyboards, one Premier drum set and you remember that expensive used Gretch electric/acoustic antique guitar which was hanging on the wall and we had it for years. Well, Lank Marvel from the 'Followers' band came on his way to the Algarve and as soon as he saw it, paid the asking price in cash! This means we will be able to put food on the table for six months. How good is that?'

Caroline was overjoyed to see dad in such fine form.

'That really is good news dad and just as well about the food because I have bought you some new kitchen equipment to replace the old tosh I was using the other day. A complete set of cutlery, a frying pan, two saucepans and a super carving knife that resembled a dagger but it is very sharp, so be careful with it.'

'That might come in very useful, as I could kill those blasted police chiefs who started the new roadside vehicle checks!' He said seriously with real venom in his voice.

'I've been stopped five times this week for document and safety checks and I'm getting really brassed off with it. I think that they only stop me because the van has Musical Madness painted on the side; I think they believe I really am mad! So the dagger may come in useful; I am serious!'

'Don't be so daft dad.' Caroline said with some concern in her voice, as she knew that Shak could be paranoid about some matters.

'Oh Flopsie I'm so sorry that in my fit of anger I forgot to thank you for the lovely thought you had in replacing the kitchen equipment. You are always so considerate and thinking of my needs rather than your own, so thank you.'

With that he hugged her and kissed her on the cheeks and felt ashamed at his insensitivity. Changing the subject and the embarrassing praise as quickly as she could she said.

'I heard from Jenny in Australia yesterday and she said that James was in Portugal in the Algarve at present on business and would we have time to see him?'

'That's nice, how's she doing, I haven't heard from her for some time and she normally phones me every week.'

'She said she was sorry she hasn't been in touch but she has been snowed under with work as James has been away for so long but she will call later in the week.'

Shak thought for a bit and suggested that he would wait until she called next time but didn't think they could meet as it was too far to travel and at the moment could not leave the shop for such a long period.

Caroline went quiet and serious for a bit and muttered thoughtfully.

'I am really worried about the amount of dead bodies I have to deal with at present. We have had three more this week and although I haven't had time to analyse them all in depth, they all seem drug related and the narcotics situation seems to be on the increase. All the information from my police contacts suggest that the heroin is being landed somewhere in the Algarve. I wonder if James has any knowledge of what's going on but then I can't think of any reason why he should. Perhaps he has said something to Jenny.'

She was thinking and mumbling aloud rather than talking to Shak.

26

Murder Plotted

'Fernando! How ya doing me Old Dutch?' Rosa called out to Fernando from the bar counter, using her best artificial Bronx accent. That was the only bit of Cockney rhyming slang she knew and had picked it up from some London customers.

'I didn't recognise you with the new Skull and Crossbones on your back.'

'I am in fine fettle Rosa and it is nice to see you again, without all the biker boys surrounding the square.'

Fernando was a member of the Faro Bikers Club and they used Rosas as a regular coffee stop. She strolled over to the three of them seated by the round table under the sun shade.

'What are you doing socialising with these old peasants, not normally your type of company?'

Hearing them being addressed as old peasants the two of them had faces like slapped arses!

'I'm not socialising Rosa, I am negotiating to fix up a contract with them to tend my garden at home,' he lied.

'I hope they are better at gardening than they are at Tilting Windmills!'

She thought this was a hilarious joke as she waddled back to the bar chortling away. The joke was lost on Fernando.

'Three white coffees on the house Fernando?' she called out.

'That is very kind of you Rosa.'

She then yet again grappled with the Gaggia coffee machine still laughing at the windmill joke.

Fernando had the face of a stone cold killer as he phrased his next question.

'I'm not spending too much time on this subject.' He said playing hardball.

'I suggest that you think very carefully before you answer this demand and remember that I have spies everywhere. What was it that Hans van Glytch whispered in your ear at the Hotel Paradise opening?'

The two politicians looked blank, were amazed and staggered at his knowledge of everything they did and were silent for a few minutes. Fernando kept his cool as an experienced negotiator; he would never break the silence after asking an open ended question. He would wait for their reply no matter how long the silence lasted.

The Prime Minister thought for a long time before he answered, then replied calmly.

'He said that the next shipment of heroin had just been delivered and my twenty five per cent will be transferred to my Swiss account the following day, provided I keep my mouth shut.'

Hearing the alarming news, which he thought was stupid in the extreme, Sr Coelho collapsed forwards with his head hitting the table, his straw hat fell onto the floor and he went into a dead faint! He couldn't believe that Rabbit has spilled the beans so quickly without a thought or in consultation with him.

Fernando couldn't believe his luck with such an open and early confession. He thought he would have to use thumb screws at least but then thought that Rabbit must have a plan, he couldn't be that reckless. He let the thought linger for a while then filed it in his memory banks for a later date.

'Then make sure that I get my fifty per cent as usual, paid into my Swiss account.'

'Agreed.' Said Rabbit.

Fernando was more than pleased with the outcome of his visit to Querenca and decided to finish the meeting immediately.

'Right you two,' he said ignoring the fact the Coelho was still out cold. 'You make sure that you keep your side of our agreement or you might find yourselves banged up for longer that you would ever believe.'

He immediately rose from the table and signalled to his two officers to holster their rifles. He mounted his Harley with a swing of his leg over the saddle, gunned the engine and with a roar, left the square with a cloud of Redex smoke belching from the twin exhausts, followed by his officers close behind.

Rabbit went to the bar, asked Rosa for a bucket of cold water which he threw over Coelho. He woke with a start and looking blearily at Rabbit said.

'What the hell did you do that for?'

'Do what?'

'Giving him all the information about the heroin?'

'Listen here you dozy little twat, what good is the news about the drugs if we are having him whacked, he can't use it if he's dead can he?'

'Don't you include me in your murderous plan; I'm having none of it!'

Rabbit was furious with the accountant.

'Look here you poxy little bean counter!' He shouted at him. 'You are in this up to your neck and you can't get out of it, you're in too deep.'

Coelho was insulted and rattled. 'Don't you keep calling me little, I can't help my size, and I was born tiny!'

'Yes you were but you weren't born stupid, now listen to the plan.'

Rabbit sat him up on his chair, replaced his straw hat, slapped him around the face, and proceeded to outline their next move.

'We are going straight away to the Horse Fair in Estoi and we will find the scumbag who will do the deed and remember that with Martins out of the way we will be fireproof. So get into the car, do exactly as you are told and follow my lead.'

The roads around the fair were packed with horses, carts, old Transit vans and gypsies wandering all over the place, so they had to park some mile away and walk to the entrance. Coelho took a haversack out of the boot as they started their trek to the Meet. They searched for a while for someone who might know who was the boss of the fair and selected a gypsy who would possibly identify the head man.

'My man, tell me who is the Gypsy King or Chief around here?' Said Rabbit with an air of authority.

'Who wants to know?' He said chewing a matchstick.

Forgetting he was in disguise Rabbit exclaimed, 'The Prime Minister of Portugal, that's who.'

'Oh yeah of course you are, and I am Marylyn Munro, so sod off and don't waste my time.'

Rabbit pulled out a large wedge of Escudo bills and said.

'Would this help you to find him?'

The gypsy's eyes came out like organ stops and gulped.

'Certainly sir, I didn't know you were in disguise, I'll take you to him immediately.'

They trouped around the grounds for what seemed like forever until they came to a traditional gypsy red painted caravan standing on four yellow steel rimmed wooden wheels. There was a flagpole and gypsy flag showing the green and blue motif with the red sixteen spoked Chagra Clan crest fluttering in the warm breeze.

'This is where the King normally lives, so do I get the money now?'

'No you don't, if we have a deal with the King, he will cut you in if he thinks it is appropriate but thank you for showing us the way.'

The man complained bitterly as he walked away suggesting in a loud voice that Rabbits parents weren't married!

Rabbit knocked on the cracked green wooden door of the caravan which was reached by walking up three wooden rotting steps and a loud voice shouted from within.

'Bugger off I'm having a rest.'

'I've need of your help for which I will pay you handsomely.' Rabbit called back.

'How much?' Came the reply.

'More money than you have ever seen in your life. I am the Prime Minister of Portugal and have to be in disguise for security reasons.' Shouted Rabbit.

There was a silence followed by a shuffling gait and furniture moving. The door creaked open as it scraped on the uneven floor and the vision of the King was frightening. He must have been six foot nine inches tall, built like a small building, wild red hair down to his shoulders with his face covered in scars. He was stripped to the waist wearing only torn trousers and no shoes and he was a bit smelly. His voice sounded similar to a bag of bricks being dragged across a cobbled street.

'Show me the colour of yer money before we go any further.'

Rabbit pulled out the wedge of notes and the King made a grab for it but Rabbit was too quick for him, he tossed it to Coelho who caught it deftly. He should have played for England's cricket team!

'What do I need to do for the money?' he grumbled.

Rabbit said they couldn't talk in the open and would have to go inside the caravan to discuss the matter further. Reluctantly the King motioned them inside. Coelho was trembling at the sight of the hulk. He really was a wimp unless he was using a spread sheet. They both walked inside of the rather stinking abode and all three sat down on the untidy hard bed. He said sternly,

'We need a contract taken out on a certain police inspector and we understand there may be a villain in your Meet who would do the job for a substantial sum. You would of course be paid a significant finder's fee.'

'How much?' Said the hulk.

'That would depend on the fee for the job but you would receive ten per cent.'

108

'Twenty.'

'Agreed.' Said Rabbit.

'You need to talk to Ivor Gonagetim, he's the man for the job and I'll take you to him.'

The three of them trudged around the Meet and every gypsy they past, deferred to the King making creeping comments in subdued voices. The must have walked for some twenty minutes before they reached a rusty decrepit old Ford Transit van which was the home of Gonagetim. The King said.

'I can tell from both your body language that you find me a bit frightening. I can understand why, as most of my clan feel the same way and that is how I keep control of them. But if you think I am a terror, wait until you see Ivor; he is far worse than me, he kills for pleasure and a psychopath to boot.'

The Prime Ministers throat felt similar to a piece of coarse sandpaper and Coelho shook like a jelly on a plate at the thought of meeting the Eastern European thug.

27

The Menorca Auction

'Mary the Virgin' was an unusual name for a boat, especially as it was painted in gold lettering on the bow and stern but with the twins Catholic upbringing they thought it was most appropriate. The Spanish lads had made such a good job of spring cleaning the old tub. It was looking the best it had in years, specifically as they had spent a lot of time polishing its name. The whole vessel had never looked so sparkling.

The twins were delighted with the enormous effort and hard work the lads had put into the clean-up of the old girl, that they not only paid the sum agreed, they gave a small bonus.

The boys were overjoyed with the money they earned and went straight back to the bar to savour the fruits of their labour, determined not to spend it all on drink but to keep the bulk of it until their next social security payment.

Paddy and Mick now had to find the Police Auction rooms which, as a local had told them was not too far from the marina where the boat was berthed. It was a beautiful sunny day in Menorca with a warm breeze keeping the temperature to a comfortable eighty six degrees. The boys were in great spirits as they walked to the site with a spring in their step, the hot sun on their faces and keen to bid for anything that would help them complete their Red Coral dive.

The auction rooms were in fact an old disused concrete warehouse and the Police had used it for many years promoting the sales of goods which they had retrieved from robberies and villains. Most of the loot was small enough to be carried away by the robbers but some were larger items; because as the sale rooms became more popular, locals would bring their unwanted household effects to be sold, hoping to make a few bob on the side. The non-profitmaking proceeds were put towards a charity for underprivileged children.

The day was disappointing for the organisers as there were not many punters bidding. Probably because it was such a nice day, they would undoubtedly be out on the beach or out in the sea, sailing and enjoying the sunshine. This pleased the twins no end, as there would be less competition for the goods they were seeking. They bid for a few housekeeping items for the boat, especially those articles which had been smashed in the storm and these they picked up for next to nothing.

What they really were desperate for was the diving equipment that they needed to replace and augment their existing kit. Luckily there was no one interested in the three complete sets of diving tackle, consisting of air tanks, weight belts, octopus air hoses, BCDs (buoyancy control device waistcoats) fins and masks. They weren't in top condition and some bits needed some repair work. The tanks were a bit rusty, the BCDs frayed and the weight belts were not complete but they got them all for a song so were best pleased.

They returned to the boat, loaded all the gear and made ready for the final part of their journey to the seas around the east of Italy, near Sardinia, Corsica and the island of Capri. They were not quite sure if they would dive on the Tyrrhenian or Ligurian sea within the Mediterranean but that decision could wait until they were nearer the islands.

Whilst they were in Ireland they had been told of the best dive sites in the area so were well versed in where to find the Red Coral.

The sailing time they estimated would take about a day and a half, if the seas were kind to them, longer if not. The best information they could gain from the weather forecast on the radio, was that all would be plain sailing with only a slight swell. They released the mooring ropes, started the old diesel engine and sailed out of the harbour into the wild blue yonder singing 'The Wild Colonial Boy' raucously at the top of their voices with a lovely Irish lilt as they sailed along.

28

Dinner Revelations

Dana re-adjusted her neckline, pulling the shoulder strap back into position in order to not show so much flesh, opened her handbag and produced James's passport.

'I came by to return your documents, as so many people leave them behind when they go home. Would you want me to run your bath now, as dinner is at eight thirty?'

'NO! I mean no thank you, I can manage that myself.'

James realised he had been too curt to her and regretted his tone and aggressive attitude but wished she would go and leave him alone.

'Very well then I will see you at eight thirty sharp, don't be late as Mr van Glytch is a stickler for time keeping.'

She smiled sweetly as she turned to exit the room, so disappointed that she could not get any further in trying to get him into an embrace. The door closed gently, James took a deep breath and a sigh of relief that he didn't have to give in to her obvious charms and overtures.

He ran his bath and allowed the hot water to permeate his tired bones and aching body. In minutes he was asleep again. Fifteen minutes later something woke him with a start, he dried himself, shaved the dark beard stubble, cleaned his teeth and rapidly dressed for dinner. He wore a rather creased white shirt with a too brightly coloured loud tie, a boring dark suit and the wrong colour shoes needed to match his outfit, as he packed the incorrect ones when he left home. He looked in the full length mirror situated by the door and thought that he looked adequate but then Australians have never been known for their sartorial elegance. If Jenny had seen him she would have said that he looked a mess!

As he went to leave the room he thought he should take a moment to admire the bedroom which he had not had occasion to so do in the rush and panic to get ready in time.

It was large enough for a small family in which to live. The floor was Italian marble and a nice touch thought James, was an enormous Arabian Rug covering most of the floor which silenced the noise of ones shoes on the floor. The four poster bed was gigantic and the whole room was fashioned in ultra-contemporary style, with Picasso and Cubist pictures on the walls. The whole room was outrageously opulent with no expense spared.

The exterior wall was framed by a large plate glass window overlooking the Rio Formosa. As the weak sun started to set across the sandy beaches, the panorama was stunning with the best multi-coloured sunset James had ever experienced in all his travels.

He looked at his watch and the time was twenty five minutes past eight. Just right James thought to himself as he picked up his Filofax, his pen and opened the door to take the lift to reception.

Van Glytch met Dana in reception and walked with her arm in arm towards the two Star Michelin restaurant. Under his other arm was a foolscap pad and pen for making notes during dinner.

'How are you getting on with Mr Richmond Dana?'

'Not as well as you would have wished Hans. I've tried everything in the book to get him into bed but to no avail. I think he is either a very cold fish, homosexual, knackered or extremely happily married. Apart from throwing him on the bed and smothering him with passion I am at a lost as to what to do next.'

'That is a shame Dana, as you know I do want to have something dirty on people in case I need it in future negotiations and for blackmail. Do your best and keep trying. Are the motion cameras up and running in his bedroom?'

'Yes I checked them myself before he occupied the room and they are set to motion start.'

'Well done Dana, I always knew I could rely on you. Now go and meet Mr Richmond at the lift.'

He continued through reception past the tinkling fountain until he reached the dining room. Hans had selected the best table in the hotel within an enormous glass pod hanging outside of the hotel showing the stunning views over the beaches and seas. He checked the table to ensure it was only laid for two, that the napery was spotless and in the correct position. Cut glass crystal was perfectly set for all the most expensive wines and there were Orchids in a vase on the centre of the table. Everything was faultless.

James pressed the reception button of the lift and he was not surprised to see Dana looking gorgeous waiting for him at the ground floor.

'Your table is ready for you Mr Richmond and Mr Glytch is waiting for you.'

'Thank you Dana, will you please show me the way.'

They walked together to the restaurant without speaking. James was still nervous having Dana so close to him. To his surprise most of the tables were taken, the diners looked very smart and up market and made him feel a bit Antipodean and colonial in his mish-mash of clothing.

117

He thought that earlier he heard a helicopter landing on the roof, so he shouldn't have been too surprised at the elegance of some of the people.

Hans was standing waiting at the table with his hand outstretched ready for a handshake. James thought it had better be firmer than the last one but is was not. Still limp wristed.

'Good evening James. I hope you don't mind first names for this informal evening do you?'

'No that's quite ok with me Hans.'

They both sat down and James admired the sumptuousness of the table and the sensational view from the glass pod in which they were seated. James opened his Filofax and the tape recorder automatically started to silently whir.

'I hope you don't mind if I make a few notes about the conference facilities Hans?'

'Not at all old chap, very professional, I wouldn't expect anything else. I'll also note the main points of our chat.'

'Now James, everything tonight is on the 'Paradise' so don't be shy with your menu ordering.'

'Thank you Hans, I am most impressed and honoured. Who will be waiting on us tonight?'

'Dana of course, as you know she is all yours for the length of your stay and nothing is too good for you.'

James inwardly groaned. He was increasingly concerned about the two of them and would have to be on his guard all evening. Dana brought the two menus and as she passed one to James, she bent forward and her Charlie's almost flopped out! James was again embarrassed and looked away. They both studied the food on offer and

James chose the flambéed lobster to start and the Chateaubriand for the main course.

'Excellent choice James my favourite, I will have the same Dana. Bring a bottle of Krug for the starter also. Oh and Dana, bring a bottle of our best Chateau Neuf du Pape for the main course and a bottle of water with gas also.'

'Certainly Mr Glytch, do you want wine in the bottle or de canted?' Dana wrote down the order.

'De canted in the best crystal carafe please Dana.'

'Now James I must tell you why I am looking such a mess. I was coming out of 'The Korpus Gentleman's Club' in Vilamoura at three o'clock in the morning; a bit of a seedy place but the girls are very accommodating, especially me being a short arse. I know that with my strange looks people call me a freak and I am the butt of all their jokes but I have got used to this over the years. 'Bear' the captain of my boat, my minder and chauffer, had gone to pick up the Bentley from the car park whilst I waited at the doorway.'

'All of a sudden two thugs appeared from out of the gloom and started to knock seven bells out of me. They stole my Rolex, the gold chain from around my neck my heavy gold wrist bracelet and my wallet which was stacked with money. All the time they were beating me they kept shouting about their grass or my grass or something about lawns. Now I know that my English is not very good but I have deliberately not planted grass around the hotel, as the sun being too hot it soon goes brown; so I had no idea what they were raving about. Bear brought the car round and seeing the mêlée leaped out of the car door and being an ex-cage fighter knocked the stuffing out of the two guys and they scarpered.'

James was even more concerned about Hans's business dealings, interjected saying. 'Hans, I think they were talking about 'Turf' not grass.'

'What's the difference, grass, lawns or turf; it just didn't make any sense.'

James decided it was prudent not too offer any more explanations about the Turf subject, so he keep quiet.

'So that explains why I am bandaged up around my arm, have a black eye and a thick lip.'

Whilst they were talking, Dana appeared silently at the table with the lobster starter, the Krug and the water, served it all beautifully and without a word left the restaurant.

The lobster was superb; Hans poured the Krug into two glasses and handed one to James. He was concerned not to have too much wine as he needed to deep a cool head for any negotiations which might follow. Hans on the other hand was determined to enjoy the wine and by the end of the first course had finished off the entire bottle, eyes going glassy by the minute. James stuck to his one glass then kept to the water and wondered and worried how Hans would fare with the main course and the Chateau Neuf du Pape. The tape continued to record everything.

29

Inside Waterfalls

Waterfalls are not commonplace in the Algarve, apart from the natural and popular 'Inferno' just outside Estoi. So to find one some thirty five feet high, surrounded by plate glass, inside a building, falling through three floors in an office in Faro, was a bit of a surprise and shock to visitors and clients. It was built by one of the owners of the law practice called 'Ilda and Ilda' just off a narrow street near the Faro Marina. Mrs Ilda was a very shrewd and well-connected Legal Eagle lawyer and had worked the Court system for decades. She was well respected, ferocious and feared by the opposition lawyers in the courtroom. Her husband Mr Ilda was a well renowned, honest and competent builder, commonly called 'Ilda the Builder' and he had created the waterfall as an unusual feature and talking point in the three roomed office.

They had worked in the legal profession and building trade for some forty years. Both had died from natural causes at a relatively young age and had left the whole business to their one and only qualified partner called Fay Raposeiras-Fox; (Raposeiras in Portuguese means Fox, so her nick name had always been Foxy) an un-married English lady who had worked in the firm for some twenty five years. She qualified as a QC after leaving university with a law degree and moved home to Portugal for a more relaxed and less pressured life in a sunny climate.

For legal issues she had an encyclopaedic memory and could recall any case on which she had ever worked and had a mind better than a filing cabinet. However, her short term personal memory was very cloudy and could rarely recall what she had for breakfast yesterday!

One of her regular clients was Katricia Hart whom she had come to know and respect for many years in her dealings with local prisoners, who Katricia had helped in her capacity as prison visitor. She had recently asked Foxy to help with two villains who were unjustly accused of a crime of which Kat believed they didn't commit. But they all say that don't they!

Foxy was an outstandingly attractive lady in her mid-fifties, but looked twenty years younger, with an unusually trim figure for her age. Five foot eight tall with long dark brown hair tied in a pleat at the back of her head and an elfin face, by now having spent so much time in the sun was well tanned. So stunning was she that she still would get wolf whistles from the guys working on building sites, which of course she ignored but with which she was secretly pleased and impressed.

There was a joke being told around the Faro coffee shops and the chattering classes. 'What is the connection between the Queen, Maggie Thatcher and Foxy,' a silence while the answer is sort. — None of them are ever seen without their handbags!

Foxy was never without her handbag, the only time it was not on her arm was when she was in Court. Many people have small fetishes or nervous afflictions, like twitching of the eyebrows, nodding of the head or constant tapping of the feet whilst sitting.

Fox's affliction was touching and rubbing a plastic bag inside her handbag whenever she was feeling nervous or uncomfortable, which she never did in her professional capacity. It was comparable to a having a child's comforter.

She was rarely conscious of the habit and could not think how, when or where it started.

30

Ivan Gonagetim

There was a patch of tall green grass outside of Ivor's Transit van at the Meet. He was lying on it outstretched with his arms above his shoulders and his hands cradling his head, enjoying the hot sun tanning his body, wearing only a pair of grubby underpants.

The King and the other two walked up to him and the King announced their arrival with a booming voice,

'I have some customers here who have need of your services Ivan.'

Ivan didn't appear to hear and continued to lay in silence. He always was a man of few words and when he did speak it was more like an inarticulate grunt. All of a sudden he leapt from lying on the grass to standing upright in one bound. The King had seen him make this move many times and could never understand how it was done but then Ivor was a man mountain and worked out every day to keep fit.

Rabbit and Coelho looked at this apparition and they were terrified. He looked more animal than man, six feet tall, solid muscle, gristle from his neck to his toes and covered in dark black hair all over his body. The guy had the ugliest pox marked face with a broken nose that they had ever seen; with a mouth full of decaying black and grey teeth. He was clearly a cold blooded killer and reminded them of a Gorilla.

He grabbed hold of Coelho by the lapels, lifted him up in the air with one hand and threw him onto the ground. Coelho was winded and thought it would be best to stay where he was in case he got another beating.

'What did you do that for?' Rabbit said with some trepidation.

'Cos I can!' Came the reply. 'Now whadaya want done?'

'We need you to take a contract out on the Chief Inspector of Police.' Rabbit replied with some anger in is voice at the way he had treated Coelho and thought what a nasty bastard they were using to do the deed.

'I've already got one pig to silence, I spose another won't make any difference, how much?'

'Name your price for a quick kill.'

'Fourteen million escudos, (about 1,000.000 Pounds), fifty per cent now and the rest when the jobs done.'

Rabbit very coolly said. 'Agreed, providing you pay the King his cut.' 'Done.' Growled the Gorilla.

'Coelho, get up from the ground and give him the money from the haversack.'

The Finance Minister reluctantly struggled to get to his feet, opened the sealed pack of notes, counted out the fifty per cent and gave it to the animal. He thought it was way over the top to pay so much but thought it better to tackle Rabbit about it later. They left the King and Ivor to split the spoils and arrange the kill.

As they ambled away, Coelho said to Rabbit that he thought the price was too high and that they should have negotiated a lower sum. He thought that half that amount would be more than enough to pay. Typical tight arsed accountant!

'Don't be such a dope; you really are as much use as a fart in a bottle! The price is a drop in the ocean to us and don't forget that we will save the fifty per cent we would have had to pay to Martins, so it's cheap at the price. I told you it would be simple. Now let's vamoose out of here pronto, get these ridiculous disguises off and get back to Lisbon.'

31

The Dive Site

Chrystal clear waters of the Tyrrhenian Sea are ideal for diving for the coral. The twins didn't consciously sail to these seas but arrived rather by accident, as they weren't very good at navigating.

They stopped the tired old engine and threw the Force Four Sea Anchor overboard, together with the heavily weighted salvage net, which snaked its way to the sea bed. They then with great excitement meticulously prepared the diving equipment.

Having donned all the air tanks, BCD, weight belts, octopus air hoses etc. they checked each other's gear to ensure there were no errors. Diving is about life and death situations, so careful preparations were essential.

'Now Paddy, do remember dat dare may be sharks down dare, so if we see dem, sink slowly to bottom and stay still until dey go away. Do also stay clear of de Fire Coral, you remember de last time you got stung by it, you suffered from skin irritation for two years.'

'Oh shut up you bloody old woman, I'm not stupid you know, I do know my diving rules.'

'Your stupidness is a matter of opinion Paddy you old fart!'

They were both laughing at their regular banter, as they always joshed about when preparing for a dive, which was mostly brought about by nervousness and the dangers of the deep.

They spat into their masks and smeared the spit around the glass to prevent fogging up, moved to the edge of the boat and both took a giants stride into the water. They sank to the bottom of the sandy sea bed slowly, equalising the pressures by holding their noses and clearing their ears as they descended.

The whole area was a magical place covered with acres of multi-coloured coral; all species of animals, kelp forests and dazzling tropical fish. Micks favourite being the thin flat pointed nosed Yellow Tang.

After searching around for some minutes, they found the target of their long journey, fields and fields of Red Coral! They gathered armfuls of their prize and swam backwards and forwards to the salvage net until it was full.

They kept checking their diving wrist watches and depth gauges, as at one hundred and sixty five feet depth their air wouldn't last long. Their deep sea watches buzzed to indicate that their tanks would be running out of air soon. They signalled to each other that time was up and started to slowly surface; stopping at twenty feet from the bottom of the boat, where they would hover for fifteen minutes in order to equalise pressures to avoid the bends.

After removing their fins, they climbed the stainless steel steps which led up to the deck of the boat, climbed out of their diving gear, and with a cowboy whoop yelled Yeeehar! They danced together around the boat celebrating their success. Then running over to the salvage net rope, hauled their prize up from the deep, over the side of the boat and onto the deck. There were sacks full of the money making gem material. They bagged up their booty into the sacks, raced to the sea anchor, raised it with gusto and then over to the wheelhouse pressing the start button. The engine burst into life, to start their journey to Morocco to sell their wares; then via The Mediterranean on to Portugal.

32

The Gangster Revealed

Dana appeared with a trolley with the steak main course and all the trimmings, which she served very professionally. James was relieved to find that nothing fell out his time! She poured the drink for both of them then asked.

'Will there be anything else gentlemen?' 'No thank you Dana,' they both replied in unison.

Hans downed the first glass of wine in one gulp, then he poured another and that also didn't touch the sides! James could see clearly that it would not be long before Hans was drunk; his speech was already slurring.

James was interested to know how Hans had amassed his fortune, so without thinking too much about it and quite pointedly asked how it all happened. Which he later thought was a bit personal and rude but the question was put and from which there was no retreating.

'It's a long story James but I'll keep it as short as possible or we might be here all night. My mother was a prostitute in Amsterdam and who my father was I have no idea but seeing my diminutive size he was probably a Dwarf! As a growing child I was left to my own devices and spent most of my formative years ducking and diving on the streets. I didn't have much of an education as you did. The only qualification I have is an Honorary Degree from the University of Hard Knocks! Most kids of my background would have had to survive with their fists, natural aggression and criminal connections but due to my size I had to live on my wits and cunning. I made a reasonable living by picking pockets, a little thieving and buying and selling what I could.'

'Eventually I made enough money, rented a night club and hired some muscly minders to do my heavy and dirty work, employed some old slappers to entertain the clients. They were then instructed to ply them with extortionately high priced drinks and other services, if you know what I mean. I made a small fortune from these activities, and then I went into importing narcotics. The business really took off and I became a multi-millionaire before I was twenty years old. In the last few years I've diversified my products and have been dealing in all sorts of the white stuff and other types of smack, grass and psychedelic pills. This hotel is fundamentally used for laundering the goods into clean money. So in short that's about it.'

James was staggered and dumbfounded at this revelation and his feelings were definitely mixed. As we all know, mixed feelings are those when one sees the mother-in-law driving your brand new Rolls Royce over a cliff and crashing onto the rocks below! His thoughts were of surprise, shock, disgust, sadness for Hans's background and what was he? An honest financial consultant, talking conference facilities and negotiating with a gangster! The tape continued to record.

'Now James let's talk about you. As I have said I did not have the benefit of a good education. But you did have a superb opportunity to become qualified. You come from a reasonably wealthy family. Your father was a lawyer and Chairman of the Melbourne Horse Racing Commission and your mother was a physiotherapist. You have two brothers and a sister. You went to one of the best schools in Australia, Welsh College in Melbourne and then went on to Melbourne University where you qualified as an accountant. Later you became chartered. You started your own company, R.I.P. when you were twenty five years old and your wife is a director and major shareholder. You have been a very successful businessman and I admire your success. If I was lucky and you would agree, I want you with all your financial expertise to be part of my drugs syndicate and business empire.'

Once again James was stunned into silence and had a face like thunder at the stupid open way Hans had divulged his dirty business so quickly to him, almost a stranger; also how he had obtained all the information about his family and background. He must have an extremely good researcher doing the checks; he didn't think he had the ability to do it himself. He thought the best thing to do at present was to continue with the meal and keep his own counsel.

The main course was perfect, comparable with the starter, it was excellent and Hans washed it all down with the rest of the carafe of wine. James had only had one glass and some of the water. He was determined to stay sober in order to see what happened next.

Hans was now swaying in his seat, slurring his speech and sweating profusely. He said to James.

'So James, I am looking for a partner to expand my business and Australia seems ripe for my products and you seem the right type of guy to join me, so how would you feel about being in partnership?'

Well, James was speechless and was lost for something to say so he tried to hide his disgust and said nothing.

Hans said. 'Think about it James while I go to the toilet.'

He searched in his jacket pocket and with sticky sweaty fingers he pulled out a white packet and passed it across the table to James.

'Its top quality stuff, class A drugs: heroin etc. I only sell the best and the imports into Australia would be worth a small fortune to you James.'

'But Han's, what happens if you get caught by the police, you will get prison for life?'

'No worries there James, I have the police and the most powerful politicians caught in my spiders web.'

Then he left the table and wavered across the room to the gents. James was alarmed but kept his cool, took his hanky out of his pocket, covered the packet without touching it with his fingers and returned both to his trousers pocket.

When Hans returned and in order to play for time, James said that it was an interesting offer but he would have to talk to his other partners before making a decision.

'That's quite understandable old boy and I would do the same in your circumstances, so take your time and we can talk again before you leave for home. Now it's nearly midnight and time to turn in for bed.'

Hans stood up, wobbled, swayed and fell on the floor with a crash trying to hold onto the table as he went. He grabbed hold of and pulled the tablecloth with all the crockery which went smashing onto the carpet. The other diners could not believe what they saw and were horrified, some of them stood up to get a better view. Dana witnessed what had happened and hurried over as fast as her high heels would allow, helping him up onto his feet. She supported him on his good arm, staggered with him, then stumbled and pushed him to reception and seated him on one of the armchairs. She called the receptionist and

136

instructed her to take Hans to his room; with that he passed out cold.

James closed the Filofax which automatically turned off the tape recorder, picked up one of Hans glasses which was one of the only ones left not broken. He then took advantage of the confusion and walked quickly to the lift. Dana saw him and walked rapidly to the lift, tried to get in with him but she was too late, as the doors closed in front of her. James again sighed with relief that he was on his own at last. As the lift was travelling to the third floor, James had a Damascus moment and saw a clear plan of action appearing in his mind. Eureka!!

33

Camel Train Terminates

The Camel Train eventually terminated in Morocco, much to the relief of Gamel. He had spent months travelling across North Africa, stopping numerous times in towns and villages; he had lost count of how many. His backside was raw and painful from sitting in the saddle. It reminded him of a book he once read many years ago entitled. 'Fifty Years in the Saddle – By Major Bumsore. He now knew how he felt!

Being in a country which reveres camels, the ghastly beast; he was able to sell it to some local Berbers who thought they had paid too much for it. But in truth, although Gamel disliked the animal, he had looked after it well and it had never been 'Bricked'. Old Arab joke. It was in very good condition. So he was glad to see the back of the creature.

The trip had been successful regarding the sale of his goods, he had made enough money together with the cash he got for the camel and had sufficient to last him long enough to get to Spain. He had also bought some excellent quality Red Coral from a couple of crazy Irishmen who knew nothing about the value of the goods or the skills of negotiation so he had screwed them into the ground on price. But they seemed quite happy with the deal having unloaded half their haul, which didn't cost them anything and had made enough money to keep them going for around six months.

Gamel thought it would be prudent to discard his Berber clothes and dress more appropriately as an out of work seaman, as he was now to get work on a ship which would take him to Spain. So he travelled by taxi to the dock area of Tetouan where there were boats ferrying to and from Marbella. He chose a boat which looked a bit downmarket and would not raise any eyebrow's when it docked in Spain. The ship was called 'The Nansea Buoy' which worried him a bit and thought he would have to be careful with some of the sailors! He called up to the captain who was lounging out of the bridge smoking a cigarette and he waved to him to come up the gang plank. So having the name of the ship in mind he minced up the wooden slope as best he could. Within minutes he had a job for the voyage as an unqualified deck hand. He thought what luck, Spain here I come!

34

Another Body Found

Praca da Ribeira Hotel in Oporto is situated right near the river Douro and is close to the Pont Luis 1St Bridge. It was a great favourite of Roly and Hedda, who had stayed there many times as it was a bit quirky, the service was superb and the food excellent. Not that was much help to them as they didn't arrive until 11.00 at night due the extended length of their journey from the Algarve. The other thing that made them late was that they had quite a lengthy boozy lunch at a beach bar in Estoril just north of Lisbon.

They checked into reception and the porter took their bags up to their rooms. Roly had chosen two rooms at the back of the hotel, as from experience he had found them much quieter than the front. They had parked the Mehari in the underground garage so their photographic equipment would be quite safe.

They all flopped into their beds worn out and tired after the long journey. Roly and Hedda crept into bed and immediately started to doze off. Hedda was reflecting on the vision of Feliciano lying on the beach at Antonio's bar and thought what a lovely peaceful man he was and that it would be so nice if he met a similar girl he could marry. He would make a wonderful husband and father.

Roly was having some trouble getting off to sleep as he could not quite understand why Hedda was encouraging him to spend more time in Hamburg, with her staying on and so lonely in the Villa. She seemed much quieter of late and lost in her thoughts. Eventually he dropped off into a troubled slumber.

Feliciano was dozing as he went to sleep and thought about the other two travelling companions who seemed to be such a lovely couple but there was something troubling them. His thoughts then turned to the reason for their trip and the Rappels Vulture and with that thought he dropped into a deep and untroubled sleep.

The next morning they awoke to a bright and sunny morning and the anticipation of one of the best breakfasts in Oporto. Although most hotels only served a continental style fare, this one specialised in 'The full English' which they all devoured with relish, washed down with plenty of coffee. They chatted for a while about the day ahead and Roly told them that the site they were travelling to would only take about an hour's drive so they would have plenty of time for studying the bird life and still be back to the hotel for one of their famous gourmet dinners.

They arrived at the disused RGZ mine and set up their hide and photographic equipment some fifty yards from a small pond which was a bit smelly, so they moved back a bit to avoid the stench.

Their anticipation was at fever pitch with the thought that they might see the Vulture before anybody else. Luckily they were the only Twitchers around so they thought that the news of the bird hadn't reached others ears. They settled down quietly to wait with binoculars and cameras at the ready. This continued for some hours and they photographed some unusual bird life but no sight of the Vulture.

Feliciano had started to doze and asked the others to wake him if anything new arrived. He had just dropped off and Hedda shook him gently as she had seen a very large bird circling the lake. After a few circuits they realised that

142

it was the Rappels Vulture they had come so far to see. It swooped down low flapping its large wings and landed on a log just by the edge of the water and started to peck at the bark. It was the most ugly bird ever seen on earth; long spindly neck with vicious eyes and an even more vicious beak which was ripping bits off the log on which it was perched. The wind blew the log into the shallows of the pond but the wind didn't worry the bird as it was intent on destroying its prey.

Cameras whirred and clicked and they shot some wonderful photos of the creature. With much excitement Feliciano picked up the binoculars to get a closer look and was frozen to the spot as he realised that the log was in fact a human corpse!

He told the others to take a look and they confirmed that it was in fact a body. Hedda felt a bit sick and Roly could not believe what he saw. Feliciano told them to stay where they were. He picked up the Motorola mobile phone and called the police department in Oporto to report the find. They said they would send a S.O.C.O team immediately and then put him through to the pathology department. The call rang out for some time and eventually Dr Caroline Fisher-Hatch answered.

'Well hello there, what can I do for you today?' she trilled.

Feliciano answered saying, 'My name is Sergeant Feliciano Neves from the Faro precinct and we have found a body laying in the water at the old RGZ mine just north of Oporto. We have notified the police and think that you should get here with your pathology team as soon as possible.'

Caroline switched immediately into professional mode.

'Very well Mr Neves don't move from where you are, don't touch anything and make sure those big footed coppers don't stamp all over the site. I will be there with my team in under an hour.'

Feliciano rang off and relayed the conversation to Hedda and Roly so they stayed exactly where they were and continued to take more photos of the Vulture.

35

Tetouan Dock Morocco

The commercial port of Tetouan in Morocco was nothing like the twins expected. They had in mind the Waterford Marina in Ireland or the small port where they berthed in the Ribera Del Puerto Marina Menorca. As they sailed into the port it seemed like another world to them. 'Mary the Virgin' was dwarfed by the ocean liners and container ships crammed into their berths and she looked as a rowing boat compared to those leviathans.

They slowly sailed around the dock for half an hour until they found a tiny berth close to a cruise ship and moored as best they could to the dock, the top of which must have been twenty feet higher than their craft. They found some wooden steps covered in slime and seaweed, which Paddy carefully climbed with the mooring rope to secure it to the dock bollard.

They now needed to find some buyers for their coral. After booking in with the Harbour Master they made enquiries with the clerks at the Masters office and they were directed to the closest Souk. They were told to be careful in the markets as they are enormous. Many strangers get lost inside and have to find a guide who would help them to find the way out. However they were not to be deterred as they arrived at one of the entrances and were indeed staggered at the size.

The Souk was a fascinating place for anyone who had not been there before. The smells and aromas of the spices and foods and bakeries were intoxicating. Plus the quality and low prices of the leather goods and the ironwork in the blacksmiths workshops could only be seen in Morocco Souks.

The traders were not normally pushy but one in particular pestered them to buy two twelve inch high black figurines of the Egyptian Gods 'Anubis' and the 'Winged Isis' claiming that they were originals found in the Valley of the Kings. He also said Anubis was the God of Embalming and Isis was the Goddess of the Moon, Love, Magic, Fertility and Healing and they would bring them untold wealth in the future. Paddy knowing that they had seen them in every tourist stall in the market said of course they were and he was related to Mickey Mouse! They were knocked about a bit and not too pricey, so they bought them just to get rid of the man.

They searched for hours around many of the stalls and shops but they couldn't find any traders interested in the coral. Eventually they came upon a traditional Moroccan coffee shop with colourful walls and wonderful aromas of spices and local coffee. Feeling very despondent, they ordered two speciality coffees and sat on the cushioned floor in silence for a while.

A heavily built Arab dressed in scruffy sailors garb was sitting on a poufy cushion by the next low table to them and enquired as to why they looked so down in the dumps and gloomy. They told him of their search for a buyer for the coral and their need to sell some before they sailed on to Portugal.

He pretended not to be too interested and reluctantly asked what price they were asking. The twins really didn't know what the coral was worth so quoted a ridiculously high price at which the Arab nearly fell off his pouf laughing.

'You must be having a joke with me,' he said still trying to suppress his mirth, 'I might be interested at the right price.'

Mick believing he was the smarter of the two thought that here was an opportunity not to be missed and tried to up-market the goods said.

'Look here, dis is not yer ordinary coral it's very rare Red Coral, der best there is for making high class jewellery, so we need a good price.'

'That well may be my old salt but I still have to move it on and as you know it's illegal to harvest Red Coral, so I will be taking all the risks.'

They did what they believed to be haggling for a few minutes and finally agreed on a price which the boys were happy with and a handshake sealed the deal.

'Now you being a local man, you can show us der way out of dis maze, we'll take you to our ship and you can haul der sacks away with you.'

They both followed the Arab through the narrow web of streets and lanes until they emerged out into the sunlight and then took him to their boat, where they exchange the money and the goods.

The next challenge was to sail on to Portugal. They slipped their mooring, started the tired old diesel, and weaved their way through the moorings and ships then out to the open sea. They had originally chosen the port of Tetouan as it was closest to the Rock of Gibraltar which they could use as a direction marker, as it can be seen for miles around. They only then needed to hug the coast all the way to Portugal and the marina in Vilamoura.

The day was sunny and warm with a light breeze blowing off the calm seas with some spume and spray playing into their faces. They sailed along past the Rock and along the coast of Spain, passing Cadis, El Puerto De Santa Maria, San Lu'car De Barrameda. Then they decided to take a shortcut across the Golfo De Cadiz giving them a straight line course to Portugal, as this would save them many hours following the coastline.

They felt very happy with themselves having just made some money selling the coral to the Arab seaman. The sea crossing was a joy and their spirits rose as they came across a school of dolphins which were weaving backwards and forwards, leaping in and out of the water across the bow of the boat.

They felt that God was in his Heaven and all was well with the world. Were they in for a shock in a few days when they arrived at their destination? They were going to need the help of God and all his Angels to get them out of the pickle they would get into once they berthed in Vilamoura!

They then realised that apart from the vibration in the propeller shaft which was getting worse, there was another problem with the boat. It was starting to list to the port side and she was settling much lower in the water than normal!

36

Frantic Phone Calls to Australia

James lay on the four poster bed full of good food and excellent wine. He was too hot, too sticky, perspiring too much to sleep, and was wide awake at the horror of the evening's revelations and what a desperate jam in which he found himself. The silent air conditioning did nothing to cool him down.

All of a sudden he panicked at the enormity of his situation. He had been socialising with a criminal drug dealer, ostensibly and overtly considering a partnership in an illicit drug cartel and had been seen to be so doing by dozens of diners in the restaurant. In addition he had in his pocket a packet of illegal heroin. What would happen if he was caught with it in his possession?

He immediately jumped out of bed, opened the bedroom safe which was concealed in the wardrobe. He set the private code number and put the drugs with the hanky and the glass with Hans fingerprints inside, ensuring that he didn't touch either with his fingers, then locked the safe door. Thank heavens he had the foresight to tape record the whole dinner conversation. That would be his salvation if the worst happens.

It was time to telephone Jenny in Australia. Because of the time difference she would just be waking up. The phone rang for a long time before her quiet sleepy voice said.

'Hello, Jenny Richmond speaking, who is calling and waking me up at this time of the day Jim? She knew that it was James time to make his regular daily call.

'Hi my love how are things going your end, I hope they are better than the day I have recently had, I'm just getting into bed totally exhausted.'

'Oh it has been hectic with you being away so long there has been so much to do and so many decisions to make but I think I am coping. How are your business meetings going?'

'I will have to give you the details later. The Spanish deals are concluded and profitable but I am having so much trouble with the conference hotel. I have been pampered by all the staff, almost ravished by my personal hostess, overfed by Mr Hans van Glytch, the hotel owner and he wants me to go into partnership running a heroin drugs importation business into Australia.'

'Yeah, ok Jim pull the other one it's got bells on. And don't you think you are going to have a bit of Rumpy Pumpy with some old tart and bring something nasty home here,' she chuckled.

'Now why would I be looking for mincemeat here when I have steak at home?' he laughed.

'Seriously Jenny, I have got involved up to my neck in this narcotics business and I can't think of a way out. Somehow we need to get this slime ball banged up in prison before he kills half the young people in the Algarve. Have you got any ideas?'

'The only thing I can think of at present, is that I could speak to Caroline, as she is in close contact with the police in Oporto and she did tell me the other day that there is an increase in drug deaths in Portugal. So the next time I talk to dad I'll ask her and see if she has any ideas.'

'Ok my love, do it sooner rather than later because this situation is very urgent. I must get off to bed now as it is past one o clock and I have a heavy day in front of me tomorrow. Sleep tight.'

With that he rang off and collapsed into bed with all his clothes on.

37

Dana Gets a Surprise

'Death warmed up' was the best way to describe the way he looked after last night's drinking binge. Sweat was running down his face and his stomach was churning like a cement mixer. He felt nauseous and sick as a parrot!

He was sitting on the Captain chair in his office in the hotel which was furnished very differently to the ultra-modern style of the rest of the building; being furnished in dark oak wood, deep pile carpets and leather upholstery. His arms were crossed on the white desk blotter, his head was resting on his arms and he was almost asleep.

He was aroused by the telephone ringing on the desk. It was Dana calling.

'How are you feeling today Mr Glytch? You weren't too good last night when we put you to bed. Is there anything thing I can do to help you with today?'

'Yes there is Dana, there is something I need to talk to you about, although I don't feel like it at the moment, it is becoming urgent. If you aren't doing anything important at present come in as soon as you can.'

Almost immediately there was a knock on the door and Dana walked in without being asked. She was dressed in a smart light blue business trouser suit, black flat shoes and with most of her flesh covered. Hans thought, well that makes a change! But then he normally decides what clothes the hostesses wear when on duty anyway. He wearily raised his upper body from the desk, sat back in the chair, tried to look awake and said.

'Come in, come in Dana, pull up a chair and get comfortable. I need to talk with you about your future. As you may well know I am not a well man. I have regular check-ups with the doctor and he's been telling me for some time that my liver is almost shot to bits and my kidneys aren't too good also. Due to my size I have also always had trouble breathing and my heart is very weak. He always recommends that I should diet, to lose weight and reduce my alcohol level. Well we both know that's not going to happen. So I could be dead within the week, next month or in five years, no one can tell.'

Dana listened carefully and quietly without interruption. As she heard the bad news about his health problems a single tear dropped onto her cheek. She really was fond of the old bugger even with all his peculiar ways and the news about his possible death shocked her and made her feel so sad.

'Oh dear Mr Glytch, I am sorry to hear about all your health problems. Does this mean that you are going to sack me and get a full time nurse to look after you?'

'Good gracious me no Dana quite the opposite, I have always needed your help and will continue to do so until I fall off the twig. You have forever been my most loyal and effective employee. You constantly do as I instruct you without question, and you support my decisions in front of the rest of the team, even when you think I am wrong. Therefore I want you to be my PA.'

'Now you may or may not know that I don't have any family or close friends to support me and when I die I don't have anyone to whom I could leave my estate. So I want you to inherit the hotel.'

By this time Dana was surprised, in shock and tears flooded down her cheeks; she had no idea that he thought so much of her. She went to speak.

'No tears Dana and no questions. Listen to what you must do. I want you to go to my lawyer in Faro; she is with Ilda & Ilda in the Ave Da Republica, Apartado 700. It's in a small street two roads back from the marina. Her nickname is Foxy and she did all the legal work when we built the hotel; an excellent women and on top of her game. Bear will take you in the Bentley. Have her draft up a Will leaving the hotel, all the land and it's trappings to you. Then get her to send it to me and I'll sign it in front of independent witnesses. Now dry your tears get along with you now and get to Faro as soon as you can.'

Dana hurried out of the office with hanky in hand drying her tears as she sped up the lift to her room. She threw herself on the bed and cried tears of sadness and of joy that eventually she was to become a millionairess. But she realised that she now wore Golden Handcuffs until Hans kicked the bucket.

38

The Crime Scheme

Dr Fisher-Hatch was the first to get to the RGZ site together with her three interns and got there before the S.O.C.O. team, who arrived some twenty minutes later. She was delighted that she had beat them to it, as if they had reached there earlier, they wouldn't have taken the care to preserve the site as well as she and her team. She instructed the internes to secure the area with 'Crime Scene Do Not Cross' tape for about fifty square yards around the 'log' then turned her attention to the three bird watchers who were still sitting quietly in their hide as they were instructed.

Feliciano was the first to emerge and looked at Caroline with awe at her ravishing appearance, even though she was dressed in her white overalls, she looked stunning. He held out his hand for the traditional Portuguese handshake as Caroline did the same. She thought that he held onto hers a bit longer and tighter than normal, even so at the same time thought what a super looking guy. Both their hearts missed a beat at the same time and their eyes dilated open wide. She thought I don't have time for this at present; there's too much work to do. This will have to wait until another time.

'I am sergeant Feliciano Neves from the Faro precinct and I'm here with my friend's for a day's bird watching,' he stammered, not being able to control his wobbly voice and legs.

'I'm very pleased to meet you Mr Neves and thank you for calling us so quickly after you found the body. We are so delighted that we arrived before the police,' she said with a quiver in her voice, as she shyly admired this handsome detective.

Hedda was watching this romantic drama unfold and thought to herself, this is similar to 'Some Enchanted Evening' from Rogers and Hammerstein's South Pacific. She would follow these two with much interest and excitement in the near future.

Caroline instructed the internes to carefully examine the site without doing any damage and look for any evidence such as footmarks, tyre tracks, shreds of clothing, cigarette butts etc. Then bag up anything they found into the plastic containers. In the meantime she was still looking at Feliciano out of the corner of her eye.

After a detailed search, one of the internes called out that he had found some boot prints in the mud near a tyre track. She called back.

'Take plaster casts of both and some samples of the white mud from the edge of the Slime Pit and put them all in the van.'

She walked over to the three birdwatchers that were standing together chatting, watching the crime scene unfold and she felt her heart racing much more than normal. As she came close to Feliciano (too close?) and thought that some help would be useful.

'Mr Neves, as you are the most senior policeman here, could you please direct the officers to carefully drag the body out of the Pit, put it in a body bag then lay it horizontally on the floor of our van.'

Feliciano was delighted to find that they were communicating easily, effortlessly and did as he was asked.

The Oporto policemen didn't have a problem with another precinct official directing their activities.

Caroline said to Feliciano that this body was the fifth she had to deal with in the path lab and her workload was increasing by the day. The interns were very willing but didn't have the experience to undertake autopsies, only minor forensic duties. Feliciano seized his chance and suggested.

'Well Caroline I have a qualification in forensic science, so if you need some help I could be of some use. I have two weeks leave to take and I would love to be of some assistance. I would of course have to be instructed by you and work under your guidance.'

Hedda was watching the verbal intercourse and said to herself. 'Well done boy, get in there and don't miss any opportunity.' Roly not being as observant as to what was going on, he carried on shooting pictures, packing up the photographic equipment and loading it into the Mehari.

Caroline thought for a bit and considered the professional implications of his offer, then said quickly.

'Thanks so much Feliciano that would be a great help to me, when could you start?'

'I don't have to go back to Faro with Hedda and Roly, so I could start any time to suit you. I would have of course to tell my boss what I was doing but that would be alright, as he would be happy to see the back of me for a few weeks.'

'That's settled then, if you could come to the path lab sometime tomorrow morning that would be splendid,' she said enthusiastically.

The police carried the body to the van, slid it into the open doors, then they continued to finish their work searching the site for clues and they found a number of interesting items which could be useful. They were glad to conclude their search as the stink from the Slime Pit was getting up their noses and clinging to their clothes. Then they left the mine area with their vehicle slipping, sliding and wheels spinning on the slimy surface. Feliciano thought that using the blaring two tone siren was a bit over the top but then he had used it in the past to get home early for tea!

Caroline and the interns returned to the van and drove out of the mine to take the cadaver to the morgue. As the police car did, they slipped and their wheels spun on the slimy surface. Fernando was full of joy at the thought of helping Caroline dissect the body, so he said to Hedda and Roly,

'I can't believe my luck, what a charming girl, sophisticated, smart, intelligent, and a lovely peaceful demeanour. I think that this may be the real thing for me after all these years of having no luck with women. Let's all get back to the hotel, shower this smell off us and get ready for a wonderful dinner.'

Hedda looked at Roly and asked if he had seen anything going on between Caroline and Feliciano. He said.

'What sort of going on? Apart from them talking about the body, I was too busy still photographing the Vulture as it flapped away.'

Hedda thought to herself that sometimes Roly was only just aware that he was alive. He was a typical mathematics professor, only interested in formulae and numbers, has never been able to understand interpersonal feelings, he was frequently absent minded and has his head in the clouds most of the time. But she still loved him to bits in spite of all his foibles.

They all finished packing up the equipment, piled into the Mehari and started to battle through the evening traffic to the hotel.

Hedda came down the stairs of the hotel looking magnificent in an evening dress, but Feliciano thought that she had lost some weight since they first met. Roly followed in his clean and expensive outfit but with a somewhat shambolic appearance; he always looked a bit like a sack tied up in the middle. He seemed to appear as a typical dotty academic. However he did give the impression of being classy, as his looks outweighed his dress. He had an aristocratic air about him, tall with an athletic build, pleasant round face, slightly balding head, large ears and a mildly Roman nose.

They strolled through to the dining room and had a superb dinner as Roly had prophesied. Through the meal they chatted comfortably about their most unusual day, what with the Vulture and the dead body there was much to discuss.

Feliciano being sensitive to any atmosphere was concerned when he saw Hedda having trouble digesting some of her food and was clearly at some time in pain. He thought he would speak to her about it when they were alone. His chance came sooner than later as Hedda needed to go to the ladies room. He suggested that he go with her as he wanted a pee. They both left the table and when they reached reception, Feliciano suggested they sit for a while and found a secluded spot with two armchairs.

'I noticed Hedda that you were having some pain over dinner. Is there anything you would want to talk about?'

The relief in her face was clear and noticeable; her eyes welled up with tears as she silently wept with her chest heaving.

'Yes Feliciano there is, I haven't told anyone about it but I have terminal cancer and don't have much time left to live. The pain gets worse by the day and the painkillers have less effect by the week. It's such a relief to be able to talk about it as I haven't and will not tell Roly until near the end.'

Feliciano felt so sad, as he held Hedda in great regard so he just hugged her and they both had a weep for a few moments and Feliciano said.

'There are no words I can say that can help you with your terrible condition but if you ever need some support or a sympathetic ear, I am always here for you.'

She held onto him for a few more moments and said with a genuine plea,

'Feliciano please do everything you can to build a relationship with Caroline, as I can see clearly that you were made for each other and remember my words. Life is very short as we get older so make the most of very day with her. That will keep me as happy as any painkillers as I fade away.'

There was nothing left to say so they used the conveniences and returned to the table where Roly was happily demolishing the chocolates and drinking his third cup of coffee.

Disregarding the chat she had in reception, Hedda pretended she was bursting to find out more about the new budding romance with Caroline and Feliciano and wanted to make a show of it in front of Roly. But before she could manoeuvre the discussion to the subject, Feliciano excitedly burst into the topic without prompting.

'I can't conceal my joy and excitement about meeting Caroline. We have arranged for me to help her in the path lab, I am starting tomorrow and with any luck I may be there for two weeks. I will certainly ask her out to dinner and this place seems a most appropriate venue for a romantic evening. This does mean that I won't be going back with you to Faro but that is good news for your Mehari as there will be less weight and you will travel faster. Also looking at the map, it is all downhill to the Algarve!'

The joke was lost on the two Germans as everyone knows they don't have much sense of humour.

However in spite of the gag, Hedda was smiling and so pleased that things were going well as she raised a glass to both of them. Roly looked confused and wasn't aware of the relevance of the raised glass said.

'What's all the excitement about?'

Hedda and Feliciano looked at each other knowing the secret, just burst out into uncontrollable laughter. Roly looked nonplussed.

39

The Twins Arrive in Vilamoura

The binoculars that the Vilamoura Capitania (Harbour master) had glued to his eyes had fantastic magnification and could see for many miles out to sea. In the early morning sun he looked eastwards and could see the fleet of around twenty five small fishing boats returning from their nights fishing and heading towards the fish dock at Quarteira. He panned further to the east and saw a solitary ship sailing towards his marina. He could just make out the name on the bow, 'Mary the Virgin.' Strange name for a boat he thought.

Paddy slowed the engine as he approached the marina, switched off the ignition and tied up at the Marine Office dock. They asked the Capitania where they should berth. He was most concerned as he saw the list to port and also on the port side deck there were suspicious looking sacks. He told them to berth at number sixteen next to the large white motor launch called 'White Ecstasy'. Once again their craft would look very shabby next to such an up-market vessel. The Capitania told them that once they had berthed they should immediately come back to the Marine Office to complete the necessary registration documents.

As the twins manoeuvred around the marina weaving in and out of the other vessels seeking their berth Paddy said.

'Mick, oi can't understand about dees documents we have to register. In de last two docks all we had to do was show our passports, oi expect it's all to do with de

Portuguese bureaucracy, oiv heard it's a bit tricky over here.'

'Na, noting to worry about Paddy, we will have to blag our way tro dis as we normally do.'

So the twins did as they were instructed and went straight to the Marine Office to register. They were met by the typical 'Cap and a book of tickets jobsworth' type official; hatchet faced, non-communicative and would only do things by the book. The Marine Office was part of the Marine Police and Customs Agency so there was nothing that could be done outside of official procedure. The office was similar to most institutionalised buildings which had never been modernised during the Salazar regime. The interior walls were a faded white distemper, a few filing cabinets, a massive photocopier, a map of Portugal on the wall, an old brown wooden desk with three rickety chairs for customers and a slightly better one for the official 'interrogator'. The floor was covered in brown linoleum which had seen better days, worn away at the door threshold showing the wooden floorboards underneath.

The boys sat down on the hard chairs and felt extremely uncomfortable as the customs official glared at then with cold unflinching eyes. Even his worn, thread bare uniform and his cap which fitted nowhere (it reminded Paddy of the Irish axiom. If you can't fight, wear a big hat!) had seen better days.

'Passports,' he grunted and they were happy to pass them over which they did without question. He photo copied the documents and handed them back to the twins without comment.

'Dare you are Paddy oi told yer, noting to it.'

'Now let's see your ships papers. Captains certificate of competency, insurance cover note and your engines make model and horsepower,' he said menacingly.

The twins looked at each other with confusion in their eyes and were speechless! Mick thinking on his feet said lying, that the papers were on the boat, knowing that he didn't have a clue as to what the guy was talking about.

'We are having a lot of trouble with drugs being imported into our country and that is why we must insist on these documents. They have to be produced, and registered within twenty four hours or you will be arrested and your boat will be impounded,' he snarled.

The twins thought that as they didn't have any of the documents that they needed, it might be better to high tail it out of Vilamoura before they were impounded. But little did they know that events would overtake them before they had the luxury of an escape. They left the office as soon as they could without creating suspicion and then slowly walked behind the building where they could talk without being heard. Then Mick thought for a bit and said to Paddy.

'We can't do a bunk Paddy as we need to sort out de vibration in de prop shaft and what is probably a leak in de boat which is causing de listing. So as soon as we can we need to go over de side and see what needs to be done.'

The Capitania was suspicious of the twins and their cargo. So he called the Marine Police in the Marine Dock office and shared his concern about the boat listing to port, the dodgy sacks on board and that they should consider some sort of investigation by the local police, as this may be a civil issue. The Marine Police called their friends in the Faro police headquarters.

The matter was passed to Jos'e Barros who suggested to Fernando Martins that as this could be a drugs problem, they should work on it together as South and North Chiefs and create a plan of action. This was agreed and they set up a twenty four hour surveillance watch on 'Mary the

Virgin', using a SWAT (special weapons and tactics) team of armed detectives disguised as local fishermen. Martins disagreed with using the team for such a trivial matter even if it may be related to narcotics, (well he would wouldn't he with his involvement with Rabbit) but as Barros was in charge of the southern area, he left the final decision to him.

40

Caroline is Excited

Caroline was so excited after travelling through the rush hour traffic to Musical Madness. When she tried to heave the Vespa onto its stand she nearly dropped it onto the flagstones in her rush to see Shak. She raced into the shop past the Cloud Jingle and shouted,

'Dad, dad, dad, I am so thrilled I think I have met the man of my dreams!'

Shak put his index finger over his lips in a signal that said be quiet, as in her haste she didn't see he was trying to sell a keyboard to a customer. She muttered sorry and quietly walked to the back room of the shop waiting for Shak to finish the deal. As it was closing time he locked up the front door. Some minutes later he came through to the back room with a smile on his face saying he had sold another keyboard.

'Now my little Flopsie what did you want to say to me and what's all the excitement about, something concerning a new man? Now tell me all the gos.'

'Well dad I can't believe it's happened. I went to the old RGZ mine to see another dead body and the guy that called it in was a sergeant Feliciano Neves from the Faro police precinct and he was up here on a bird watching holiday with two friends. He is drop dead gorgeous, a lovely gentle man and he is also qualified in forensic science. It really was a magical moment when we met, a bit like when you and mum got together. I am sure he feels the same way about me as he was all of a dither and tongue tied. As I am totally overwhelmed with work he has offered to stay in Oporto and help me with my workload. Is that good news or not?'

Shake gritted his teeth, which Caroline was too excited to notice and forced a smile, as this was the moment he had been dreading for years. He knew at some point he would lose his girl to a man, because someone as lovely as Caroline could not and should not stay single for the rest of her life, even though she had decided to be a bachelor girl. It seemed that he may lose the only other love in his life and that would be a hard cross to bear.

'That is wonderful news Flops,' he said as his heart missed a few beats. 'When do I get to meet him and give my seal of approval to the match? Are you sure this is the one for you, its early days yet.'

'Dad I have never been so sure of anything in my life, both our body languages confirmed that this will work. I'm certain that within the next two weeks he will ask me out to dinner somewhere, when he does you will meet and I know you will like him. He's just your type.'

'Ok my love if you are sure, then it's alright by me and you have my approval and blessing to take it further. Now let's get you down from cloud nine and plan what we will do tomorrow; Sunday.'

Caroline had already arranged that she would stay the night and cook him his favourite Sunday lunch, a roast chicken meal with all the traditional trimmings which she had bought and was in her bag on the scooter.

They opened a bottle of champagne to celebrate the news, chatted all evening about the new man, his German friends and the Slime Pit episode. Finally both of them were exhausted and with tongues sore, they hit the sack around ten-o-clock, with Caroline dreaming of her 'Some Enchanted Evening.'

The telephone rang in Caroline's room at nine-o clock in the morning and woke her up with a start. She had slept the sleep of Sleeping Beauty without waking all night long. It was Jenny, her step sister on the phone from Australia.

'Hi Caroline I am calling to talk to dad, as I haven't spoken to him for so long but before you put me through to him, I need to chat with you about a deadly serious fix that Jim has got into in the Hotel Paradise in Faro. Apart from being almost ravished by one of the hotel hostesses, which he can deal with no problems. He's been offered a partnership in an illegal drugs syndicate which he believes goes right to the top of the Portuguese Government, Politicians and an Inspector of Police. He's terrified that he's getting sucked into a situation which he might not be able to handle. Do you have any contacts that might be able to help him out of this hole?'

'Well Jenny, what a coincidence, I met yesterday a very noble and conscientious detective sergeant who works with the Faro police and he is so yummy it's unbelievable. He will be working with me for the next two weeks on some forensic analysis, so I'll see if he would have any solutions which might help and will get back to you in double quick time.'

'Oh thank you so much Caroline that would be such a help and I'll tell Jim that we may have some help at hand. Could you please now pass me over to dad?'

When Jenny and Shak finished talking, Shak brought Caroline a large mug of tea almost as big as a 'bucket' to her room which she drunk while still in bed. This was one of the little luxuries she loved when staying with her dad, as she lived on her own and never has the chance of being so pampered and spoiled.

They had a light breakfast, saving their hunger for the lunchtime meal. Caroline busied herself preparing the food and Shak went down to the shop to unpack some new deliveries. The smell of the chicken cooking as it permeated the whole flat was something they loved, as it reminded them of their home in England. She laid the table as usual as though they were dining at the Ritz. The wine was Shaks favourite German wine, Liebfraumilch which was far too sweet for her taste but Shak loved it so that was all that mattered. The chicken was cooked which she left to rest for half an hour, then looked for the carving knife with which to slice the meat and it was nowhere to be found. She called down to Shak.

'Dad have you seen that new carving knife I bought you recently, I've looked everywhere for it and I need to carve now.'

'Sorry Flops I can't hear you, give me a minute and I'll come up, I've nearly finished. Ok I'm here now what was it you said?'

'I said have you seen that new carving knife I bought you recently; I've looked everywhere for it and I need to carve now.'

Shak looked a bit uncomfortable and muttered under his breath and absentmindedly that he had not seen it for a while. He might have used it in the shop but not to worry anyway, just use the old one and let's get on with the meal. Caroline was a bit miffed as she bought it especially for these occasions. The matter was soon forgotten and they thoroughly enjoyed the lunch,

41

Ava Hotel Faro

Swimming pools were not common in the Algarve and there were certainly not many on the roofs of hotels but the four stories and 134 rooms Ava Hotel in Faro had one of the first to be built in nineteen sixty. There are wonderful views from the roof looking over the marina, which led out to the sea but only for small boats, as they had to navigate under a low railway bridge, the track of which ran close to the hotel.

The pool terrace had been beautifully designed with multi coloured floor tiles, planted out all over with Palm trees, sweet smelling Jasmine and Tobacco plants laid out in Morocco style planters and many wooden pergolas which gave shade. The fragrance from the flowers was overpowering in the evenings and it was a most relaxing place where one could chill out and listen to the tinkling of the fountains playing into the pools.

Foxy was lying on a white sun lounger with a blue padded cover by the light blue tiled swimming pool, enjoying sun bathing in the briefest red bikini which showed of her well-formed body beautifully. The day was hot, around ninety five degrees with a slight warm breeze. She was the only person on the roof so the silence was most welcoming. This was one of the rare days off from her legal duties and a longed for respite from the hubbub of the courts. Her always present handbag was lying close to her on the floor by the sun lounger.

Her sojourn was broken by Roberto the waiter appearing out of the roof top lift. He walked over to her and said quietly.

'I am sorry to disturb you madam but Mr Jos'e Barros the Chief Inspector of Police is in reception and he wants to have a word with you, shall I send him up or will you come down to the desk.'

Foxy was mildly irritated by the interruption but this was all part of being a lawyer so she had got used to it over the years.

'No I won't come down Roberto, please ask him to come up and also please hand me my towelling wrap. I don't want him to see me half naked, as we all know about his reputation with the women.'

She smiled a knowing smile at Roberto and he responded with a meaningful wink.

'Roberto, could you also bring up two freshly squeezed glasses of oranges and a bowl full of nuts and crisps for Mr Barros and me.'

'Certainly madam will you need anything else, some more filling snacks or a light lunch?'

'No thank you Roberto that will be all and please tell Mr Barros that I'm a bit pushed for time so he will have to be brief.'

Foxy lay back on the sun lounger to enjoy the next few minutes, comfortable now that she was well covered by the towelling wrap. Without thinking she put her right hand into her handbag and stroked the plastic bag.

Her peace didn't last long as the lift doors opened and out strode Jos'e in full uniform carrying the refreshments which she had asked for. As he walked over to her he said.

'What do you think of your new waiter Foxy; I've taken over from Roberto to save him the journey. Do you think they would give me a job? And how is the most beautiful lawyer in Portugal today?'

'Well first of all I think you would make a lousy waiter as you are too fat to serve between the tables and secondly, you can cut out the flattery because you've used it all on me before. I told you last time you tried it on that I am not available because I am married to the job!' she said laughing. 'Now what do you want you pain in the bum and make it quick because this is my day off.'

'Alright but you know me, never miss an opportunity, keep trying and you never know, you might change your mind someday but then again probably not.'

'I must be serious for a while. As you know we have an increasing problem with imported drugs coming into the Algarve, we think via Vilamoura. So for the past year we have been particularly vigilant with any new vessels docking there. Yesterday a strange boat called 'Mary The Virgin' sailed in and the port authorities thought the boat, the guys on board and its cargo were a bit suspect. They haven't provided any documents apart from their Irish passports and have been given twenty four hours to produce them. So we have organised a SWAT team to watch them under cover and if we have to apprehend them you may have another court case on your hands. So I thought it would be best to let you know so you can be prepared.'

'Thanks for keeping me informed Jos'e. Now drink your orange, eat the nuts and leave some for me, then bugger off. This is one of the only days holiday I have and I want to finish my sunbathing.'

He knew she wasn't being rude, just their normal friendly banter; it was just the way their familiar relationship had formed over the years. They were very fond of each other and both respected each other professionalism.

Jos'e wandered over to the lift in mock disappointment that again his amour had been rejected and disappeared down the lift to reception. Foxy took off her wrap, carried on sunbathing and fell asleep surrounded by the sweet smelling flowers.

42

The Morgue and Path Lab

Feliciano woke early as he didn't sleep well thinking of what he might find the next day and hoping he doesn't put off Caroline for any reason. He showered, shaved, covered his face in aftershave, dressed in the best clothes that he had with him in double quick time and walked down to the breakfast room to say goodbye to Hedda and Roly. They were nowhere to be seen so he had a light continental breakfast with coffee, left a note with reception to bid his farewells then left the hotel.

It was only a short walk from the hotel to the morgue and the path lab, so he strolled casually with a spring in his step, drinking in the warm sunshine and the green trees lining the road. He arrived at the morgue exactly at nine o clock ready to help Caroline. Was he excited and his stomach was turning somersaults!

He had always hated the atmosphere in morgues as he had to work in them when he was training for his qualification. They always looked so depressing with stone flooring, rows upon rows of grey filing type cabinets three high which held the dead bodies. Morgue attendants who looked so bored with their tasks and cadavers waiting to be cut up ready for the pathologist's scalpel he found depressing. Even though they were refrigerated, there was always the scent of death in the still air. The path lab was so much more acceptable to him as the air was cleaner and the equipment all new and shining. He quickly walked through the morgue to see Caroline working.

She was already at her tasks and dressed in her scrubs, still looking gorgeous. She had no time for small talk so without a hello or good morning showed him the latest cadaver on the stainless steel slab, which was the one they found at the Slime Pit. The interns had covered it with a sheet.

'Right Feliciano, I am giving you an opportunity to test your pathology skills and forensic knowledge, so you have ten seconds to tell me how this poor soul died.'

She pulled back the sheet and Feliciano couldn't help roaring out with nervous laughing as he saw a large kitchen knife sticking out of the centre of the poor man's heart. He now knew just what a whacky and black sense of humour Caroline had. In the midst of death she could see the funny side of an awful situation. He thought now I know she is the girl for me. They both chuckled with each other then broke out into uncontrollable hysterical laughter for several minutes!

The three interns also dressed in scrubs, ready for work, looked on in surprise and amazement at what they had witnessed. Caroline called across to them.

'Come on you lazy lot stop goggling at us, get back to the tasks I gave you with the other three bodies before they get stiff with rigor mortise.'

They knew by the tone and chuckle in her voice she was only joshing but they did get back to their jobs pretty quickly. There was an uncomfortable embarrassed silence between the two of them and Caroline said that they were both out of order and should be ashamed of themselves for treating the corpse with such disrespect. Feliciano agreed and looked highly embarrassed. They walked slowly to the path lab office and sat down at Caroline's desk.

'Feliciano, thank you so much for offering to help with my workload, I don't know what I could have done without your help. We need to agree between us how we split the tasks. I suggest that I will carry out the post mortem on the Slime Pit victim; if you could do the research on the tyre treads, the boot print and the mud sample, as these will be terribly time consuming and detailed tasks. How do you feel about that?'

Feliciano would have licked the morgue clean with his tongue on his hands and knees if she had asked, so anything was fine by him.

'Caroline I'll do anything you ask of me, as you are the boss, far more qualified than I and I am happy to take on those three issues. Perhaps if I start with the tyre treads, first by photocopying the casts, then sending the copies to the all the tyre manufactures in Portugal and could do the same with the boot prints. The mud I will leave to the last as I have an idea what it is and the research wouldn't be so time consuming. I could analyse that while waiting for the replies to the other two. Is that ok by you?'

Caroline was delighted with the suggestion as it would reduce her workload significantly and she preferred to work on the cadaver, as she found this type of analysis much more interesting. Feliciano went over to the cupboard which held the samples and immediately set to work on his projects.

Looking at the knife sticking out of the body made Caroline's blood run cold, as a shiver ran down her spine; she had some distant memory that the knife seemed somehow familiar but couldn't recall why. She put the memory to the back of her mind and continued with the post mortem. The body hadn't been cleaned as she had instructed the interns and it didn't half pong. So she took samples of the slime and then cleaned the man from top to bottom on his back sides and front.

The cause of death was obvious but the biggest problem she found was the lack of identity, as the body was naked, the fingers had been cut off, all the teeth had been yanked out and the face had been beaten so badly it was unrecognisable. In addition as he had been in the acid Slime Pit for so long, all the body and the face were badly bloated.

With all of the excitement of meeting Feliciano and the discovery of the body in the Slime Pit, she suddenly remembered that she should have spoken to him about her conversation with Jenny about James's drug problem. So she left the post mortem for a while and called him back into her office.

'Feliciano I need to talk urgently with you about some family complications we have with a relation from Australia. At some point I need to fill you in about our family history so you would understand the details but don't have the time at present.'

At that point Feliciano jumped in and suggested that he should take her out to dinner one night and discuss the family. Caroline was overjoyed at the prospect and agreed immediately. He said they could go to the hotel where he was staying as the cuisine was excellent. So they made a date there and then. Caroline suggested that she could pick him up on her scooter and go to the hotel as she knew short cuts through the traffic. Feliciano was appalled at the thought and said that he would pick her up from Shaks flat in a chauffeur driven limousine at eight o'clock on the chosen date. Caroline was so impressed at the importance he was giving to the occasion.

'So getting back to the problem we have. I'll keep the background short for the sake of brevity. I have a step sister called Jenny and she is married to a financial consultant in Australia called James Richmond. He is on a business trip in Spain and Portugal and at present staying at that posh new hotel near Faro called Hotel Paradise. Completely by accident, he has got entangled with a drugs cartel which involves the top politicians in Portugal and the highest level police inspectorate, all of whom are in on the racket. James is at a loss as to what to do next and I said to Jenny that you might be able to help. What do you think we should do?'

'Crikey, that sounds a tough nut to crack especially as there is police corruption involved, I could be getting into very hot water sorting this one out. Let's talk some more over dinner and in the meantime I'll try to find a solution. As it happens I might be able to speak in confidence with my uncle who is the Chief Justice Minister of Portugal. But give me more time to think about it and we can discuss it again.'

Caroline was delighted that their relationship was developing and the warmth and interest they had both shown in each other was reassuring. The offer of dinner was the icing on the cake and she was even more convinced that Feliciano was the man she had dreamed about for years. She stopped her thoughts racing and returned to the autopsy.

43

The Twins Discovery

The twins were panicking. They needed to rush to get the boat repaired so they could escape from the marina without having to show their documents before the twenty four hour deadline expired.

Mick helped paddy into his scuba diving gear with instructions to find the leak in the hull and repair it with a two part waterproof sealing compound, which when mixed together could be packed into the leak and would set hard as rock within minutes. Mick would then be operating the bilge pumps which will empty the sea water out of the bottom of the boat and cure the list to port.

'Dare is no need for full diving gear Paddy as dare is very little depth in der marina, so only one air tank, and mask is needed. No BCD, weight belt or fins needed. So make it as quick as possible.'

Paddy stuck up his thumb in agreement as he donned his mask and thrust the air hose into his mouth, tested the oxygen flow, and stepped down the stainless steel ladder into the warm and cloudy marina water.

The leak was indeed as they suspected in the joins of the planking of the hull and was probably damaged when they berthed in Morocco. The split was about six inches long along where two planks butted. Paddy worked as fast as possible and had the leak fixed in about fifteen minutes. Mick was already operating the bilge pumps as Paddy climbed the steps back onto the deck.

Within an hour the boat was losing its list and was almost level in the water. They were extremely pleased with their repair and decided to celebrate their task with a pint of local beer and a rest lying in the sun on the fore deck. Neither of them noticed the SWAT team disguised as fishermen watching them through binoculars as the boat fully levelled itself.

'Now Mick all we have to do is to sort out dat vibration on de prop shaft and we will be off out of here like a rat up a drainpipe!'

They were much more concerned about the prop repair as it had been dodgy for ages. They estimated it would take much longer to fix than the leak and would need both of them underwater for some time, that is if they had all the tools to hand for the overhaul. They were still concerned about the twenty four hour deadline as they only had about eight hours left.

They both donned their partial diving gear and did a giants stride over the deck to save time. They swam to the rear of the hull to find that the prop shaft was only supported on one side of the hull and the other was missing its bolt which held it onto the keel. The most difficult repair would be replacing the bearing which had slipped out of its housing and was dangling around the propeller shaft. They had a spare on board but it would take hours of hard graft to refit a new one.

By sign language they decided to go back to the deck and plan how to undertake the repair work. As they went to surface, Paddy pointed to a pile of brown waterproof packages individually tied up with string lying on the sea bed underneath the 'White Ecstasy's' enormous hull. Mick swam over and picked two of them up and passed one to Paddy. They then surfaced, climbed up the ladder and threw the packages on the deck. Then removed their diving gear and stared at the packages.

'What do yer tink they are Paddy, dare must have been hundreds of dem under dat big ship?'

'I dunno Mick, let's get dried off and open dem and find out.'

As professional divers they were used to finding strange objects on the sea bed and the boat was full of their treasures, so it was nothing unusual to bring debris to the surface and didn't think too much more about their discovery.

They went below to shower off and decide what to do next. They hadn't been in the wash rooms for more than a few minutes and there was a hell of a commotion above them. It sounded like an army of heavy boots, there were many bumps and thumps with much shouting and calling in Portuguese tongues. They were terrified and thought they were under some kind of attack, possibly by pirates or terrorists! Unbeknown to them the SWAT team had swooped onto the deck!

They swiftly pulled on some shorts and with great fear and trepidation slowly crept up the companionway which led up to the floor above. They peered through the glass window of the doors and could not believe what they saw. There were at least half a dozen fishermen with black balaclavas over their heads with only slits for their eyes, pointing machine pistols and sub machine guns at the poop deck door behind which the twins were crouching. Standing behind them was Feliciano and Fernando Martins who was in full uniform. One of the two packages had been opened and there was white powder spilling out everywhere.

'Dis is not de time to be playing de heroes as in de western cowboy films Paddy, let's get out dare with our hands in de air before we get shot.'

185

They walked slowly onto the deck with hands in the air as Martins shouted to them to lie on the floor with hands on top of their heads. They did exactly as they were told as one of the fishermen handcuffed them together.

'What de hell is going on, we ain't done noting wrong so what's all de guns and masks for, were just ordinary divers trying to repair our boat.'

Martins walked over to them and said that the team had taken photographs of them bringing the packages onto the boat. That they were under arrest for drug smuggling and they would be taken to the Faro police station, then on to prison to await court proceedings. Paddy shouted out.

'But we have told yer dat we were repairing our boat and found dose packages with a load of others on de sea bed and brought dem up to see what dey was.'

'Yes of course you were, so why was it that soon after your boat levelled itself after you dumped your cargo of drugs onto the sea bed, that you innocently brought some samples onto the boat? You can save your excuses for the judge when you are in court. Meantime you boat and all its cargo is impounded,' snarled Martins.

With that he ordered them to get dressed, they were taken off the boat at gun point and manhandled into the back of a large black van with metal grills at all the windows. As they were hustled into the back doors, they slammed shut and were locked; they were still shouting and protesting their innocence.

Feliciano told the team to stand down and congratulated them on a job done well, that they could now take off their masks and set their guns to safe mode. They all then left the ship to resume normal duties.

Feliciano and Martins had a quick tour of the ship to look for more evidence but the only material of any substance was the sacks of Red Coral. There were all sorts of treasures that the boys had scavenged from the sea beds plus small statues and artefacts they had bought in Morocco. There was of course the diving equipment which Martins had his greedy eyes on. So he suggested that the sacks should be taken to the evidence room in the Faro police headquarters but the diving gear which was no good to anyone, should be transported to his home and stored in his garage. Feliciano thought that was a bit odd but as he had so many other things on his mind relating to the arrests he thought no more on the subject.

The whole of the ships entrances and exits were then covered in 'Police Do Not Cross' tape and two uniformed officers were instructed to guard the boat until further notice.

Feliciano and Martins sat together in the rear seats of the police car driven by a uniformed officer, as they returned to Faro from the Vilamoura crime scene. There was clearly a frosty atmosphere between them. They had always had to work together but they disliked each other with a vengeance. But for some unknown reason this crime had almost cemented their dislike. They travelled in silence until they reached the Faro police station, where Martins broke the quietness saying that all the administrative matters related to the twins were now firmly in Feliciano's Southern department; as he was now deputising for Jos'e Barros and it was no more to do with him. He opened the car door and slouched away rubbing his head which was bent down and undoubtedly painful, as he returned to his Northern headquarters. He was clearly displeased with some aspects of his day. It reconfirmed Feliciano's understanding when he told people that Martins was only miserable when he's awake!

Feliciano entered his Southern office and went straight to the duty desk sergeant where new villains are registered and recorded and asked if everything about the twin's crime had been entered correctly. He didn't need to re-check the register as he had known the duty sergeant Vitor Gomes for many years and his attention to detail was impeccable. The sergeant said.

'You know sir, I have been doing this job for nearly thirty years and it still amazes me how many felons although having been caught red handed, still protest that they are innocent as the Irishmen did. I put them into separate cells, they were interviewed by our detectives and they both gave the same story. So we took their statements, they signed them, still shouting and protesting that they had done nothing wrong, then we sent them both to Faro prison.'

Feliciano smiled a knowing look and winked at the sergeant which said everything to him and he continued walking wearily to his private office. On his desk was a pile of paperwork which needed attention before he finished for the day. When this was completed he switched off the lights, walked back to Vitor's desk and past pleasantries with him, asked him how his wife and family were and how his ill father was progressing in hospital. He then walked out and disappeared into the humid gloom of a Faro night.

Vitor watched him as he walked away and thought what an excellent boss he would make instead of Jos'e Barros, who could be an excellent leader. He was fair, friendly, firm and very professional. If only he could be faithful to his wife and leave the young girls alone, he would be perfect.

44

A Romantic Evening

Mercedes Benz limousines are probably the best cars to impress a girl on her first date with a new man. This one was black all over with light cream seats and interior fittings. It was chauffer driven and he wore a dark grey uniform with matching cap. Feliciano sat in the rear seat feeling very apprehensive and nervous about the forthcoming dinner date with Caroline, as he wanted the evening to be perfect and doubted his ability to ensure its success. His hands were sweating, his heart was beating faster than normal and he had butterflies in his stomach.

He instructed the chauffer to drive slowly as there was plenty of time to kill and gave him directions on how to get to the Musical Madness shop. Then he was to wait outside until Caroline and he were ready to go to the Praca da Ribeira hotel where he had booked a table for dinner.

He walked up to the door of the shop and rang the bell. On hearing the unusual 'Cloud' jingle it make him smile but he was still worrying about the evening and even more so meeting Caroline's dad for the first time.

He could hear her running down the stairs to the shop and she opened the door with a big smile on her face. She looked stunning in a powder blue evening dress down to the floor, with a v neck just showing the slightest cleavage. She always said she didn't like showing her bits off in public. There was thin gold edging around the neckline hemline and arms. She wore her mother's single row of pearls and earrings. Anyone could have seen the love light in her sparkling eyes. Feliciano was dumbstruck with her beauty and for a while was lost for words. Recovering with a bow, he produced the bunch of red roses he had concealed behind his back.

'Oh how lovely and thoughtful of you, I have never had a dozen red roses bought for me, ever!'

'What makes you think they are for you? They are for your dad,' he joked. 'And there aren't twelve there are thirteen, as a little bird told me your lucky number is thirteen. I am only joking of course they are for you.'

She clutched them to her chest as they walked up the stairs to meet Shak. He was standing in the sitting room, upright by the fireplace with his left hand on the mantelpiece and right hand holding the lapel of his coat in mock Victorian father pose.

'Oh come off it Pops you never stand like that, you'll scare the pants off the poor man.'

'Well if I am to meet the first suitor my daughter has ever brought home to meet me, I thought I should look the stern father part,' he chuckled extending his right hand.

Feliciano hadn't met many English people but he had heard that they were very formal on first meeting so he had rehearsed in detail what he should say in these circumstances. He gripped Shaks extended hand in a firm handshake and with great formality and a small bow said.

'Good evening Mr Shaking Shak, I am so pleased to meet you and to gain your approval to take Caroline out to dinner. I have been looking forward to seeing you ever since I met her. I would also want to take this opportunity of seeing your music shop if that is alright with you?'

Caroline and her dad were shaking with laughter inside but dared not show that they found his formality so strange.

It was almost Victorian in its structure but also a welcome and refreshing change from the casual approach of most young people these days.

Shak took the opportunity of showing Feliciano around the shop, explained the number and variety of different instruments in stock and the approximate prices of some of the more rare pieces. Feliciano was genuinely interested and asked all the right questions about the business. Shak was openly impressed with the young man's social skills and his ability to converse comfortably in exceptionally perfect English. After about fifteen minutes, Caroline called down to say that time was pressing and they should be making moves to go to the hotel. They both returned to the flat where Caroline had made herself ready.

Feliciano again shook Shaks hand before stepping down the stairs with Caroline following. As she stood on the top step she turned to Shak and mouthed 'What do you think of him dad,' Shak stuck up his thumb in a sign of approval and mouthed back with a smile on his face, 'I approve of him!' She was overjoyed with his consent and skipped down the stairs to catch up with Feliciano and they both rushed out to the Mercedes.

Shak sank into the battered old leather sofa realising that there was magic and magnetism between the two of them and burst into uncontrollable tears. He could see that he had just lost the second love of his life, and then cried himself to sleep.

They sat in companiable silence in the back of the car, both lost in their own thoughts about the meeting with Shak. Feliciano thought it had gone very well and Caroline could not have been more pleased with the whole situation. They stayed in this reverie until they reached the hotel.

The car pulled up outside the large opulent doors of the hotel and the uniformed doorman quickly walked to the

Mercedes and opened the rear door for the couple to exit. Feliciano paid the driver with a sealed envelope containing the agreed sum and ushered Caroline into the foyer. He took her arm and walked her to the restaurant where the Maître de was waiting to check them in. He showed them to the secluded area that Feliciano had previously chosen. They sat around the small square table laid with freshly laundered white linen napery and a waiter handed them the menu and the wine list. As in all fine dining restaurants the ladies menu didn't have any prices printed. She felt very cosseted and was most impressed.

They both studied the menu in silence then Caroline said quietly.

'I need to talk to you urgently about the Slime Pit Man; I am having enormous difficulty with the autopsy and need your help.'

'Now Caroline, this is our first dinner together and work is not on the menu. Whatever you need to discuss can wait until tomorrow. But I will tell you now, I have a plan which will involve talking to my uncle but this also can wait until tomorrow. Agreed?'

She knew that he was right and agreed to leave all discussions about work until tomorrow. They then ordered their chosen food. Caroline always thinking of her figure selected Lobster in brandy for starter and a Caesar Salad for the main. Feliciano's choice was the Sea Food soup and Dover Sole. He also ordered a bottle of white Quinta Cabris wine and a large water with gas.

They then talked none stop about their backgrounds and family lineage with Feliciano doing most of the asking and she talking nineteen to the dozen. Nothing new there! He knew how well qualified she was in her job but was interested to find out more about her childhood days. She told him in great detail about her mum going missing, sometimes with a tear or two in her eyes. He asked what type of education she had and she went into great depth on this topic. She told him she was educated in a private Convent school run by Catholic Nuns in her home town of Reading in Berkshire. His heart dropped down to his boots. He thought Oh no! A Catholic God Botherer, a Bible basher. Just what he didn't need after the problems he had with religion.

'What's up with you Feliciano, you're looking so glum, what have I said to upset you?'

'I have had so much trouble with 'God' in the past I really didn't want to get involved and get close to a religious girl'

'Religious? Not me, I couldn't stand the Convent or the nuns, the sanctimonious old biddies. They were more than a pain in the butt and I couldn't wait to leave and go to university. They were so bigoted and favoured the Irish or Catholics students and had no time for me being C of E. I nearly got expelled twice for bad behaviour. Once I put some tampons covered in red ink in a Nuns umbrella. When it rained she got covered in the things. Then next possible expulsion, I bought some small red Penis and Testicle lapel badges when I was on holiday in the Algarve and gave them to all the girls in my class, which they wore to church and of course I had to take the rap for that! Religious? Not me!'

'I can tell you that Shak was not a happy bunny when he had to have an interview with Mother Superior about expelling me but he did manage to keep me in the school for the rest of my education, probably because they wanted to retain the extortionate fees. It wasn't all bad news though, as I had an extremely good music teacher who taught me to play the flute and the piano.'

Feliciano's mood changed within seconds and they laughed until the tears ran down their cheeks. He was so relived and loved her sense of fun and humour. He told her about his entry into the police force as a motorcycle cop, his promotion to detective and his difficult relationship with his boss Martins. Then they realised they had so much in common. They were passionate about Ballet, Classical Music, and the Arts and clearly they were both Culture Vultures. Caroline's favourite piece of music was Spiegel im Spiegel played on the piano and Feliciano's was Brahms Symphony number four in E Minor Opus 64. They both promised each other that would take in a Ballet as soon as they could but Feliciano said that in Portugal the adverts for them normally only appear after the show had started! Then they were off again laughing a bit too loudly for the other diners.

The evening was a resounding success, the food was sublime but it had to come to a finish around eleven thirty and as they both would have busy days tomorrow so they decided to end the meal there. Feliciano really understood what a classy and refined woman Caroline was. Then he went to the men's room, paid the bill at reception and they left the hotel. Then walked arm in arm to Caroline's flat which was not far from the hotel. She was convinced that Angels were dining at the Ritz and he was sure he heard a Nightingale singing in Berkley Square? When they reached the entrance Feliciano said nervously,

'Are you going to ask me in for coffee?'

'Certainly I am not; I'm not that sort of girl! Besides you had three cups with your meal so why would you need another.'

She tapped him playfully on the nose with her index finger and said.

'Not so fast Romeo, we will have plenty of time in the future for coffee in my place so don't be so impatient. We need an early start in the morning so I'll see you there sharp at nine o clock. By the way I love the Whistle, did you hire it from Moss Bross?'

She entered the entry code on the apartment door, turned, kissed him lightly on the cheek and giggled at him as she disappeared into the darkness of the hallway. He was worried that he might have gone too far on the first date and would fret about it all night. He hoped that tomorrow he would be able to explain that he wasn't used to dating and that in all the films he had seen, the boy always asks if he could come in for coffee. He could never think why, as he was not too keen on coffee anyway! Also he can't whistle so why had she mentioned it and thought some of the English catchphrases were confusing and just didn't understand about the whistle.

45

Faro Prison

Opposite the municipal theatre in Faro, is Faro prison which is a dreary dull building totally secure and resembles an eighteenth century workhouse, except in a workhouse at some point, one can come and go. Its home to around one hundred and fifty inmates, all men and nearly forty per cent are foreign. Fifteen nationalities including English, Scottish, French, Brazilian, Western European, African and Chinese as well as Portuguese, make up the residents. So it was nice to see the Irish twins representing Ireland! Administration is divided into three departments – security – clinical – and education, so the twin's needs would be well catered for, especially education.

The prison is not somewhere most people would want to go to unless it was to visit an unfortunate friend who had broken the law. Someone jailed and incarcerated in a place where time at worst almost stops, at best grinds itself to a gut wrenching standstill, the days merge into weeks, weeks into months, then years and routine takes a robotic hold on daily life.

Mick and Paddy were kept in a small twelve foot by twelve foot cell, with one small barred window. There were two beds, a toilet, small chest of drawers and a washbasin. Worn whitewashed walls complete with previous inmates graffiti and writing decorated the confines and completed the sparse designer look. The whole prison atmosphere reeked as Paddy put it, of Eau de Pisserear. Not exactly the Hilton Hotel. They continually shouted their innocence of the drug dealing crime and consistently appealed to have a lawyer to visit and represent their case. They were told that the legal professionals were few and far between and would take some time to arrange a date. However there was a regular prison visitor who could see them at short notice and her name was Katricia Hart. They jumped at the opportunity to talk to someone English. An appointment was made and she would visit them in two days' time.

Kat was told of the need for the twins to have a visit by her local Vicar. So she pitched up on the appointed day and time and saw the boys seated at a small table in the visitor's room along with a dozen other inmates sitting at tables with wives, girlfriends and relations. The room was guarded by three officers armed with batons. The doors were locked and barred with grills once the visitors had entered.

'Good morning to you both, my name is Katricia. I understand your names are Paddy and Mick O Leary, I have been told that you are here for drug smuggling is that correct,' said Kat.

They agreed with the introduction and asked Kat to call them by their first names to which she agreed. Then pandemonium broke out with the two of them both gabbling at the same in a strong Irish accent protesting their innocence, they sounded like a group of fish wife's all talking at once.

'Whoa whoa, slow down you two, now tell me in detail why you are in this place and what can I do to help you.'

They related their tale in depth, from leaving Ireland to berthing in Vilamoura and finding the packages on the sea floor. Then the SWAT team invading the boat and they had been photographed bringing up the two packages. They insisted that they hadn't dumped the other drugs over the side and that the reason for the boat being levelled was the repair to the planking and the sea water being pumped out of the bilge.

'Honestly Kat dat is de Gods truth. We are just adventurous divers and dats what we do; pick up tings from der seabed as souvenirs. Now Kat can you get us some legal chap to represent us co.'s we are innocent of the de drugs ting. Ok we are guilty of stealing de Red Coral but dats all.'

This saga took up most of the visiting time and although Kat was used to hearing that most prisoners were not guilty of anything, she tended to believe their version of events.

'Now boys, my job here is to listen to you and give moral support, I am not a legal advisor nor can I give you any advice. But I do believe you are telling the truth. I have a very good lawyer friend who might be able to give you some help. So when I leave here I'll go to her office and see what I can do. We have now run out of visiting time so I must leave you until next time. I also have to get back to my husband who is incapacitated in a local care home.'

'Well tank you Kat it's nice to know dat somebody believes us and we look forward to meeting dis lawyer lady. We are so sorry to hear about your husband and if ever we could help you with him we would do anything to assist. Tanks again and goodbye,' said Mick.

Kat had plenty of time on her hands and walked straight to the Ilda & Ilda offices which were only half a mile from the prison. It was a lovely sunny day with a warm breeze blowing in her face so the walk lifted her spirits after the smell and the depressing atmosphere of the prison.

Luckily Foxy was in the office preparing for her next courtroom appearance. Her secretary welcomed her in the foyer and rang through to Foxy to see if she was free.

'Of course I am free if it's to see my old friend Kat, she's always welcome here and she's good for a chat and a laugh. Come in and take a seat Kat. Two white coffees please Ana,' she called out. 'Now what can I do for you Kat.'

'I've just seen two new inmates at the prison and have listened to their tale of woe and I really do think they have been jailed unjustly and I wondered if there was anything you could do to help them get a fair trial?'

Kat then outlined their story as they told it to her without missing any details and thought that the photographic evidence might be a good place to start.

'I would need much more information about their case before I could take it on. As you will know I am snowed under with clients at present but this one does intrigue me. Initially I'll go and see my good friend Inspector Barros to see what proof he has of the drug dealing.'

Kat thanked her for her help and for the coffee and made her way home to see John in the care home. She was genuinely concerned for the twins and more so that there may have been a miscarriage of justice in arresting them. It would be much cleaner if the matter of the drugs could be cleared up before a trial. She did think though that they would be charged for the Red Coral matter.

Foxy thought she would use her lunch break to quickly chat with Jos'e, so strolled to the precinct where she met the duty desk sergeant Vitor, who she had known for many years.

'Hi ya Vitor how are things with you today. I've come to see that old reprobate Jos'e, is he around today?'

'Hello Foxy. Yes I am very well but we haven't seen Jos'e for some time, I expect he's taking some leave. But detective Feliciano Neves is deputising for him perhaps he could help. I'll give him a call and you could make your way to his office just down the corridor, third on the left, I am sure he will see you.'

Feliciano opened his office door to greet Foxy who he did not know too well but knew her by reputation.

'Good morning Feliciano, I need some information on the Irish twins arrested recently; I understand that they may have been unjustly detained.'

She believed that some photos had been taken prior to the arrest and asked Feliciano to show her the file. He obliged and they both looked at the twins emerging from the water with the drug packages in their hands. She asked what proof there was to make the arrest for smuggling. Were there any photos of the drugs actually being dumped overboard? Feliciano said he was familiar with the case as he was on the boat when they were arrested but couldn't find any more photos other than the two they had already seen.

'Thank you very much Feliciano, you have been a great help. I'll now consider taking on their defence. Give my regards to Jos'e when you see him.'

Foxy returned to her office, telephoned Kat and told her she would take on the twin's case.

46

The Final Autopsy

Thank you notes were a way of life for Caroline as it was drummed into her as a small child that if she didn't write notes to thank people for Christmas presents, she wouldn't get any gifts for her birthday which was in the following January. So when Feliciano walked into the path lab, one was thrust into his hand before they had a great big hug, to the embarrassment of the three interns. He asked what the letter was for and she said it was a thank you for a fantastic evening they had yesterday. He was very surprised as nobody had ever thanked him so formally for anything.

'Well that's what happens when you meet a nice lady, who has been well brought up in a convent,' she chuckled quietly.

'Now Feliciano we must get down to analysing Mr Slime Pit. It is a curious case as there are no distinguishing marks, moles, or warts etc. As you will know, the face has been battered beyond recognition and the Vulture has pecked the eyes out leaving only the sockets. The finger tips have been cut off, so no fingerprints, the teeth also have been ripped out. But there are some unusual bruises around his waist, a dozen or two square marks each around four inches square in two parallel rings something similar to belts. The only other strange matter is that from the top of his breasts to the bottom of his feet on both sides there are two sets of parallel scabs which looks as though he was dragged on his front over some rough concrete. The marks are formed over the breasts, the hips, the thighs, knees, and shins. Most odd! I've removed the knife from the heart and there weren't any fingerprints showing, it was clearly wiped clean. My real concern is it is the same type of knife as the one I bought for my dad!'

'How have you got on with your three bits of research Feliciano, the white mud, the tyre and boot prints?'

'Well Caroline, I have had some results from the manufacturers of the tyre and it's from an old Renault vehicle but the tread is so bald they couldn't identify the car. The mud, I thought I had seen some in my research when I was training for my forensic qualification so I phoned the manufacturer and it was as I thought. It is called Bentonite. It was named after Wilbur C Knight in 1898 after the Cretaceous Shale near Rock River Wyoming. It is used mainly as a drilling mud, consisting of Potassium, Sodium, Calcium and Aluminium. But it's more common use is for sealing and lining ponds, canals and lakes to stop the water leaching away into the ground. So it must have been used in the Slime Pit to do just that. Once it is layered on top of the earth it sets similar to concrete.'

'Well you have been a busy little bee haven't you, I am impressed. Now how does that help us with our killer, what about the boot prints?'

'I've very good news there. I phoned dozens of boot suppliers because I didn't get any replies to the letters I sent and one came up trumps. The boots are quite rare and expensive, are made by Timberland. There's only one boot they make with the tread that matches and the model style is called Zalando. It is unusual in that it has fourteen lace eyelets and it is the only boot they make with that number. All the other Timberland styles only have twelve. Looking at the cast of the boot and comparing it with the Timberland model, it is a size eleven. That would indicate that we are looking at quite a big man with normal size feet or a small man with big feet.'

'Wow that does tell us something doesn't it. This means that if we can find the boots we have the killer! Presumably if the mud sets as concrete then it will be stuck firmly onto the boot soles. Our challenge is that if we want to find the villain, we need to find the identity of Slime Pit Man and at the moment we are stumped. If we could find who he is, we could then search for the people with whom he mixed and might find a motive for the crime.' Caroline was quite excited about the discovery.

'You are absolutely right Caroline and if it is any help I have a ten point list which I have used in other murder cases which helps to find the reasons why people murder.'

To keep a secret – Revenge – Frustration/Hate – Money/greed - Sex/Jealousy – Property dispute – Personal Vendetta – Class Conflict – Narcotics – Urge to protect.

'If we can find his identity though a list of his colleagues, family and friends we could match them up against the list and this might lead us to some suspects.'

'Feliciano, this is an excellent checklist that we can use in all our autopsies. I knew the minute I met you that we would make a good team, not only in our personal life but professionally too. So let's get cracking in depth in both those areas.'

'Caroline I must leave you to continue with your Slime Pit Man autopsy as I have to go and see my uncle in Lisbon, to see if he can help with this drugs problem that James Richmond has found at the Hotel Paradise. I think he may be able to give me some special authority to investigate some dodgy influential people. Also I need to visit the Valbrucks to update them on their robbery so we will have to keep in contact for a while by telephone.'

'Oh bugger! I would much rather you stayed with me to help and that we could fix another evening date. But as my parents always said, work must come first or there is no money to enjoy our leisure time. So off you go and get back as soon as you can. Love you lots!!'

They hugged for a while and she kissed him on the lips for the first time. He stepped out of the morgue feeling like a King and felt like he was walking on air!

47

Parliament Palace

Palacio De Sao Bento was the home of the Assembly of the Republic, which is the parliamentary seat of the Portuguese government in Lisbon. It was constructed on the ruins of the old Sao Bento Benedictine Monastery which was built in the seventeenth century. It was a magnificent white marble fronted building bosting sixty eight front windows together with twelve Doric columns supporting neo classical porticos and the triangular pediment roof.

The President of Portugal was Vasco Da Gama Fernandez and his Justice Minister was Lino Gonzales, Feliciano's uncle. The Prime Minister's office and his residence are housed in the adjoining Sao Bento Mansion which is not where Sn Rabbit received his disastrous letter from Fernando Martins. That was in his other Lisbon office.

Feliciano had travelled by train from Oporto to Lisbon earlier in the day, a journey of some four and a half hours, arriving at the Marques De Pompal railway station in time to see his uncle that day. The first class ticket was extremely inexpensive and the breakfast which was served by white coated waiters with black tie was excellent. He took a taxi from the station to the Palacio.

As he walked up the wide spacious steps of the Palace he felt both nervous and excited at the same time. Nervous because he had never been in such magnificent building being the seat of power in Portugal and excited because the meeting with his uncle could be the start of solving one of the biggest crimes and scandals in recent Portuguese history.

The elderly retired soldier dressed in army uniform was the doorman of the building and he directed him to the Justice Ministers office which was some three hundred yards from the reception area which was enormous. It was laid with marble floors and lined with statuary of famous Portuguese noblemen. His uncle's secretary was seated at a massive oak desk in front of the tall mahogany double doors to the office. She was a typical stern faced elderly lady, locally known as the gatekeeper, whose job it was to stop anyone seeing her boss unless an appointment had been made in advance. She had seen it all and heard all the excuses before. She would have been more suited in an SS uniform complete with a sub machine gun.

'Good morning madam, I have come to see the Justice Minister on a very important mission.' said Fernando politely.

'Have you an appointment, as nobody is allowed to see the minister without one,' she growled with a stern look on her face.

'No I have not but this is a police matter of national importance and he will see me as I am his nephew; trust me he will see me.'

He flashed his identity warrant card with his photo on it. She took it begrudgingly and studied it for some time, looking up at him and down at the photo several times. While he was waiting for her to decide whether he was genuine or not, she made him feel as a ten year old schoolboy standing on the naughty step.

'I'll see if he is in and taking unannounced callers.'

She lifted the telephone slowly as if it was too much effort.

'Good morning Minister, I have a policeman here to see you without an appointment and he says he is your nephew,' she said with great self-importance.

There was a short silence and while she still had the phone to her ear, the double doors burst open and his uncle marched through them and gave Feliciano a great man hug. She put the phone down and looked really thwarted as she saw all her perceived authority and power disappear like a snowball in the summer!

'Feliciano I am so glad to see you, long time no see. Come in, come in my boy and tell me all your news. Hester, please rustle up two light lunches and a bottle of my favourite Borba white wine.'

Hester hated being treated as a servant or waitress. She scowled at them both as they walked into the office and said with great venom,

'Certainly Minister I assume there will be nothing else.'

They ignored the sharpness of her voice, closed the doors and sat in two easy chairs in front of an enormous marble carved fireplace. Feliciano thought how cosy it would be in the winter with a roaring log fire to sit beside.

'Now my boy tell be all about the news and scandal that you normally get involved with. How's your parents and family and have you found a nice girl yet, you crusty old confirmed bachelor?'

Feliciano looked around the room and was mightily impressed with its stately appearance. An enormous desk filled one end of the room and in the centre was an antique conference table with twelve chairs. The floor was all white and black marble with Persian rugs scattered in strategic places. Hanging from a central point in the ceiling was a gigantic crystal chandelier. The walls were mostly lined with polished oak panels and there were many paintings of past ministers and Presidents but he noted there was not any of Salazar. No surprises there. In the many alcoves there were busts of famous past Presidents.

He looked across at his uncle who had aged significantly since he last saw him but he still had the gentle mild humorous look on his face that he always remembered. He was about five feet six tall, thick set with a square face and chin with his slightly balding head shining in the light. His hair was going silver grey at the temples, was hanging over his ears and he wore horn rimmed spectacles. His tummy was much larger than it should have been and he suspected it was due to too many expense account lunches.

'Well uncle let me answer your last question first as we may not have time for the others. I have met the most fantastic girl I have ever seen in my life. Her name is Caroline; she is English and is drop dead gorgeous. She is intelligent, witty, and classy, refined and has a really whacky sense of humour. She is the pathologist in Oporto and is part of the reason that I must talk with you. She has a sister in Australia and her husband is staying at the Hotel Paradise in the Algarve. He has accidently got himself embroiled in a drugs cartel which wants him to be an agent in Australia. He is not interested but does have tape recorded evidence that senior politicians and someone high up in the police force are part of the gang. I feel that if you could give me special authority to go under deep cover, I could flush these villains out and get them arrested.'

Lino walked over to the tall window overlooking the rear gardens which he stared out of, with his hands clasped behind his back and thought for several minutes without saying a word. Then he turned and looked Feliciano straight into his eyes and said in a serious tone.

210

'Does this tape recording mention the names of these people and you do realise that a recording taken without consent is not always admissible in court.'

'I don't have full knowledge of the conversations yet, so I don't know about the names and I do know about the legal situation. But the tapes are a good place to start in order to stop these bastards.'

'I do have the authority to give you special powers but this situation is so serious it may well cause repercussions throughout parliament and could bring down this administration. Therefore I must talk with the President before we make any more moves.'

He immediately left the room to go to the President's office, leaving Feliciano to finish his lunch and drink a couple of glasses of his uncle's favourite wine. Lino was gone for over an hour and when he returned his face was serious, unsmiling and ashen.

'The President was furious and I have never seen him so angry with the news and it took me a while to scrape him off the ceiling. But he did agree that you should have authority to go ahead but on the express condition that you obtain the names before you start and send written confirmation of them to me. You do realise that if you go ahead with the project and it fails, your job and mine will be finished and we will both be on the scrap heap!'

Feliciano understood the gravity of the task, was delighted and terrified as the full responsibility of the whole situation as it dawned on him and understood that it would be him in the hot seat if anything went wrong.

Lino then called in Hester and dictated the authority that Feliciano needed. When it was typed he passed it to his nephew saying.

'Don't forget my boy, you mustn't use this document until you have the names and have sent them to me.'

He then read out the statement which was typed on official parliament headed notepaper:

This document authorises detective sergeant Feliciano Neves the authority to work under deep cover to command any police officials, no matter what position they hold, to obey his instructions to the letter without questioning his authority so to do. They will not tell anyone of his plans which must be carried out with the utmost secrecy. Those who ignore his instructions will be severely disciplined in person by me. The Justice Minister.

Anyone questioning his authority or plans can contact me immediately at any time, day or night for confirmation of these instructions.

Signed:
Lino Gonzales. The Minister for Justice.

'Agreed uncle and thank you for your help. Now don't forget to finish off the wine and eat your lunch. Please thank Hester, it was very nice and just what I needed.'

'Now off you go Feliciano and do take special care, these people who deal in narcotics are nasty vicious individuals and care not about anyone but themselves. They will probably be armed and life is cheap for them.'

'Oh and by the way, it was so nice to hear about Caroline, she sounds absolutely gorgeous and I look forward to meeting her. Also give my best wishes to your parents and apologise for me for not keeping in touch; life is hectic at present.'

He smiled and left the office and nodded to Hester who curled her lip at him, and then he caught a taxi to the station to travel to Faro.

48

The Nude in the Bed

James decided he would have an early light evening supper. He expected Dana to be waiting at table but another lovely girl was waitress. He asked why Dana was not serving and she said that she thought it was her night off. What a relief thought James. The meal as usual was excellent and again he had too much to eat and drink. So he decided to have an early night and catch up on some paperwork.

He retired to his room around eight thirty and after opening the door he could not remember leaving the dimmer light on low. But being a bit forgetful these days thought now more of the matter. Walking past the four poster towards the bathroom he couldn't believe his eyes. Lying stretched out on the bed in a Playboy centre fold pose was Dana, totally naked wearing nothing but a smile! He had to confess that she did look sensational with all her figure going in and out in the right places, together with a well-trimmed Brazilian strip.

'Good evening James, I thought that we might have a little bit of comfort together, as nobody would know and I am rather good at this sex business.'

She had remembered to turn on the hidden camera which was facing the bed.

'Dana, this is something in which I am not interested. I am a happily married man and I don't want to jeopardise that relationship by being unfaithful to my wife. So I think you ought to get dressed, go away and leave me to my work.'

'Oh come on James, don't be a prudish spoilsport, it won't take long. I know I would be the best screw you will ever experienced and as I said, it will all be a secret between us.'

James knew that the only way out of this dangerous situation was to play his trump card. Although he was a full red blooded Australian stud and in the past had been a wow with women, he would have to play the homosexual role.

'Dana you don't understand, I am a left footer, and I play for the other side, a Poof, a Pansy, a Queer. I can't think of any other way to describe me, I prefer sex with men and women are a big turn off for me. Now you must get dressed and leave my room.'

She was so angry and disappointed and knew that Hans would feel the same, as this was the last chance they had to get James compromised. She leapt out of the bed with all her bits jiggling up and down, threw on her wrap and flounced out the door with her nose in the air slamming the door as she went.

She went straight to the lift, pressed the button for the ground floor, ran direct to Hans's office and without knocking strode into the room with her negligee flowing behind her showing her lengthy legs. Hans looked up in surprise and said that that must have been a quickie! She was absolutely fuming and shouted.

'I knew it right from the start, from the day I met him, how he dare turn me down, he's a Nancy Boy a Friggin Faggot! He told me so; he almost threw me out of the room. So we will have to find another way to blackmail him.'

'Slow down and don't upset yourself Dana; it's not the end of the world. I've thought of another way to hold him in my grasp, it will just take a little longer and will be just as effective. You have done your best, now go and lie down in your room, get a good night's sleep and forget about everything.'

James thought he had done very well in convincing Dana that he was Gay and let out a big cowboy Yippee!! Then the phone rang next to his bed, he raced across the room thinking it might be Jenny but the voice on the other end said.

'Good evening my name is Mr Neves' ----

Before he could say any more James interrupted and said quickly.

'Yes I know who you are and you are seeking to join our financial conference that we are delivering next year. I am a bit busy at present, please give me your telephone number and I'll call you back in five minutes.'

James had already found the hidden camera and suspected that his phone was also tapped so he made haste down to reception where he could use a pay phone with an outside line. He phoned Feliciano back on the number he had given.

'Hello Mr Neves, I'm sorry about cutting you short on my room phone. I'll also keep this short. Are you free tomorrow, if so can you meet me outside Faro train station at eleven o clock. I will be wearing a blue tee shirt with a large yellow Kangaroo printed on the front. I will explain all when we meet.'

Feliciano confirmed that the arrangements suited his plans for tomorrow and he would be at the station at eleven. He was mystified as to why there was so much secrecy about the meeting but he was sure all would be revealed in due course.

James went to bed and mused over the day's events and felt quite pleased with himself now that he had stopped Dana in her tracks. For the short time he had known her he had come to like her. She had a pleasant personality and was certainly one of the most beautiful girls he had ever seen. She was intelligent, had excellent social skills and a good sense of fun. He just couldn't understand why she was always trying to seduce him. It wasn't as though he came across as a film star type sex god. He was also looking forward to meeting Feliciano. He knew through Caroline and Jenny that he was a detective but could not really understand how he fitted into the jigsaw. With that though in mind, he fell into a deep troubled sleep.

He woke the next morning to a clear blue sky with a slight chill in the air. He opened all the windows to breath in the cool breeze which cleared his head somewhat from the troubles and mysteries of last night. He dressed in his Kangaroo tee shirt and shorts which didn't match, also his dark hairy legs didn't do too much to set off the ensemble, which turned a few heads as he walked into the dining room which was now set for breakfast. Some of the folks eating their full English thought it was not quite the appropriate garb to wear in the morning but then he was Australian, so they would make allowances for his poor dress sense.

He finished his early morning repast and walked through reception to find a taxi in the rank outside. He saw Dana tip tapping in her high heels walking through reception in his direction with her nose so high in the air it almost touched the ceiling! As they passed each other James said good morning, which she ignored but muttered just loud enough for James to hear, Faggot! To be fair he did look a bit precious in his unusual garb, as he had his man bag hanging over his shoulder, similar to a woman's shoulder bag. He had his Filofax cum tape recorder inside together with the drug packet which Hans gave him and the wine glass with the fingerprints which he would give to Feliciano. So to complete the illusion he minced very slightly out of the main hotel plate glass doors to hail the cab.

49

Hedda Dies

Two days prior to Feliciano's telephone call with James Richmond, he caught the train from Lisbon to Faro. This is not the normal train journey as one would expect because there was not a train to Faro from the station in Lisbon. There was a short fifteen minute walk from the rail terminal, across the Praca do Comercio to catch a ferry across the river Tagus, to the other side of the river where the train leaves for Faro. The two railway lines would not to be joined up for another thirty years until another railway bridge was built across the river.

The service on the train was just as good as the one from Oporto with excellent food. Feliciano relaxed after his meal and slept for most of the journey, as the strain and excitement of the past few days were catching up with him.

He arrived at Faro much refreshed and decided to walk to the police precinct some mile and a half away. Although the sun was shining the weather was getting decidedly chilly so he thought the walk would revive him after the stuffiness of the train. He picked up his unmarked police car from the pound and drove to the Hill and Casa Crao to tell Hedda the good news about her robbery. He parked in her driveway, ambled to the front door and rang the doorbell. When Hedda opened the door he wasn't prepared for the apparition he saw framed in the doorway. Hedda was a shadow of her former self. She must have lost at least three stone in weight, her clothes hung off her skeletal frame, her face resembled a skull and her hair had almost disappeared with only a few wispy strands hanging over her shoulders.

'Feliciano, how nice to see you, do come in and let me get you some refreshments, would you prefer coffee or tea?'

Her words came in short breaths as she struggled to talk, which sounded similar to a croak. He was lost for words for some time as the shock of her appearance sunk into his mind.

'Hedda please don't bother yourself, go and sit down and let me do that for you as you look absolutely exhausted, how long have you been as bad as you are now.'

He went over to the kitchen which was part of the living area and boiled the kettle to make the coffee. He found the biscuit tin and took it over with the coffee to the settee which was set in front of the fireplace. Hedda was sitting huddled with a blanket around her and shivering in front of the roaring log fire and although it was quite warm outside she was clearly suffering from the cold.

'Feliciano, thank you for doing that for me. The cancer has now spread over the whole of my body, the pain is unbearable and I only have a few days to live. I'm freezing cold and cannot get warm. Roly is in Hamburg and he's fully in the picture as to what is happening. He's flying out to take me home tomorrow so I am not here for much longer but before I go back to Hamburg to die, I have some things to do here and I also wanted to see you.'

Feliciano was devastated at the news and to see her in such a dreadful condition. Over the time they had known each other he had become very fond of her, had come to love her in a human way and he felt so wretched to know she was dying such a painful death. They sat close to each other in front of the fire and hugged for a long time saying nothing, while tears ran down both their faces.

As the sobbing ceased and they became more controlled, Hedda asked.

'Anyway Feliciano what is the reason for your visit today, surely not to see me in such a miserable situation?'

'Well, my calling has almost lost its point seeing you in your condition, as I wanted to tell you that we have found the guys who broke into your house. They were two gypsy lads and a Portuguese drug addict. They were found at the Estoi horse fair with a small stall trying to sell the goods they had stolen from other properties. Your safe was among the items recovered, the rear of the safe had been cut open and the front still locked, which meant it would have been no good to anyone. But of course their fingerprints were all over the safe. So they were compared with those found here at your house and they matched. They were arrested and are now in prison waiting for sentencing. I expect they will get a slap on the wrist and be told not to do it again, or am I getting too cynical?'

Hedda looked and sounded sorrowful as she quietly said.

'Well, at least that episode is over and done with. It is a crying shame that some people have such wretched lives that they have to steal from others. But there's not much we can do about that, it seem that these days it's the drugs that cause them to commit such awful crimes against other folks and their property.'

'But moving on, Feliciano I am delighted that you have met Caroline and I know that you are made for each other. I also know from my experience of life and affairs of the heart that you will get married and will be very happy together. Both Roly and I want to help you on your way so we have decided that when I am dead, we want to give Casa Crao to you both and to have it for free, to give you a start in your married life.'

Feliciano was speechless and his throat went dry. He couldn't believe that for someone who he had known for such a short time would be so bighearted.

'Hedda that is so generous of you but we cannot accept. You have two grown up children who would expect you to leave a nest egg to them. Caroline and I will be able to make our own way in life. She is well paid and I am on a reasonable salary, so thank you so much but no thank you.'

'My children are very comfortable and financially well set. Our son is a senior engineer with BMW, my daughter is a financial director of a large manufacturing company and they already own their own houses. They also do not have and do not want any children, so there's no one else who would need the house. It would be no use leaving Casa Crao to them as they don't enjoy the sun and are not very keen on the Algarve. But I respect your independence but I cannot think of another way to help you. Oh and by the way, I have finished my book which chronicles Roly and my life together, warts and all. You may also wish to know that you and Caroline are mentioned in some of the chapters. It's at the printers at present and Roly will send you a copy.'

Feliciano was so impressed with her generosity and her stoic approach to her death. As there wasn't much more he could do or say in the circumstances, he asked her if there was anything he could do for her and she thanked him but said there was not. They hugged on the doorstep with more tears. She closed the door and with a heavy heart and with a lump in his throat, he drove away down the drive to go back to the precinct. He knew that this would be the last time he would ever see her.

Hedda limped and dragged herself into her car and drove down to Santa Barbara De Nex'e. Every move she made caused pain all over her body and she parked outside the estate agents office called Algarve Casa's. She was determined to ensure Feliciano and Caroline would inherit the house, no matter what Feliciano had said to the contrary.

She knew the agent George very well. When he saw her he was also shocked at her appearance.

'No time to talk about me George it's far too late for that. I want you to do something for me. As you can see I am dying and my last wish is that I want you to give Casa Crao, lock stock and barrel to Feliciano Neves, a detective with the Faro police and his intended wife, Dr Caroline Fisher-Hatch. You will take your normal commission plus any other expenses you may incur. Here are my written instructions to expedite the sale, which has been agreed between Roly and me. Any other directives you need you can get from Roly in Hamburg. He is in full agreement with the deal. I am now going back home to die. Do exactly as I ask. Goodbye.'

She struggled and limped back to the car and drove back to Casa Crao leaving George open mouthed and bewildered. Hedda was never seen again in the Algarve.

50

Lady Susan's Restaurant

There were two green roofed taxis waiting at the stand outside Hotel Paradise and James continued mincing up to the first one but there was not a driver to be seen. He asked the other driver if he was able to use him as the first driver wasn't available and he agreed, asking where he wanted to go to. James sat in the back seat and told the man to drive away and he would tell him where as they travelled. He was still concerned that somehow he might be overheard. Eventually he told the driver to take him to Faro railway station and they arrived around ten forty five.

James stood outside the dilapidated grey station entrance which could well do with some renovation. He was amidst the usual platform smells of diesel fumes, oil and stale fish. He was watching the mass of humanity ebbing and flowing in and out of the station with their multi coloured suitcases and personal belongings; from the wealthy up market business men in natty suites to the almost down and out scruffy travellers. He thought nobody should ever be bored whilst they could watch this fascinating parade. It was almost as good as a professional stage show.

An elegantly dressed, full dark bearded Portuguese gentleman in a spotless dark grey two piece suit and sober tie walked up to him and in faultless English with a cut glass accent said.

'Sir, I wonder if you could help me, I have lost my wallet and I need to get to Lisbon urgently on a legal matter and I cannot think of any other way to get there other than asking people to help me. Just a few thousand escudos would help?'

James thought for a while and a distant memory reminded him that Shak had told him about this con man many years ago and it was clear that his patter hadn't changed at all. Just as he was telling him in his best Australian twang to get stuffed, Feliciano arrived in his liveried police car. As soon as the guy saw the policeman he was off like a long dog!

Feliciano proffered his hand which James shook warmly, motioned to him not to speak, then opened the front door and he sat in the seat next to Feliciano. Not until he drove off did James start to talk.

'I can only apologise profusely about all this cloak and dagger stuff but I'm under constant surveillance by some very nasty hoodlums. I've found a secret motion start camera in my bedroom and I am sure that my phone is being tapped. I have been repeatedly compromised by my personal hostess, who tries to get me into bed and have been asked to join a drugs cartel to import narcotics into Australia. In truth I am terrified as to what will happen next and I am in desperate need for some support from you, your team and anyone else that could help.'

'I've been told some of this from Caroline who has been talking to Jenny as a result of your chats with her. I think the best plan is if we go somewhere quiet and you can give me chapter and verse. We'll go to Lady Susan's restaurant in the back streets of Faro where we can talk privately. I've known Robert and Susan in their restaurant for years and they have always been totally discreet.'

This time of the day there is always a parking space outside the restaurant, as lunch wouldn't be served for at least another hour and a half. As they sauntered through the entrance, Susan walked towards them immaculately dressed, tall, blond and as upright as a pike staff.

'Feliciano, so nice to see you again I hope you are well and who is this Antipodean gentleman?'

James was not too happy to be called Antipodean but the tee shirt was a big give away, as back home that would have been seen to be quite an insult but as she didn't seem to mean to be rude he let it pass.

'I am well Susan thank you, this is James Richmond a friend of mine here on business from Australia and we are in a bit of a rush. So if you could serve us a ham and cheese toasted sandwich and a large bottle of water with gas, we would be most grateful. We would prefer to sit in that corner over there as we need to have a quiet chat.'

Susan went off to the kitchen and busied herself with the order. The restaurant was one of the most unusual and successful in Faro, in that it served truly international food. Whereas most others were churning out traditional vegetable soup, fish, boiled potatoes and vegetables, which had been the staple diet of the Portuguese since Henry the Navigators time.

The seating arrangements were unique with ten horseshoe shaped white leather banquet seating, arranged around round tables with white napery and silver cutlery. At the end of the narrow eating area was the bar zone with an imitation red tiled roof overlapping the serving space and next to that was the seats where the two of them sat. They were happy that this was a very private place.

'Now James fill me in about your troubles at the hotel, some of which I know already but repeating it would be useful for the sake of completeness.'

227

Feliciano had a naturally quiet soft manly voice so James had to listen carefully to hear him speak.

'I came to the hotel as part of my business trip to Europe, as I was looking for a venue for our next year's conference. The owner of the hotel is a dubious character called Hans van Glytch, a dwarf Dutch multimillionaire. He and one of his hostesses treated me as royalty and she - well at this point we should draw a veil over her antics! Everything I wanted was on the house and I didn't have to pay for a thing. It became obvious later why this was so, as he not only wanted the exorbitant fees for the conference facilities and the marketing opportunities I would provide but also wanted me to be part of his narcotics cartel importing drugs into Australia. I have a tape recording of our dinner together, where his openly admitted when he was drunk that this was his business. I also have a sample of some of his heroin and a wine glass covered with his fingerprints.'

'That is excellent information James, so it would probably shorten our chat if we heard the tape in its entirety, I'll make notes and stop you if I need any clarification.'

James started the tape and the longer it ran the wider Feliciano's eyes opened. He stopped the machine several times for amplification and when it ended he was well satisfied.

'This gives us a wonderful place to start but we can't always use the tape as evidence in court. Did he give you the names of the other people who are part of the cartel, as this would be vital for us to use in a prosecution?'

'No he didn't but he did say that the other guys were at the top of the government and the police force and I suspect that some of his hired muscle is also party to the deal.'

'James, it is vital that we get their names as I have special authority from my uncle who is the Justice Minister. He is backed by the President, enabling me to override all authorities in Portugal to crack this drugs cell wide open. But the only condition is that we know the names of the co-conspirators before I can start SWAT operations. Can you think of any way that he would tell you who they are?'

He showed James the letter of authority and he was impressed to see that he had such high level contacts.

'Apart from the fact that I am increasingly becoming involved and terrified, I could try trapping him again using my tape recorder. I do have another meeting with him tomorrow when he will show me the conference facilities, so I will try then, see what happens and I'll get back to you.'

'Splendid James, rather than using the telephones, lets meet here at Lady Susan's at the same time the day after tomorrow and we will see how you got on.'

James agreed. There was no need to pay the bill as Susan said it was on the house as she walked them to the door. Feliciano dropped James off some quarter of a mile from the railway station as he didn't want to be seen alighting from a police car. He then hailed another taxi from the station rank which took him back to the hotel.

51

Judge Antonio Da Silver

Foxy had telephoned Kat and told her that she had made an appointment to talk to Judge Antonio Da Silva about the twin's illegal arrest and asked if she would like to come along to add additional weight to her argument with the Judge. Kat was more than pleased to be of help and Foxy agreed to collect her from her house in Gorjoe's near Santa Barbara De Nex'e.

They drove along the narrow country side roads on the way to Faro, bumping up and down on the uneven and potholed surface. Neither Faro nor Loul'e councils would re surface the tarmac, both claiming that it was the others responsibility. Apparently this is quite a normal political practice in Portugal.

They arrived in Faro at the Av.5 Outubro, well before the appointed time and sat in the car park of the Tribunal Judicial De Faro, which is the main seat of justice in Southern Portugal. They looked at the Court House with disgust. An unfortunate looking building evidently built in the early sixties in the Estado Novo architectural style, which was strongly influenced by the Italian fascist design. It was used widely in Portugal between the end of the Second World War and the early seventies, especially in public buildings. The architect was Raul Rodrigues Lima. It was a most ugly building with twelve light grey matchstick looking columns holding up the uninteresting plain flat roof. He must have designed it following a nightmarish dream!

Foxy looked at Kat and said with a voice laden with distain and a chuckle in her voice.

'If I couldn't have designed something more beautiful than that I should have left it alone. Lima should have been hung drawn and quartered for his efforts!'

They both laughed and agreed. Then they then chatted about the possibility that Judge Da Silva might look favourably upon their argument that the Irishmen albeit a bit stupid, were not narcotic dealers but genuine deep sea divers, totally out of their depth. If you will excuse the pun!

Their appointed time arrived and they walked arm in arm, with Foxy's other hand holding her handbag, out of the car park through to reception, which was just as ugly as the outside. They booked in with the receptionist, who directed them to Judge Da Silva's chambers.

They knocked on the massive tall mahogany panelled doors and were welcomed by a booming voice telling them to come in. On entering the chambers they noted that the decorative style was just as boring, dull and bland as the exterior of the building. Apart from his large antique desk there was very little furniture, only just a few upright uncomfortable chairs. There weren't any pictures on the walls, only multiple bookshelves full of legal books.

The judge stood up when they walked into the room with an outstretch hand offered to Foxy, which he shook with great enthusiasm and asked them to sit on the opposite side of his desk.

'Who is your lovely companion Foxy, why is she here with you. I wouldn't have thought you needed any support especially after I have seen you decimate oppositions in the courtroom?' he said with a hearty laugh.

He had a wicked waspish sense of humour which Foxy was well used to but that hid a sharpness of intelligence and wit which the legal profession had witnessed many times in court.

'This is Katricia Hart a very old and trusted friend of mine who has been a regular prison visitor for many years. I thought it would be as well for you to hear her version about the Irish twins who are currently in prison. This of course is why we are here.'

The judge was a tall dignified, thin rakish figure of a man with a long narrow face topped with a mass of silver grey hair which hung down to his shirt collar, clearly in need of a cut. His black eyes were deep set into their sockets and he had a thin hooked nose giving the impression that he looked similar to an eagle. His voice was deep and gravelly. He evidently didn't miss a thing as his gaze swept over everything he saw.

'Now Foxy, I hope you haven't come here to pervert the course of justice by trying to persuade me that the two villains are innocent all charges?' he said with a wry smile.

'Come off it Antonio, you know me better than that. It's just that both Kat and I have interviewed them separately in depth and we have come to the same conclusion, that they aren't guilty for the reasons for which they were arrested. We thought it would help their case and also help you in the courtroom to hear why we are convinced of their innocence on this charge. I have also talked with sergeant detective Neves and he has shown me all the evidence that is on the case file and there are significant gaps and omissions which lead to my deductions.'

'Fair comment Foxy I have always respected your intellect and intelligence in all your legal cases, so off you go and give me all the reasons for your view.'

'There are a number of inconsistencies in the reasons for their arrest.

Number one: The Capitania, the Marine Police and the SWAT team all assumed that as the boat was listing to port it had an alleged cargo of drugs which had had shifted and caused the list.

Number two: The boat in fact had a serious leak in the planking on the port side and the sea had flooded in and caused the list. If the Marine or Police divers checked the timber on the port side, they would find a recent repair.

Number three: It was assumed that as the boat righted itself, the twins had thrown their drugs booty overboard. If the forensic team check the bilge and the hold, they wouldn't find any evidence of drugs but they would see the dirty sea water line showing the level of the water indicating the list.

Number four: The police did photograph the twins bringing aboard two packets of drugs which they found on the seabed but there wasn't any photographic evidence of them ditching the alleged drugs overboard. Nor were there any witnesses to this fact.

Number five: When the Irishmen found the drugs on the seabed, they insisted that the haul was not in fact under their boat but dumped under the 'White Ecstasy' which was berthed next to them. I suspect that if the forensic team checked this boat they would find traces of Heroin and different narcotics in its hold.'

'Well Foxy that is quite a lot of evidence to suggest their innocence, even if some of it is opinion and not proven in fact but there is enough to suggest significant and reasonable doubt.'

He had been taking copious notes throughout Foxy's diatribe. He stood up from his chair, walked around to where Kat was seated and plonked himself on the desk in front of her. He looked her straight in the eyes for a few seconds and Kat felt extremely nervous due to his stare.

Her palms started to sweat and she shifted anxiously in her seat. His body language seemed quite threatening.

'So Katricia, do you concur with everything that Foxy has told me, without any deviation?'

'Absolutely I do, I wouldn't vary anything, in fact it is exactly as the boys suggested and I'm convinced of their innocence of the charge. But I do believe that they are guilty of illegally harvesting the Red Coral and trying to enter the country without the correct papers and authority.'

The Eagle stood up and strolled around the room with his head bowed, deep in thought for at least five minutes. There was an uncomfortable embarrassed silence which pervaded the chamber which made the ladies feel uneasy. Foxy once again had her fingers in her handbag nervously fiddling with the plastic bag. He stopped pacing, stood upright and boomed.

'Very well, you have both made me think that there have been many mistakes made in this case and I will use your testimony to help me decide the issues when the twins come to court. Thank you both very much for your time and inputs, they were well thought through and succinct. Now I must say goodbye as I have a mountain of outstanding legal work to complete.'

He glided to the chamber door which he opened for them, shook both their hands gently, made a small bow and bade them farewell.

They strolled to the car park glad to get a breath of fresh air after the stuffiness of the chambers and were elated with the old 'Eagles' response to their version of events. They decided to go to the nearest bar to celebrate with some wine and nibbles.

52

The Plot Thickens

James paid the taxi driver and thanked him for his steady and relaxed driving from Faro, as some of the motorists driving in Portugal made his hair stand up on end. They hurtled along the roads as though the Devil was on their tails!

He was pleased about his chat with Feliciano but even more troubled that he was getting deeper embroiled into something over which he had no control and lacked understanding of the vicious underworld of drug dealing.

He sauntered uneasily into the reception of the Paradise Hotel, almost sure that somehow Hans would know where he had been and that he had been talking to the police. However he need not have worried because Hans was chatting to the receptionist in a most relaxed way. He turned and saw James and a large smile broke over his face. Not the best expression for him, as when he smiled his ridiculous moustache wobbled and swayed up and down resembling a ferret in a fit!

'Hello James, how has your day panned out. We've missed you today and I wanted to discuss with you our plan for tomorrow, when we can have a tour of the conference facilities to see if it suits you needs.'

James felt a bit more relaxed seeing Hans in such a jovial mood so he suspected that he didn't have any idea about where he had been. Just as they reached each other,

Dana tottered by on her high heels and ignored him with a look of disgust.

'I've had a very good day thank you Hans doing touristy things in Faro,' he lied. 'I had a super Portuguese lunch, ambled around the marina and the back streets looking at all the gift shops and bought a few bits for my wife as souvenirs. Yes, that's a good plan for tomorrow; shall we say we meet at ten thirty here in reception?'

Hans agreed and James took the lift back to his room, very relaxed now that he knew that Dana wouldn't be trying to get his trousers off any more. In preparation for his meeting tomorrow, he fitted new batteries into his Filofax tape recorder and checked that all was in working order. He didn't fancy anything to eat so he piled into his figures and paperwork and had an early night.

The next morning was very similar to yesterday, warm, sunny with a cool breeze which he felt when he opened all the windows. He often though it would be good for him to go for a long walk or a run on the beach before breakfast. But Churchill's rejoinder always came back to him when he thought about exercise, when he said in an interview: *'Every time I feel the need for exercise I lie down until the feeling disappears.'* So he forgot about the walk or run and went and had hearty breakfast full of cholesterol and all the wrong things for healthy diet!

Hans was waiting for him in reception at ten thirty on the dot, dressed for business. They had the customary warm handshake and good mornings and took a brisk stroll to the conference facilities which were only a short walk from the main building of the hotel.

Hans had prepared the complex well in advance to ensure all the amenities were in tip top working order. All the electrical gismos had been checked and double checked and there was a coffee machine filled and working in each of the facilities.

They examined the two main conference rooms first and James was overwhelmed at the size of the halls and the up to date equipment. There was high quality flip chart supports, electronic projection screens, state of the art overhead projectors, a Bose sound system complete with as many microphones as require for multiple orators, three lit rostrums for speakers notes and electric blinds at all the plate glass windows for darkening the room for film shows.

'Hans this is just the size and quality of services that my delegates would expect, I am impressed. Can we now look at some of the syndicate rooms as these are most important for our workshop and think tank activities?'

'I am glad that you find it all to your satisfaction James, we've invested enormous amounts of Escudos to achieve perfection. Now let's move through to the syndicate facilities all of which have the necessary functions for your break outs, tea and coffee sessions. In addition you will have your own personalised hostess for each room who will attend to your every need.'

Having experienced some of Hans hostesses attentions he wasn't too sure what he meant by 'every need' but it was good to know that his clients would be catered for in every eventuality.

They entered the first syndicate room and as expected it was to the same standard as the main halls with similar electronic equipment and multiple flip chat stands. There was a large table in the centre of the room with seating for twelve delegates and soft boards on the walls to hang flipcharts. Hans closed and locked the door quietly and sat on one of the chairs and said casually.

'James, have you thought any more about our business proposition?'

James hadn't been prepared to discuss the cartel at this stage as he thought that would have taken place in Hans's office in complete privacy. He suspected this was why Hans had locked the door. So thinking quickly on his feet he said.

'Hans, before we discuss the cartel business lets conclude the minutiae of the conference contract. If you don't mind I want to take some notes before I forget what we agreed earlier. As you know I do have a head comparable to a sieve and tend to forget the details.'

Hans didn't have a problem with that so James opened his Filofax and the tape recorder started to silently record their discussions. Hans outlined the contract conditions, the price per delegate, the options for food and dining and the importance of booking well in advance to secure the dates which James required. James made notes of all the main points in his Filofax. That being concluded Hans asked the same question again.

'James I ask again, have you thought any more about our business proposition?'

'I have, I have also spoken to my partners in Australia and they showed some interest but were reluctant to agree to any deal as they needed to know the names and more about the other people who are involved in the syndicate. They felt that as you are the only contact we know about, they were suspicious that you might be a one man band.'

There was a long silence as Hans considered his response. He moved to the end of the room, sat down with his head cradled in his hands with his elbows resting on the table. He stayed in this position for almost five minutes deep in thought. Eventually he turned to James and he was horrified at how Hans's appearance and demeanour had changed. Gone was the 'mine host approach' the 'hail fellow well met bonhomie.' His face looked dark and evil in the extreme. He appeared as venomous as a snake with cruelty written all over his phizog. Even his stupid moustache was frozen to his top lip. James felt that the room had taken on a gloomy and ominous feel and it terrified and panicked him. His hands started to perspire and he could feel the sweat running down his spine.

Hans moved over to where James was sitting and with a voice which sounded gravelly he growled.

'Right James this is the deal! If I give you the names and you with your partners decide not to join our family, and you speak one word about this conversation to anyone; in the business I am called the Magician as I can make people disappear. You will all find yourselves fitted with concrete boots at the bottom of an ocean feeding the fishes! If I can't inspire love between you and Dana, believe me I can cause fear!'

'If I choose not to give you the names, our relationship ends here and you better leave for Australia first thing in the morning before something nasty happens to you. Alternatively, I give you the names and you all become part of our business with multiple benefits and money that comes with being part of our family. It's your decision which I need now!'

The tape recorder was still humming away and James hoped that the knocking of his knees and the trembling of his hands didn't show but he knew he didn't have any choice. Feliciano needed the names so he could execute his plan to catch these bastards. He said hoping the quavering in his voice didn't show.

'Ok Hans, my team have given me the authority to proceed and the decision is mine - so let's have the names and we will join the party.'

Hans demeanour changed immediately back to his old bumbling 'mine genial host' approach.

'Right, they are Sr Rabbit the Prime Minister, Sn Coelho the Finance Minister and Fernando Martins the Chief of Police. They all receive a cut of the profits for their cooperation in greasing the wheels of our operations and sweeping Portuguese bureaucracy aside. I'll talk with them to decide how we divide the cake for your percentage, which I can assure you will be substantial and you will have more money than you could even dream of. Welcome to the club.'

James asked if the products would be delivered to Australia from Hans's base in Holland, to which he agreed. Then said James, knowing the Australian coastline well due to his hobby of fishing, suggested that the best importation drop off point would be Bathurst Island, just north of Darwin. It's an extremely wild and desolate part and it would be easy to move the goods from there to the mainland. At this point he was really getting out of his depth and hoping that this load of bullshit would fool the Dutchman.

He congratulated James on his knowledge of the best landing point, gave him a big man hug, slapped him on the back and shook his hand vigorously. James felt most uneasy and sickened at this close contact with the scumbag. So he closed his Filofax and they strolled back to the main reception of the hotel, mutually pleased with the result of their negotiation. But both for very different reasons!

53

Slime Pit Man's Identity

Still a Mystery

Slime Pit Man's body was now stiff as a board as rigor mortis had set in, making further identity much more difficult. Caroline realised that there was no point in trying to find the cause of death, as a kitchen knife thrust in the heart was a real give away. There was also not much need in removing and dissecting the internal organs other than for professional completeness. But she did so in case there was any question from other people who might challenge her competence. No other cause of death was found there.

She was puzzled and intrigued by the dragging of the body which left the scabs all down the front of the cadaver and it continued to raise her curiosity. Why if the killer had done the deed would he then drag it naked and cause the scabbing? She decided to call Feliciano for another opinion. Not only that, she was desperate to see him again. She realised that she had fallen for him, hook line and sinker! She called his office number at the Faro precinct. He answered the phone in his normal soft voice.

'Sergeant Feliciano Neves here, how can I help you?'

'You can easily help me Romeo by coming up here to Oporto and giving me a hand with Mr Slime Pit. Not only that, I am pining for you so get yer skates on and get up here quick,' she said in a voice full of yearning.

'Oh Caroline, it's so lovely to hear your voice and I have missed you so much, although I have been snowed under with work, you have never been out of my thoughts for a second. I think I love you! I have so much news to tell about my first visit to my uncle. I've talked with James and we may be able to get concrete evidence about the drugs cartel but I will save all the news until I see you. Could you book another dinner at the same place at the hotel where we went last time, two days from now and I can't wait to see you?'

'But I have to see James first to see if he managed to discover the other names in the drugs cartel. Then I have to visit my uncle so I'll come up to you the same day.'

Caroline was delirious with joy at the news and called the hotel straight away to reserve the same table for the dinner.

54

Feliciano Meets the President

He ate a continental breakfast. After the enormous full English he had yesterday and with his burgeoning stomach, he thought 'light' would be healthier. He finished it all and washed it down with two cups of black coffee. James slunk out of the hotel hoping nobody saw him leave and got into the first taxi in the rank outside. Again ensuring that he wasn't heard, after they had travelled some distance, instructed the driver to take him to Faro.

As agreed he met Feliciano at Lady Susan's restaurant and they sat at the same secluded table. Susan had not started work and was still at home but Robert was holding the fort and made them welcome with coffee and sticky cakes.

'Well James how did you get on with Sr Van Glytch, did you manage to find out the names of the other members of the cartel?'

'Yes I did but only at the risk of my partners and I being murdered. I can tell you that I was petrified at our meeting and still am! The man is an evil raving psychopath and he'll stop at nothing to keep his foul racket from being discovered; including murdering anyone who gets in his way. You should have seen his face when he threatened me; he looked like the Devil incarnate. He would have scared the pants off of you, and he certainly did me. I had to agree to join the cartel before he would tell me anything about the other members of the gang. You may not be surprised to know that one of them is your boss, Fernando Martins!'

'That doesn't shock me. I knew that he was creaming off some of the motoring fines but I had no idea that he would be so debased as to be involved in narcotics. I always knew he was an evil scoundrel but I never thought he would stoop this low.'

James played back the tape recording of the whole meeting and Feliciano's jaw dropped and he was staggered at some of the revelations. He was thrilled that they had the evidence to show his uncle and the President and he would now have the go-ahead to start his undercover work.

'James from now on do be extremely careful when dealing with Van Glytch, he would have you rubbed out before you could say knife. Avoid as much contact with him as you can and if the situation arises for any reason that you meet my boss, don't drop your guard and keep well away from him, as it could be fatal for you.'

'No worries on that score Feliciano. I'll avoid them like the plague and stay in my room as much as possible until you snare them all.'

They left the restaurant, James took a taxi back to the hotel feeling very vulnerable and Feliciano boarded the train for Lisbon at the Faro terminal. Apart from the normal luggage required for a three day trip he had stowed away James's tape recorder in his overnight bag. The train journey to Lisbon was as usual uneventful, apart from the customary superb lunch after which he dozed for an hour or so. On reaching the end of the line he was not particularly keen on the river crossing across the Tagus on the ferry especially on a dull rainy day. Although seeing the enormous differences of the people travelling across the water, was a treat for anyone interested in people watching which he was. They resembled the League of Nations with all shapes and sizes, nationalities and a cacophony of different languages, it sounded similar to the Tower of Babel, so it did help to pass the time.

The taxi journey from the dock to the Presidential Palace only took some fifteen minutes and he was feeling much more confident than the last time he visited his uncle. So he leapt up the wide steps to the reception desk feeling like a young gazelle. That's just how being in love made him feel. Hester was much more amenable when he strode up to her desk and she almost managed a smile but he thought it might have been flatulence, as she said.

'Good afternoon Mr Neves, it's so nice to see you again. Your uncle and the President are in conference in his office but they said for you to go straight in when you arrive.'

Gone was the gatekeeper attitude and the sour face and he guessed that she might now think that he was someone important and worth cultivating.

He knocked on the mahogany doors and walked in without being asked. As it was a cool wet day, the carved marble fireplace was now lit with a roaring log fire, which made the whole room look inviting and cosy. The President and his uncle were sitting in large leather armchairs around the fire, deep in conversation. They stood up and greeted him as a long lost friend and pulled up another armchair for him to sit next to them.

'Feliciano, so good to see you again and I hope you have brought some good news with you. Let me introduce you to Vasco Da Gama Fernandez our President, which is a bit of a mouthful, so our friends call him Fernandez.'

'Good afternoon Mr President, I feel very honoured to meet you. My uncle has told me a lot about you and I would rather have met you in more favourable circumstances but I am sure when you have heard my news you will be much relieved.'

'Hello Feliciano so nice to meet you. Your uncle has told me of your rapid career history, your homicide successes and the difficulties you have had with your boss, Fernando Martins. He sounds quite a handful. I also hear that you have met the lady of your dreams, well done and I wish you every happiness.'

Feliciano was surprise to see that the President being the most powerful man in the land appeared to be such a normal and genial gentleman who immediately put him at ease. In a crowded street he wouldn't have looked at him twice. He was of medium height, medium weight with light brown hair and not at all striking as one would expect for a President. However he did have the reputation of being a clever astute political genius, especially when dealing with the opposition parties and other national leaders.

'Now Feliciano what information do you have for us, I hope it's valuable and of some use to stop these maniacal narcotic dealers in their tracks.'

'Then I am happy to say that all the news is good and positive. I have James Richmond's tape recording of his conversation with the Dutchman when he named all the members the drugs gang. I must say that he put himself in mortal danger to get the information. They are Sr Rabbit the Prime Minister, Sn Coelho the Finance Minister and my boss Fernando Martins.'

There was a shocked silence in the room as the enormity of the information sunk into the two ministers. Feliciano didn't break the mood. The President was first to speak in a visibly controlled voice.

'That bastard Rabbit. As there were not many well qualified applicants for the post, I proposed him as the least worst candidate as Prime Minister. He always came across as an over smooth oily operator which I was never very comfortable about but I never would have thought he would turn out so bad. As for that little creep Coelho, the slimy measly mouthed bean counter; he was never my choice but Rabbit wanted him in his team. As you may know your uncle appointed Martins, although he was universally disliked, he was good at his job. So now let's hear the content of the tape recording.'

All three of them sat in silence listening to the recording. The only other sound in the room was the crackling of the log fire and the rain beating against the windows. Nobody said a word for the whole length of the tape. There was another long hush as the quietness filled the room and the machine stopped with a click. Lino was the first to speak.

'Feliciano my boy, you and James have done a first class job. I'm immensely proud of you both and I'm sure that when your parents hear of your deeds they will also be delighted. You now have all the authority you asked for to undertake your covert operations. Anything you need, resources in men and equipment is yours, you only need to ask.' Fernandez also echoed his gratitude for a job well done. Feliciano appreciated all their praise and savoured the moment.

'As the President of Portugal I cannot stress enough the importance to this country of what you are planning to do. If you foul it up for any reason, it will be the end of your career and the end of your uncles and my ministry. It could bring down our political party and let those opposition rascals ruin all we have worked for over the years. Remember that we three are a secret phalanx committed to resolving this mess. Take your time and plan with meticulous detail, leave no stone unturned, deeply involve whatever team you build and ensure your communication with them is concise and faultless. Then send a copy of the plan to your uncle. He won't attempt to change or modify your decisions; it is just that we will want to know what

249

will happen and when, so we can be prepared for any questions from those nasty press people. Above all, we offer you the very best of good luck and success to you and your team.'

'Thank you Fernandez, I will do as you say. Before I start any planning or any operations I have to go to Oporto to help Caroline with a puzzling murder which she is struggling with, so this may take a few days. I will take sufficient time to plan properly. I already have some ideas formulating in my mind and I guess the detailed schedule will be with you within two weeks and I'll send you a confidential copy by secure courier.'

They all shook hands and Feliciano left the two of them sitting by the fire discussing the contents of the recording with a look of unbelief and scorn on their faces.

Feliciano left the Palace with the substantial burden of responsibility weighing heavily on his heart. He then hailed a taxi and caught the next train to Oporto.

55

Bi Lateral Metal Knees

On the train to Oporto a plan started to formulate in his mind. He was conscious that nothing should be rushed and detail was the watchword, but one overriding thought kept crossing his mind. He must have the full cooperation of the Captain who is in charge of the SWAT teams in Faro, as they will have to play a major part in the capture of the gangsters. He must involve him right from the start at the planning stage and get him to buy into and help with the plan. The more he tried to think through the issues the more the swaying of the train kept interfering with his thinking. In the end he succumbed to the rocking of the carriage and fell into a deep sleep. He dreamt of meeting Caroline again and realised that he was drunk with love for her and Mr Slime Pit was not the most important issue on his mind. Caroline was and he knew that she was the most wonderful person and exquisite lady he had ever met.

When the train terminated in Oporto, he was still asleep and the conductor had to wake him up. However the sleep did him the power of good and he was refreshed and ready to meet the new challenges he faced. He had booked a three night stay in the Praca Da Ribeira, the same hotel that the Valbrucks and he had stayed while bird watching and where Caroline had arranged the second dinner for them both.

He arrived at the hotel around 22.00, checked into his room and before going to bed and decided to call Caroline at her apartment. The phone rang for ages before a sleepy voice said.

'Hello Dr Fisher-Hatch here what can I do to help.'

This was her standard answer, as she was used to getting emergency calls at all times of the night and day.

'Hello Dr, I am in desperate need of a cuddle and someone to talk to about this fantastic girl I have met but it sounds as if you are in bed.'

'Feliciano! So nice to hear from you, where are you calling from, I've missed you so much. I can get out of bed and come round to see you, are you in the same hotel?'

'Yes the hotel where you've booked for dinner, I've just arrived and wanted to hear your voice before turning in. But no, you stay in bed and get some more beauty sleep, not that you need it, you are beautiful enough already.'

'Flattery will get you everywhere you old smoothie. Ok I will see you at the lab at 9.00 and we can catch up on all the news then.'

He was pleased that he had made the call and heard her voice, even though he had woken her up from her slumbers. Although he felt physically refreshed from his nap on the train, mentally he felt weighed down with the responsibility he had shouldered taking on the narcotics gang. However he undressed, got into bed and slept for a full eight hours.

Looking out of the bedroom window he was pleased to see the morning brought a chilly sunny day. It was refreshing to know that the rain had stopped and the streets looked scrubbed clean, gleaming through being washed and all the weeks of dust was now settled.

He skipped breakfast as he thought the enormous lunch he had on the train would see him though most of the day.

252

He was more interested in hurrying to the morgue and the path lab to see Caroline and help her with Mr Slime Pit Man. As he entered the lab he could see her already dressed in her scrubs and peering at the body. She heard the door squeak and turned around, ran across to him and threw her arms around his neck and they both had the most enthusiastic hug. Even a kiss full on the lips!! Wow! Things were moving on at a pace.

'That's enough of that.' They both said in unison laughing. 'There's work to be done.'

Feliciano dressed in his scrubs and they both stared at the body for some time deep in contemplative thought. Feliciano was the first to break the silence as he said almost absentmindedly.

'You know Caroline ever since I saw Mr Slime Pit, I've had a nagging feeling at the back of my mind that something is familiar about him but I can't think what it is? - Oh never mind let's get on with it. These scabs are intriguing me, they just don't make sense. Let's both scrape them off; you take the left side and I'll take the right.'

They set to work starting from the top of the body and slowly working downwards. Caroline was working faster than he as she was defter with the scalpel. She cut the scabs off the knee and shouted out loud.

'Bingo! This guy has had his knee replaced. It must help us with identification. Have a look at your side to see if it's the same.'

He cut away at the knee scab and the tell-tale scar was the same as the other side and she was right. A bilateral knee replacement job!

'Look at this Fernando, I've cut away all the flesh and muscle around the knee and if I can remove the stainless steel joint we may get an indication of where it was made.'

They both hacked and sawed the joint until they worked its way free. They washed and cleaned the steel and sure enough there was some numbers and figures engraved in a straight line. It was too small to see with a naked eye. So out came the magnifying glass and there was the clue. FARJ220442B. That also didn't make much sense. Caroline muttered.

'It is either a manufactures code number, an indication of the hospital that did the op or the surgeons trade mark. It will take for ever to trace this lot.'

Feliciano thought for a while and suggested that the three internes could do the research on the hospitals and the manufactures to see if the numbers made any sense. Caroline called out.

'Come over here you lazy lot of shirkers, come here and earn your keep instead of pretending you are doing something important. Now I want you to split Portugal into three sections and take one each. Then telephone all the hospitals and prosthetic manufactures in your area and see if they can identify the marks on this metal. There's no rush as long as you get the result within the next hour! The one that finds the answer first gets a Mars Bar. Now off you go, chop chop and get yer fingers out.'

They all laughed and chuckled as they were used to her sardonic humour and her pretend rudeness to them but boy did they respect her professionalism.

'Righto Romeo there's nothing left for us to do here until the team come up with some results, so I suggest we take the afternoon off. I'm knackered and you look shattered so let's meet at the hotel for dinner tonight. I can make my own way there and you are there already. No need for a limousine, so see you there at eight thirty.'

Feliciano couldn't argue with that so he agreed. He kissed her on the cheek and they went their separate ways.

56

They Get Engaged

The hotel Maître d' was an elderly gentleman in the true sense of the word, a dying breed in this fast moving world. He was meticulously dressed, dignified, respectful but not servile. He immediately recognised the pair as they walked into the restaurant and stood by the entrance waiting to be shown to their seats. It was difficult for him not to identify them as they looked so stunning. They turned the heads of the other diners and could have been mistaken as fashion models.

'Good evening Sr Neves, I have reserved the table Caroline requested, if you would follow me.'

As all waiters do for the ladies, he offered Caroline the seat with her back against the wall so she could see everything which was happening in the restaurant, so she thanked him but chose the seat facing the wall. Feliciano was mystified.

'Why didn't you accept the seat he offered you, ladies always prefer to see what is going on?'

'When my parents were bringing me up they set great store ensuring I had respect for other people, excellent manners and fine social skills, as they also did in the Convent. The most important for me was correct table manners and the etiquette of eating food. I find that the majority of people these days don't know or care about how they eat at table and I can't bear to watch them. So I always sit facing the wall.'

Feliciano had never thought about such a practice, as in his family of eight children it was a matter of eating the food before some other greedy kid gobbled it down!

'I'll remember that in the future and will always seat you so. Now what is your favourite meal for tonight?'

Feliciano passed her the menu, again without prices. They studied the options in silence and they gave the order to the waiter.

'Now Caroline I want to know so much about you, I don't know where to start and the first thing that puzzles me is why your dad calls you Flopsie.'

'Well, when I was in my early teens I was growing resembling a weed and I became thin, gangly and very tall for my age. I was the tallest girl in the Convent so I used to stoop and flop about, especially when at home so Flopsie became my nick name and it stuck.'

'Now it's your turn, the last time we were here and I mentioned Catholicism, you nearly fell off your chair; what was that all about?'

'I was born into a very poor family of eight children and my parents believed that 'God' decides how big the family should be. As I grew up and could understand these things better, I couldn't accept the concept of a God or the Pope deciding our future; when he lives off the fat of the land, receives money from the poorest in society, lives in luxury in a palace and has his own helicopter. So to cut a long story short, I became a Buddhist. So that explains my reaction to your Catholic Convent schooling.'

She felt very humbled by the explanation of his background and it helped her to understand how he had become such a nice caring, thoughtful and peaceful person. She would later want to know more about Buddhism. It was no wonder she had fallen so deeply in love with him.

'I am worried about you since the last time we were together, you seem troubled, preoccupied and you look distant and worried. What's gone wrong in your life since we last met?'

'Under normal circumstances a homicide detective is one of the loneliest jobs in the world, always snooping around in other people's private lives and sometimes accusing them of things they haven't done. Now I have the greatest challenge I have ever faced and it worries me.'

He went to on to briefly explain the task he was given by the President and his uncle. How it all must be kept secret and if he fouls it all up, he would be out of a job and the country would be in a political turmoil. Caroline was shocked and surprised at the gravity of his situation, especially as he had been given the task at his lowly rank of detective sergeant. He showed her the letter of authority from the Ministers and it stunned her into a long silence as she felt so helpless in this situation.

'Oh dear my love, no wonder you are so down in the dumps, what can I do to help you?'

'Not much really, only just be yourself and give me as much emotional support as you can, that's the best you can do. Now let's get away from this difficult situation and talk of nicer things. Let me tell you what's been happening since we last we met. I called in to see Hedda Valbruch, you may remember her, she was with me when we met at the Slime Pit. I went to update her about her robbery and she was in such a state, in fact she was dying from her cancer. She only had a few days to live and was in dreadful pain. She made such a generous gesture to us; she wanted to give us her villa for free when she died. Of course I could not accept as I said we should make our own way in the world.'

'Oh dear Feliciano you have had such a difficult time and what a magnificent gesture to make especially as we have only know her for such a short time. What a start that would have given us. But you were quite right to decline.'

'I also had lunch with James Richmond and he has two tape recordings of a conversation he had with that millionaire Dutchman who owns the Hotel Paradise, admitting that he was a drugs dealer and wanted James to be part of his cartel. After I played the tapes to the President and my uncle it was then they gave me the authority to go under deep cover to bust the drugs ring.'

'Blimey you have been a busy boy, no wonder you are so stressed. My life seems quite serene compared with yours.'

They had been talking so much they hadn't realised they had almost finished their dinner as the coffee course arrived. Feliciano said there was one more thing he had to do before they left the restaurant. He fumbled in his jacket and pulled out a small leather box and gave it to Caroline which she opened.

'My goodness gracious Feliciano an engagement ring! And look at the size of the diamond. Yes, yes I will oh yes I will!'

'Yes you will what; I haven't asked you anything yet?'

'Yes of course I will marry you as soon as possible, yes, yes, yes, just name the day.'

Feliciano called the waiter over and ordered a bottle of Krug to celebrate the occasion. They clinked glasses in a toast and Caroline had tears of happiness in her eyes. As the diners closest to their table had witnessed the proposal and they all stood and applauded the happy couple.

After they had polished off the whole bottle of Krug they were both feeling a bit squiffy so they decided to walk back to Caroline's flat hoping the fresh air would clear their heads somewhat. When they reached the door of the apartment she said.

'I suppose this is where you ask me if you could come in for coffee as you did last time and I said no. Well this time you don't have to ask, come on in.'

They took the lift to the top floor and went into the flat which he thought was beautifully decorated if a bit alternative and eclectic. She swayed a bit too much into the kitchen and made the coffee. Her head was still swimming a bit from the champagne.

'There we are my intended, the coffee you always lusted for even though you had more than enough with your dinner. Drink up and then you must go, we have another hard day ahead of us tomorrow.'

After he finished his drink, she took him by the arm pushed a small envelope in his coat pocket and said not to open it until he got into bed. They stood up had a most passionate kiss and embrace then she hustled him out of the front door, shut it and bolted it securely. He stood outside the door and thought; again that's not how it works in any of the films I've seen! He took the lift to the ground floor and walked back to the hotel, again totally confused.

He was so pleased and excited about the way the evening had gone and he walked back to the hotel as if he was floating on a cloud. All the heavy responsibility of his job seemed much lighter now.

He said a very good evening to the Maître d' who was waiting outside of the restaurant doors and he gave him a broad smile and a wink in recognition of his engagement.

His bed had been turned back and there was a chocolate and a miniature bottle of champagne on his side table with a note from management congratulating him on his engagement. What a nice touch he thought as he undressed for bed. Then he remembered the envelope which Caroline had slipped into his jacket pocket. He opened it and inside was a small red plastic credit card sized note which read:-

I Love You

I love you so much
and in so many ways
for so many reasons
you brighten my days,

I love you so much
and I always will too
I'll always feel lucky
because I found you!

He was overwhelmed with the thought she had put into this simple gesture and then slept better than he had in weeks.

57

Slime Pit Man Identified

HONK, HONK, came the sound which startled him as he walked to the path-lab the next day. With a screech of brakes her Vespa came to a stop right next to him.

'Hop on Romeo I'll give you the ride of your life to the morgue so hold on tight.'

He did 'hop on' as she said and immediately wished he hadn't. As a motorcycle cop he had been used to some hairy riding experiences but this was one of the worst he had suffered. She rode as mad as a Hatter! Riding up and down pavements and ignoring red lights, scattering bicycles and pedestrians asunder, they arrived at the morgue in one piece!

'Did you enjoy that?'

She said as she heaved the bike onto its stand, watched it for a while to ensure it didn't fall over as it sometimes did.

'Well it was certainly different to my motorcycling days. Really, as a policeman I should book you now for dangerous driving. Remind me sometime to give you some police training riding hints; they might save your life!'

They both had a hug and a good laugh at the experience and opened the path lab door to see the youngest intern, the one who washed the cadaver by mistake, standing there with wide grin on his face and his hand outstretched, palm upwards.

'What are you looking so please about squirt?'

'I want my Mars Bar, I got really lucky yesterday. I only had to phone four hospitals and got the right one. It's the Gambelas Hospital Particular in Faro near the airport and they identified the numbers immediately.'

'You clever young man, have you told the others to stop searching and wasting their time?'

'Not until I get my Mars Bar.'

'You'll get it when I am good ready, when you give us the code and not before, you cheeky little toad.'

With that she reached into her handbag for the bar and tossed it over to him which he deftly caught in mid-air. He laughed out loud, went over to the other two internes, cut the bar into three and shared it with them.

'Righto tow rag; give us the code, numbers and name of Mr Slime Pit Man,' she said shaking her fist at him.

'Its quiet simple really; FAR is the Faro area, J is the first letter of the patients name, 220441 is the birthdate and B is the last letter of the last name. So their records show; Jos'e Barros, born twenty second of April nineteen forty one.'

'Bloody Hell, he's my missing boss - Gollum! We all thought he'd run off months ago with Floralegs Pinto,' cried Feliciano. 'I knew there was something familiar about the body but couldn't bring it to mind, I recognised his hair! He was an excellent boss. If only he had left the girls alone he would have been superb. Much better than the miserable old git I have as a boss at present.'

Caroline told the internes to tidy up poor old Jose's remains and put him back into the refrigerated drawer and they repaired to her office through the glass door partition which overlooked the path lab and morgue. They sat down at her desk both in silent thought for some minutes.

Feliciano was clearly upset to find that his boss, for whom he had so much respect, had been butchered in such a callous way. He was the first to break the silence.

'Well Caroline, at least we have somewhere to start and something to work with and we can now piece together some of his associates, friends and enemies, of which I know there were many. Remembering Motive Means and Opportunity, I can list some of the people he was tracking, as I was working with him on some of his cases.'

Caroline was pleased to know the identity of the poor soul and was also concerned to see Feliciano so upset, even though he seemed to recover quickly and moved into professional mode so rapidly. She started by almost stating the obvious.

'Whoever did the deed, we can discard the 'Means' as the knife, without fingerprints, is one that anyone could buy over the counter, so that leaves us with 'Motive' and 'Opportunity'. Also we can't rely on the time of death as the body has been in the Pit for so long and the decomposition so bad, we weren't left with any clues as to the date of the murder.'

Feliciano then started to list the most obvious culprits, not in any particular order of importance.

'The most obvious person must be his **Wife Rosa**. She had the ultimate motive of frustration/hate and she knew that he was always playing away from home. She also had opportunity as she was with him most of the time.'

'Then there is the **Gipsy King**. He would have hated the fact that Jos'e was having a thing with one of his most beautiful gypsy girls, who he himself may have lusted after. So his motive could have been desire. His opportunity was always there as Jos'e spent a lot of time in the camps trying to crack the drugs scene.'

'**Ivor Gonagetim:** He is a psychopath, mad as a March hare, a trained stone cold killer who would do anything if the price was right. His motivation would have been money. The rumours around the camps were that he had two contracts out, both on policemen. Opportunity would be easy as again Jos'e was frequently in the camps.'

'**The Prime Minister**, Sn Rabbit. It could be him as Jos'e was on his tail for corruption with regard to the motorway scam. His motive would be to silence Jos'e because he was getting to close to his bribery. Opportunity would have been difficult as he was mostly in the public domain and surrounded by his bodyguards.'

'Then there is **Fernando Martins.** His motivation could have been to rub out the competition for the top job. Opportunity would have been easy as they worked together for a lot of their time.'

'**Hans van Glytch** is also in the frame. After listening to James's tapes, he is well into the drugs scene. If José and Martins were working together and if Jos'e discovered that Martins and Glytch was masterminding the cartel, what better motive for killing him. As for opportunity, he wouldn't have got his hands dirty. He would get one of his muscles to do the job. He has a particular nasty bit of work who was a cage fighter so he would probably use him.'

'Lastly there is your dad **Shak.** He says he can't find the knife you bought him which was identical to the one found on the body. His motivation could have been a violent rage, as you said he was incandescent about being fined five times in a week. You did say he would kill the guy who introduced the fines. Opportunity would need to be looked into in more depth.'

'So there we are Caroline seven suspects, which we need to analyse in much more depth.'

'Oh come off it Feliciano, you can't really put my dad on the list, he only said what he said in a fit of temper. Lots of people say they would kill someone for something they have done, but don't in reality do the deed!' She sounded decidedly frosty.

'Well as you well know Caroline, my job is to look at the facts without fear or favour. The best option for taking him off the list would for you both to find the knife at his home.'

Caroline was most upset that he would even consider putting him on the list as she knew that her dad was such a gentle person and she was determined to help him find the knife. Feliciano was deeply concerned that he might have damaged his relationship with her but he had his job to do even if it distressed her.

'Now my love I have to go back to Faro and start planning my undercover work. We will have to come back to the suspect list when I have completed it and sent a copy to the President and my uncle. In the meantime, if you can think of any other motives on our list, that would be very useful. Also if you and Shak could find the knife I would be delighted and we could take him off the list.'

He gave Caroline a big hug which he thought was not reciprocated as she normally would. He then took a taxi to the station and would worry himself for days over her coolness.

58

The SWAT Team Plan

Giovanni Antonucci is an unusual name for a Portuguese police Captain. His parents were born in Italy and moved to Portugal when he was five years old, just in time for him to start in the Portuguese schools. So he was fluent in Italian, Portuguese and English languages.

Despite the difference in authority levels, between Giovanni and Feliciano, he being subordinate, they were very comfortable as colleagues and were happy to mix socially as well. Giovanni was a typical Italian looking man. He had olive skin, was thick set and muscular, rugged rather than handsome, dark wavy hair swept back and always immaculately dressed in his uniform and a force to be reckoned with in his fatigues when on an assignment.

Feliciano arrived early at the Faro precinct hoping to avoid his boss. So he sloped past his office as quietly as he could. But no such luck! Then he heard the shout.

'Oh so you've decided to come back at last have you Neves. About time too, perhaps you can now get on with some of our routine detective work. I suppose you've found a bit of skirt up in Oporto. You're getting close and closer to riding that motor bike again!' He was in a particularly bad mood today as the pain in his head was getting worse and the painkillers were having less effect.

'Yes sir, yes sir, certainly sir, I will do as you say right away sir.'

Fernando had developed skilful coping strategies in replying to his bosses sarcasm and verbal abuse but he never realised that in his replies he was taking the mickey. So he continued on past his office and on to see the Captain of the SWAT teams.

Feliciano breezed into Giovanni's office and with a cheery hello, asked if he would want to pop out for a coffee in the café overlooking the marina opposite the police station, to which he agreed. Feliciano bought the drinks and they sat on a bench in the warm morning sunlight watching the tiny boats bob up and down in the slight swell. Feliciano spoke in hushed tones.

'Giovanni, I'm going to tell you something about a mission I've been given by the President and the Minister of Justice, which will rock the foundations of our government. Secrecy between us is of vital importance and if anything leaks out, then we will both be in the deep cakey stuff. Nobody but us must know about it until the day we make our move.'

He showed Giovanni the letter of authority which he read very carefully, twice. He was flabbergasted and speechless for a few minutes as the enormity of the information seeped into his consciousness. Finally he looked at Feliciano with disbelief in his eyes.

'Do you mean to say that we can't even tell our boss Fernando Martins?'

'You are correct, especially him, as he is one of the guys we will be investigating. We've tape recorded evidence which proves that two senior government officials, narcotics Baron Mr Big and Martins are part of a drugs syndicate, so at this stage it's probably best if I keep the other names under wraps until the last minute.'

'What we need from you is four teams, all armed and in different places at the same time. We need two men dressed in business suits in the Sao Bento Mansion in Lisbon lightly armed. Another two again armed and dressed in business suits, who are used to flying in helicopters, and they will arrive at the Paradise Hotel. Another six guys in disguise at the Vilamoura marina and another four heavily armed, ready to move quickly, silently, with maximum surprise, near Santa Barbara. They all need to be briefed for violent action but not told the final destinations or the targets until the last minute. Do you think you could arrange this in secret?'

Giovanni had a similar temperament to Feliciano; he was thoughtful, quiet, studious and a fine detail man. He considered Feliciano's request for a good ten minutes before replying.

'I think it's all doable, so give me three days to produce a plan, I'll put it in writing and you'll have it, say by Friday, how does that fit with your strategy?'

'Excellent; good man, I knew I could count on you. I have to send my proposal to Lisbon within ten days. Not for approval but to let the President know what will be happening and when, so he can handle any flack. The timing of your proposal will fit into the timeframe perfectly. I know we will make a tremendous team and thank you so much for your help and support.'

They shook hands and thought it would be best if they went back to their offices separately, hopefully so that nobody would have seen them in discussion. But nothing gets past Martins. As Giovanni passed his office he heard the familiar voice shouting out.

'I suppose you've been chatting with Neves about his fancy woman in Oporto, he seems to be spending most of his time up there these days?'

Without stopping he called back in an equally loud voice.

'Yes I have and by all accounts she is a bit of a corker, fizzing with personality and drop dead gorgeous. Lucky bugger!'

Feliciano skulked past Martins door this time unnoticed. He stopped to listen as he heard him talking in a foreign language he didn't understand, interspersed with English as he said angrily, 'I've paid you too much already you blackmailing bastard.' Not understanding what that was all about he hurried up the two flights of stairs, slid into his office and locked the door. It was time to start putting his plan together. Firstly he phoned Heliair, the helicopter hire company at the Alvore private airfield and provisionally booked a four seat Robinson R66 turbine helicopter with a date to be agreed. Then he called Dr Humtie Sago the vet based in Montenegro and enquired if he could be booked with a rifle and a barbed tranquiliser dart, which would stop a dangerous dog in its tracks. He then continued to blueprint his plan.

His thoughts kept returning to Caroline's coolness and he jotted a note to himself to call her as soon as he was out of Martins earshot.

59

The Nightmare so Real

Twelve matt black ocean going tugs were jostling around for the best position outside the warehouse, in the dark cold muddy waters of the river Tagus in Lisbon. The name on each boat was that of the twelve Apostles. They were reminiscent of cocky strutting starlings arguing over the best place to roost in a tree at dusk. Their crews all dressed in black moved silently around the decks identical to ghostly shadows. It was a dark moonless night and black clouds scudded across the skies. At midnight there was a cacophony of hooters and whistles from the boats, which was deafening and smoke was pouring from their exhausts as they bumped and bored across each other.

The inside of the concrete warehouse on the edge of the dock was cold, damp, smelly and covered in seaweed and slime. The rusty iron twelve foot tall sliding door was locked shut and was bolted inside at the top and bottom. There was no way out. There were a dozen or so tea chests scattered around the floor, some upright and some knocked over on their sides, all full of human bones and skulls bleached white. The skulls seemed to be laughing at the victim. The temperature was twenty six degrees Fahrenheit, well below freezing point.

Caroline was propped up against one of the cast iron roof supports with her hands tied together with Gaffer tape behind the post and her feet were also bound with tape in the same fashion. Her dress was torn to shreds exposing parts which should not be seen. Some of her long hair had been torn out by the roots. The extreme low temperature was causing the dripping from her nose to freeze into an icicle as seen in a stalactite. Her face was covered in blood, with a frozen look of horror and her black eyes were wide open in a distant stare.

The powerfully built body of the killer, hardly recognisable, due to his dark waterproof clothing; his head was covered by an enormous hood. Only his eyes showed, throwing beams of light as from two torches playing on her face. He chuckled to himself as he wielded THE knife above his head. As he brought it down for the killer blow; she tried to scream but the filthy rag smelling of oil and petrol which was stuffed in her mouth and throat stifled any noise and she passed out cold in a dead faint.

Feliciano's whole body jumped some inches from the bed as he screamed out; the nightmare disappeared as quickly as it had appeared. He was cold sweating all over and the bed was soaked. He laid there for a few moments trying to recover from the dreadful experience. He thought thank goodness that was just a dream. My poor Caroline I must call her straight away.

He picked up his brick of a Motorola phone and dialled her number forgetting that it was only six o clock in the morning. He heard a sleepy voice say.

'Good morning, this is Dr Fisher-Hatch, what can I do for you?'

'Oh you could do so much for me my love but I'm just calling to hear your voice, to thank you for that lovely poem and to tell you about the horrific nightmare I had last night where you were killed by THE knife. It was traumatic in the extreme and upset me no end.'

He then described in fine detail the pictures and images in his mind which the nightmare left on his consciousness.

'Oh dear that sounds so horrid, I hope you are fully recovered. If the vision doesn't leave within the next few hours, perhaps you should take some tranquilisers to calm you down. You can buy them over the counter at any pharmacy without a prescription.'

'Any way, I have some good news for you. Dad and I scoured the whole flat looking for the knife. We looked in drawers, wardrobes, kitchen cupboards, even under carpets and sofas but no knife could be found. We searched dads shop and as your know, that is always a right old mess – nothing. After you put dad on the suspect list he was really panicking. We both knew that he hadn't done the deed and he wasn't too happy that you thought he might have done. Then he had a thought. He was using the knife to cut open some packaging wrapped around a new drum kit, so he flew outside just as the bin men were arriving and he found it stuck in the cardboard. So take him off the list Romeo.'

'Wow, that's a relief and it narrows the list down to six. I can't understand how we or probably I missed the obvious. It's a possibly that when I'm with you my brain is so fuddled. Anyhow I think I'll give the tranquilisers a miss at present and see how it goes.'

'Yes and another thing Sherlock, dads shoe size is a six and a half, he has small feet and the boots we found were size eleven. How could we miss that evidence? Also we put Jose's wife Rosa on the list and I checked her shoe size which is a five! So unless she clomped around in boots far too big for her or got someone else to kill her husband, we should take her off the list as well.'

'Well done Caroline, if you keep this up you'll have the killer behind bars in no time and old Martins would really have a good reason for giving me the sack!'

'I've started on the plan for the President, involved Giovanni the SWAT Captain and he will have his team's objective ready within the week. So we should be ready to go within ten days.'

'Oh Feliciano do be careful, this could be the most dangerous project you have ever attempted. I don't want to lose you now we have found each other.'

She hung up the phone and went back to sleep worrying about how the assignment would end and thinking that finding Jos'e killer would have to wait until Feliciano's mission was finished.

60

The President Calls Hans

'Find Dana my PA and tell to come to my office immediately, its most important,' shouted Van Glytch to his head receptionist. She was on the phone immediately trying to locate her.

As she entered Hans's office out of breath and wondering why the hurry, as he is normally so laid back about most things to do with the Hotel. Dana said with her chest heaving.

'What's all the panic about Hans, I was busy making myself look wonderful for a new group of guests arriving this morning.'

'No panic Dana, just excitement. I've just had a call from the Presidents secretary saying that he wants to deliver his next annual party political conference in our hotel and he needs to have a look at the facility next Sunday! So as my PA I want you to deal with all the detailed arrangements for the day. Organise lunch in our best restaurant with the finest menu and most expensive wines. Check that all the conference room equipment is working correctly, spotlessly cleaned, etc. No stone left unturned. How about that, the President himself is coming here, we really are moving into the big time. One of the reasons he wants to use us is that we have a helicopter landing pad which is ideal for the top brass security.'

'That is wonderful news Hans, I'll get too it right away. You know you can always rely on me to get things organised.'

The motorcycle courier had delivered Feliciano's confidential plan to the President and the Justice Minister exactly on the day to which Feliciano had committed. Lino's secretary told the messenger to wait for a while in case the there was a reply. She supplied him with refreshments and commented that he must be cold on the bike as the weather had cooled down a bit. Then she took the package into the office.

The President instructed her to ensure that the courier was well fed and watered and for him to wait for a reply to be typed.

'I have already given the courier refreshments. Will there be anything else sir?

Knowing that there would not be anything else she disappeared to continue with her duties.

They sat in front of the fireplace which again was lit due to the chilly weather. They both studied the plan separately for well over and hour and together came to the same conclusion. Both Feliciano and Giovanni's detailed blueprint was perfect in every aspect. Lino was the first to speak.

'Well Fernandez, I know I shouldn't be the first to praise the work they have done, especially as he is my nephew but I think it's brilliant and has covered every contingency. If anything goes wrong on the day it won't be their fault.'

'I agree and while we did say that we only wanted the information as a courtesy, I'll send a letter of congratulations to them encouraging progress and to go ahead in their own time when they are ready, without any further contact from us.'

They called Hester in again to dictate the reply. The letter would be typed, signed and passed to the courier who was now much refreshed and somewhat warmer. He would then be off on his long journey back to the Algarve with instructions that the letter must be handed to Feliciano Neves only and the receipt signed by him.

Feliciano had hired a basement room in the Hotel Faro to ensure secrecy and was now briefing Giovanni fully on the names and details of the operation which will be carried out on the next Sunday.

'I've chosen a Sunday, as people are much more relaxed and probably not so aware that a sting would happen on the day of rest. All four teams must strike at the same time; that is twelve noon. This will make sure that none of the villains can communicate and get any support from each other.'

'The Prime Minister Sr Rabbit and his Finance Minister Sr Coelho are involved in the drugs cartel and for bribery and corruption in connection with the new motorway. They will be working in the Sao Benton Mansion in Lisbon. The President has given them a financial project which they must complete by the following Monday so we know they will be there. He has also told their bodyguards to stand down and take the day off. Two of your team will be introduced as financial consultants who have been tasked to help them with their figures. So you shouldn't have any problems arresting them.'

'Another two of your team, dressed in business suits will arrive by helicopter on the roof of the Hotel Paradise. They will pose as bodyguards for the President who is supposed to be visiting the hotel to take a look at the conference facilities. Of course he will not be there but his secretary will, to give authenticity to the plot. We expect Mr Big, Hans van Glytch who is the owner of the hotel and the ringmaster of the drugs cartel will be on the roof waiting to greet the President, together with his PA Dana. It's unlikely that his hired thugs will be there as they live on his yacht in Vilamoura and Van Glytch will want all the glory of meeting the President on his own. But your men should be ready for anything unforeseen that might crop up.'

'The next difficulty is that of the hired muscle on the yacht. I suggest that you lead this team as it is likely to be the most dangerous. They will probably be armed and the most hazardous will be Bruno, an ex-cage fighter and a real brute, so with you and six of your team you should make short work of them but it will probably end in a fire fight.'

'Lastly I'll lead the team to arrest Martins in his Villa. We know that on Sundays he spends most of the day relaxing and sunning himself. He shouldn't be a problem with your team of four armed men but I expect he will put up some kind of resistance.'

'Does all this make sense and fit into your strategy Giovanni and is there anything I have missed out or something you would want to add or amend?'

'No, everything is absolutely clear. I knew that you said this was a high level operation with some big names involved but I never would have thought that the government would be so involved. I am staggered! I'll give my teams their last briefing late on Friday night. This will give the Lisbon team time to get up there for the Sunday.'

They were about to conclude their meeting when the courier came into the room with the letter from the President.

'I went to the precinct looking for you to deliver this package but couldn't find you. So I asked Fernando

Martins and he said he would sign for it but I said it could only be signed for by you. He was mad as a box of frogs and said 'who the bloody hell does think he is' so I got out as fast as I could and spoke to your secretary who told me you were in the Hotel Faro. Did I do right?'

'Thank you so much for thinking on your feet. You did absolutely right. I didn't want Martins to know where we were so you did well. Now off you go and get some warm food and drink down you, you must be frozen to the bone.'

Feliciano shook his hand and palmed enough Escudos for him to have a substantial meal. Then he opened the letter and read it out to Giovanni.

They were most impressed with the wording of the text and the warm thoughts penned from the President and that he had taken the trouble and time to contact them. Then Feliciano said in frustration.

'It's a bit of a bugger that Martins knows about the letter; let's just hope he doesn't get too suspicious. At least the courier didn't let him know who it came from.'

They shook hands, had a man hug, a slap on the back and wished each other the best of fortune for the Sunday operations and left the basement to go back to the precinct office.

61

The First Sting

The two classically dressed businessmen with their black briefcases strode into the mansion with an air of confidence, with pistols in their shoulder holsters and were greeted by Sr Rabbit with warmth and enthusiasm.

The policemen were overwhelmed with the opulence of the Mansion. Never had they been in such a palatial building. There was more antique Ormolu furniture, Persian rugs and old master paintings than they had ever seen anywhere. All the windows were glazed with old float glass and beautifully decorated with scenes from Portuguese history.

'Welcome to you both, the President told us you would be coming to help us with our accounts, audits and spread sheets, so come in and sit down near us.'

He extended his hand in welcome and as he did so and before he could move, the handcuffs were on his wrist and in a flash the other end was on Coelho's wrist at the same time. They were dazed into silence as the officer said.

'Sr Rabbit and Sr Coelho you are both under arrest for bribery, corruption, and being part of a narcotics drug cartel. We have tape recorded evidence when Mr van Glytch admitted that you were involved. You do not have to say anything but anything you do say will be taken down and may be used in evidence against you.'

The next explosion of expletives was not expected by either of the two officers as Rabbit raved purple faced.

'You stupid little half-witted twat, you assured me that all the money dealings were safe in Switzerland and that dopy drunk Dutch Dwarf would keep everything secret, now he's spilled the beans on tape!'

'DON'T CALL ME LITTLE! If it wasn't for your big mouth shouting about at the Gypsy Fair when you paid that bastard Ivor Gonagetim fourteen million to kill Martins, we wouldn't be in this mess now.'

The two officers looked at each other in amazement. They weren't prepared for this revelation, as they thought the arrest was about narcotics and corruption. But without ado they took out their notebooks and wrote down everything that was said about the murder.

'Right you two; let's get you both down to the local nick and get you processed.'

They bundled them into the police car and the two were still arguing and blaming each other for the arrest. The local station was a short drive and the pair was taken to the duty desk sergeant who wrote down their particulars. They were then taken separately to the interview rooms and statements taken and signed. Next port of call was the Lisbon prison and that was a surprise for both of them.

The building looked similar to a mediaeval castle rather than a prison. It had twelve foot high double oaken entrance doors criss-crossed with thick narrow oak slats held in place with black square iron headed bolts. Under a stone archway with its round castellated towers flanking the doors, were eight arrow slit windows on each side, together with Gothic widows and two sentry boxes in which were standing armed uniformed policemen.

The pair thought this looks quite comfortable, similar to a hotel rather than a prison. But they soon changed their minds when they were banged up in the cold featureless cell with one openable barred window, two iron beds, a chest of drawers and a toilet.

The first sting had been completed without incidence just as planned.

62

The Second Sting

Flying helicopters was the greatest occupation in the world thought the pilot as he circled above the Hotel Paradise. He was his own boss, loved flying, was paid excellent fees and saw the whole world with a bird's eye view. In his opinion the Bell helicopter was the best aircraft to fly as it was so compliant and did exactly what he wanted it to do at the right time.

As he looked down he was most surprised, as the hotel looked much larger from the air and covered more acres than the view showed from his maps. He flew two circuits over the hotel to check the wind speed and watched the hotel roof wind sock which was showing a slight westerly breeze. He adjusted his height and approach to suit the conditions and started to descend. He called over the intercom to check that his three passengers were ready for the move towards the white heli-pad cross, to which all three gave nervous nods. He could see a tiny man and a tall slender figure of a woman standing next to him and signalled to the two policemen that there were no other people on the roof.

Van Glytch was over the moon with excitement as he puffed his chest out, trying to look taller than he was at the prospect of meeting the President. As the copters wash from the rotors hit the two of them, his silly hair comb-over flapped up and down like a trapdoor and Danas long hair blew all over her face.

The pilot set the machine down and landed with hardly a bump and he switched off the engine to minimise the noise.

The Presidents secretary was first out, followed immediately by the two policemen who looked every inch the bodyguards. They were dressed all in black suits, black ties with white shirts and dark sunglasses. They had white curly leads running from their ear pieces finishing under their suit to the communicators tucked in their belts. Under their armpits were the shoulder holsters with quick fire 9 mm Glock pistols which they hoped they would not have to use.

Hans hurried up to the three of them with a broad grin on his face, his moustache quivering in the wind resembling a nervous rat caught in a trap. He was crouching low to avoid the remaining wash from the rotors with his hand outstretched in welcome. Before he had the opportunity to speak, in a heartbeat the two policemen handcuffed his hands behind his back.

'What the hell's going on, where is the President. I have heard that his security was pretty tight but why the handcuffs?'

The policeman said in a loud voice to overcome the remaining noise from the helicopter,

'Sr Van Glytch, you are under arrest for narcotics smuggling and being the mastermind behind a drugs cartel. You do not have to say anything but anything you do say will be taken down and used in evidence against you.'

Hans was surprised and speechless at the speed of the arrest. His heart was pounding far too fast for a man with a poor cardiac condition. He knew that there was no use in protesting or struggling as with his diminutive size he couldn't fight his way out of a paper bag even if he was free. He just wished he had thought of having his four hired helps with him, as Bear would have made short work of the two policemen. But isn't hindsight is a wonderful thing?

Dana just watched the whole scene unfolding with disbelief as she had no idea about his drugs involvement. So as quickly as possible she hurried to the rooftop lift, travelled down to her office and told reception what had happened but said not to tell any other staff until more information was available.

The police frogmarched Hans into the helicopter and sat him down in the rear seats next to the secretary, pleased that they had not needed to use the Glocks. They took off with a fast ascent which made everyone's ears pop. They flew over the sea towards Faro which was only a few minutes away and landed in the Old Walled Town car park which had been cleared by the local traffic police ready for their landing. Here a car was waiting which whisked them away with sirens blaring, taking them to the precinct.

As with the same procedure used in Lisbon, the duty desk sergeant Lino, wrote down Hans particulars, took fingerprints, then he was then taken to the interview rooms with statements taken and signed. Next port of call was the Faro prison where the twins were incarcerated. That was an exceedingly miserable moment for Hans after living the high life in the hotel.

The second sting had been perfectly executed.

63

The Third Sting

The team approached 'Mary the Virgin' which was moored next to the 'White Ecstasy' one by one with two minute gaps, disguised as holiday makers. They boarded the boat and waited in the saloon until all were present. Giovanni was the last to arrive and gave them a final five minute briefing.

'Good morning team. This is going to be the most dangerous of the four operations we are attempting today and you must all be prepared for some violent action which may result in gunfire. So if this happens do make sure you hit the deck fast to flatten your body profile. The worst guy on the ship is Bruno, known as the Bear. He is a nasty piece of work and will have no hesitation of killing anyone. As far as we know he will be the only one armed, the other three will be less of a problem. Work in pairs and I will lead with one of the two teams who will tackle the Bear. Does anyone have any questions?'

There was silence from the team as they had been well briefed over the past few days and understood clearly with what they were tasked.

'Ok men it's now 12.00 noon, so off you go as quietly as possible to keep the element of surprise. So on with your balaclavas and the best of luck.'

The team silently left the saloon of 'Mary the Virgin' and stealthily climbed aboard the big white yacht.

Bear was always aware of any movement of the ship and noticed that it had started to sway with the weight of the boarders. He quickly grabbed his machine pistol, raced up the companionway and ran to the prow of the boat. He saw the team spreading out all over the deck and started to spray the area with bullets. The teams split up leaving Giovanni with his two men to face him on the bow of the boat. The other four hurtled down to the lower decks to deal with the remainder of the crew.

There was much confusion below deck as the teams searched for the other three crew members who they eventually found hiding in the engine room but not armed. They saw them crouching behind the engines but they didn't offer any resistance when they saw the fire power of the machine guns the police were carrying. They raised their arms in surrender and were quickly overpowered and handcuffed.

Giovani and the other pair were in a very different situation. Even though they were lying flat on the deck, the Bear had shot one man in the leg and another in the shoulder so they were out of action. Giovanni was well protected by a vent pipe, with a clear view and when bear was reloading his clip, with one shot hit him in the head. He screamed out in pain and fell backward over the bow handrail into the water with an enormous splash. If he wasn't dead by the shot to his head he would drown in minutes.

Giovanni ran to the two injured men and applied dressings to their wounds which were only superficial and called to the ambulance which he had arranged to be on standby on the dock soon after twelve-o-clock. The wounded were immediately taken to hospital where they were treated as heroes and kept in overnight for observation.

Giovani gathered the remainder of the team together on the dockside, (to the amazement of the goggling crowd which had been watching the saga unfold) and apprised them of the battle, congratulating them on their professionalism, skill and summarising the injuries to their colleagues.

They were then tasked to search the yacht and large quantities of various narcotics were found together with a watertight trapdoor used for dumping the contraband onto the sea bed, which is how the twins had found their packets of heroin. Once the crew realised that the Bear was dead and Van Glytch had been arrested, they admitted everyone's involvement in the drugs syndicate.

One of Giovani's prime duties as a leader was to care for the welfare of the team so he immediately drove to the hospital to visit the injured officers. When he arrived he found them in high spirits, well bandaged and the nurses laughingly said they have never had their bottoms pinched so many times. They also said they were very flattered! So he guessed the guys were feeling fighting fit and recovering well!

The third sting again had been perfectly executed.

64

The Fourth Sting

Two unmarked police cars and a vets van were parked under three enormous Alforoba trees at the bottom of the Hill. The fallen carobs lay as a carpet and crunched underfoot as Feliciano briefed the team for the last sting where they were to arrest Fernando Martins.

'Ok team gather round, this shouldn't be a difficult arrest. The most dangerous aspect is the man-eating dog, a Rottweiler called Bruiser. Martins uses it as a guard dog and because he's so sure that nobody would try to enter his property because of the animal, most of his gates doors and windows are left unlocked and open. So we have with us today our vet Sr Sago who will try to shoot the animal with a tranquillising dart. He will be working with me and two of you and if the dart fails, I'll shoot the beast dead but that means that we will lose our element of surprise. So let's hope the dart works.'

'The other two of you will sneak around to the back of the house and creep up to Martins while the three of us will be arresting him. We must move as silently as we can up to the top of the Hill, trying to keep out of sight amongst the trees. Martins is normally lazing around and sunbathing on a Sunday. He will have his weapon somewhere in the house but it is unlikely to have it with him near the pool.

Now, has anyone got any questions or anything to they think they want to add to improve our plan?'

The team thought for a while and nobody had anything to add but they were all hyped up and ready to go, so off they went up the twisting concrete road all very excited and full of adrenalin.

Feliciano and Sr Sago were the first to arrive at the wire fence which was covered in foliage and surrounded the property. This gave them excellent cover and they saw Bruiser lying asleep on the front porch just in front to the main door. All was quiet in the noonday sun other than a few farmyard dogs baying in the distance and the sound of the crickets screeching in the trees. The vet poked his rifle through the fence, took careful aim, and silently fired the rifle. The dart struck the dog exactly where he wanted, right in the neck. The brute gave a quiet painful howl, stood up and then fell over on his side with a thump, well sedated. There was no sound coming from Martins other than the splashing of him swimming.

Feliciano pushed the massive ornate cast iron gates which opened with a creak. He visibly strolled looking more confident than he felt, up the tarmac drive which was densely lined with mature Eucalyptus, Cypresses and Olive trees. These gave superb cover for the two armed policemen as they silently moved from tree to tree.

His emotions were mixed as he was excited because he wanted to get Martins convicted but nervous as he didn't know how his boss would react, knowing he was his subordinate officer. His palms were moist, his heart was racing faster than normal and he could feel sweat running down his back. He didn't know if this was a result of the heat or just mild fear.

He stepped over the comatose dog and rang the bell which sounded all over the Villa. The two other policemen secreted themselves out of sight on each side of the door. The splashing in the pool stopped and moments later Martins opened the door standing there dripping wet with a large bath towel wrapped around his waist.

'What the hell do you think you are doing Neves disturbing my Sunday day off? Whatever it is, it could have waited until tomorrow at the station. Nothing can be so important for you to interrupt my peace and quiet.'

'Mr Martins, I am here to arrest you for corruption and being involved in a narcotics cartel. We have tape recorded evidence given by your friend Van Glytch that you are part of his drugs ring. You do not have to say anything but anything you do say will be taken down and may be used in evidence against you.'

'You go and fuck yourself you long streak of piss and get out of here before I set Bruiser onto you and he'll rip you to shreds!'

He looked down at the dog and thought it was strange that he was asleep, as he normally kicks up a racket when anyone walks up the drive. Then puzzled he noticed the dart sticking of the animal's neck and immediately thought something was wrong.

'What in damnation have you done to my dog and in any case by what authority do you come here trying to arrest me on this trumped up charge?'

By this time the two back door policemen had stealthily and silently entered the rear door and unbeknown to Martins were standing some two feet behind him with pistols drawn. Feliciano took out the letter of authority signed by the President and Martins read it with shock and awe. Feliciano looked over Martins shoulder at the two who were ready to handcuff him.

'Don't you use that hackney old trick pretending there is someone behind me you poxy Boy Scout; I've used it too many times myself!'

He raised his right hand in a fist to thump Feliciano and as he did so the handcuffs were on him in a trice and the other two of the team appeared with guns drawn. The arrest was fast, effective and complete. Martins was shouting abuse at all of the team as they laid him out on the floor and bound his feet.

Feliciano called the team together and tasked them to search the whole premises, including the garage and to look for anything unusual or suspicious especially any narcotics.

'You've no right to go poking around in my house without a search warrant, you're getting too big for your boots Neves,' he shouted loudly laying on the floor and writhing about.

Feliciano produced the search warrant that the Eagle had signed and held it close to his face while he was lying on the floor, which he read and then spat in Feliciano's face. Inside Feliciano's stomach was churning with rage. He was tempted to kick his body all over the floor for the way he had treaded Hedda and Roly and also for the shabby way he had treated him in the past. Then he remembered a phrase he picked up from his uncle; 'Revenge is best served cold' and he calmed down and reverted to his normal professional self.

The team of four searched diligently the whole house and the garage, while the vet went down the road to pick up his van. The dog needed to be further tranquilised before taking him to his surgery. It took all of his and Feliciano's strength to lift the brute into the van and Sr Sago drove off down the drive with the dog snuffling on the floor.

Feliciano sat down on the tiled floor next to Martins and said in a very cool detached voice.

'Right Martins, you must know by now that you have no place to hide and don't have any defence for your crimes. So now give me the key and combination to your safe and if you don't, we have enough explosives to blow it open and possibly you with it at the same time.'

He realised by now that the game was up, there was little point in struggling further and there was no advantage in making any more waves, so he gave the combination; 17061944, said the key was on a chain around his neck and the safe was behind the Picasso in the bedroom.

Feliciano telephoned his uncle on his 'Motorola brick' to say that all the arrests had been successfully concluded. There was one villain dead and two officers slightly injured but not life threatening and they would be out of hospital within days. Lino passed the information to the President who was delighted at the news.

The fourth sting had been perfectly executed.

65

Celebrations at the Palace

Diario de Noticias

The oldest newspaper in Portugal. Est: 1864

Prime Minister, Finance Minister & the Chief Inspector of police arrested for corruption & narcotics smuggling

FULL STORY ON PAGE 2.

PAGE 2.

According to our crime reporter Mrs Joa'n Pires, the Portuguese President Sr Vasco Da Gama Fernandez, some months ago authorized an undercover covert operation to infiltrate and smash a narcotics cartel operating out of Vilamoura and the newly opened Paradise Hotel.

The assignment was carried out by the Southern Portugal Police Force under the leadership of a young Faro homicide detective sergeant, operating together with a crack SWAT team.

Four areas of interest were targeted.

One was in the Prime Minister's office at the Sao Bento Mansion in Lisbon where he was later arrested.

Another involved a helicopter which was used to apprehend the owner of the Hotel Paradise near Faro where he was found to be the leader of the drugs cartel.

A further exercise was launched against a luxury yacht which had been used to import drugs from Holland, in which one gang member was shot dead and two officers were wounded; although not seriously.

The last was at the home of the Chief Inspector of Police, where incriminating items of corruption were discovered along with millions of Escudos acquired by his corrupt activity. Police are still at the property and are investigating other matters of a more serious nature.

All suspects are now under arrest in the respective prisons and are awaiting trial.

The President praised all officers involved in the Sting and stated that, 'Young people are now safer from these vicious drug pushing criminals.'

The President and the Justice Minister were in the Sao Bento Palace reading the press reports with enormous satisfaction and were immensely impressed with the detailed organisation, efficiency and speed with which Fernando and Giovanni conducted the operation.

'I must confess Lino that I was apprehensive about Feliciano's ability to successfully bring this dreadful drugs business to a satisfactory conclusion. But he has excelled himself and surpassed all my expectations.'

'I can understand your concerns Fernandez but I had no doubt that Fernando had the ability, integrity and maturity to come up with the goods. As you would expect I have known him for his lifetime and he has always impressed me with his ability in all sorts of fields. He has fine leadership qualities, has enormous respect from his team and everyone he has contact with in the force. He's a great communicator; he is fair, friendly and firm, takes the hard decisions and has empathy for the victims of crime. In addition, he is qualified in forensic science in which he has a degree, is highly intelligent and his clean up rate is the best in the force. He treats everybody with courtesy, dignity and respect. I just don't know where to fault him. This brings me nicely to my next request. Now we don't have a Chief Inspector of Police for the whole of Portugal, as Martins is in jail, I would like to propose that Feliciano is given the job.'

'Well I don't think we should be too hasty with the promotion, as Martins hasn't been convicted or jailed yet; many a slip between cup and lip! But in any event the decision would be yours and yours alone, although if there becomes a vacancy, Feliciano would have my vote and my blessing. You must also consider that there might be criticism from the opposition party of nepotism!'

'Yes you are right but I guess that when the public learns that he was the master of the day in the drugs bust, I think the matter of nepotism will fade into the background. I also think they would view him as a folk hero.'

'You are probably right but getting back to the newspapers. I believe we have made significant political progress from what seemed to be a negative start with the Prime Minister being involved, which could have dropped our popularity in the polls. As it happens the general public seem delighted that we have been pro-active and foiled the narcotics ring. The press also have been giving us praise, which is unusual for them. Although to be fair, the 𝕯𝖎𝖆𝖗𝖎𝖔 𝖉𝖊 𝕹𝖔𝖙𝖎𝖈𝖎𝖆𝖘 is one of the more positive papers and normally reports the facts rather than the gutter press with their overblown headlines designed to sell newspapers rather than communicate news!'

66

The Safe Tells All

Feliciano climbed the black wrought iron spiral staircase to the bedroom and removed the Picasso from the wall. He pressed the combination numbers on the safe and turned the key. He was a bit concerned that Martins being the nasty, spiteful, malicious bit of work that he was, might have booby trapped the safe; especially as he had been so compliant in giving the key and combination without hesitation. Therefore he checked all around for any signs of tampering but could not see any. So he held his breath as he opened the door and was astounded at the contents. It was jammed packed with millions of Escudo notes to the point that it must have been difficult to shut the door. He pulled out the notes and called for one of the officers to witness the haul and help him count and record the sum.

Then hidden under the notes was the key to the Swiss deposit account box and a large foolscap brown envelope which he removed and laid on the bed with the money. Just as he went to open the envelope there was a shout from downstairs.

The officer who had searched the garage had called to tell what he had found. He was a PADI qualified diver so was very interested in the dive equipment of which there were Martins set and the other sets which Martins had liberated (stolen?) from the Irish twins boat. He was intrigued to find that the twin's equipment was missing two lead dive weight belts. So he told Feliciano of the missing belts which didn't seem too important to him but it did to

Feliciano as he remembered the bruising around the waist of Jos'e Barros. More importantly the officer was holding a pair of brown leather Timberland boots the treads of which were imbedded with hard white clay! Feliciano recalled Caroline's words in the path lab. 'If we can find the boots then we have the killer.'

Feliciano thought that so many parts of the puzzle were now falling into place. The boots were only a part of the evidence needed to convict the murderer. Still thinking of the jigsaw, he returned to the bedroom to open the envelope. Inside was a clear plastic bag the contents of which made his blood run cold. He was stunned shocked and horrified at what he saw!

The team had made a thorough search of the house, grounds and garage and nothing of importance could be found apart from the guy who searched the garage. He found a number of sacks of Red Coral and being a diver, recognised that this must be an illegal haul. So he entered the items on his search list and passed it to Feliciano.

Feliciano tasked two of the team to bring the cars up from the main road. The August noonday heat was getting oppressive and sticky so he said for the team to take Martins and tether him into the car with another pair of handcuffs secured to the driver's seat. Then gave them enough money to go to Tony the Waterman's bar in Gorjoe's and have a beer each. He said with a chuckle in his voice.

'Do make sure that you only have one each, we don't want you done for drunk driving and make sure that Martins gets a bottle of water not beer. Otherwise he may try to sue us for police cruelty!'

The team left Feliciano alone in the Villa as they bundled Martins into the car without ceremony, deliberately banging his head on the car door opening, him protesting and swearing oaths at his rough treatment. They drove down the twisting concrete road and near the bottom, they saw Maria the maid sitting underneath an Olive tree covered in ripe black olives. She was sat on the whitewashed stone wall bordering the perimeter of her house and garden. She was enjoying the heat of the sun as most country Portuguese do in the summer weather. She waved the driver down and asked why there was so much activity up and down the hill. He said that he was not at liberty to say at present but she would be told what had happened in a few days.

As she looked through the car window she saw Martins handcuffed to the seat looking very forlorn, glum and embarrassed. She was perplexed and confused to see her boss in such a sorry state. He looked at her and shrugged his shoulders and said it was all a mistake, he would see her soon and would she please look after the Villa and make it secure until he returned. She said not to worry and toddled back into the house to tell her husband the news.

Feliciano made a last tour of the property to ensure nothing had been missed in the search. He looked around at some of the tacky, vulgar, ostentatious and overpriced furnishings and recalled a Gay interior designer friend of his saying 'No taste is better than bad taste' and he thought Martins had both of these in spades.

He then took samples of the Red Coral, the money, the safe deposit key, the Timberland boots and the plastic bag which had repulsed him earlier. Put them all into separate transparent evidence bags and labelled them with dates and times for use at the trial.

He then thought he should call Caroline to update her on the progress of all the arrests. So using his Motorola, he called and she answered straightaway. She was over the moon at the results, delighted and relieved that he hadn't suffered any injuries and was safe and well. He suggested

305

that when the offenders came to trial it would be interesting to for her and Shak to come down to Faro and they could all sit in at the court cases. She agreed immediately and said that Shak was due for a break and that he had a musician friend who could mind the shop for a few days. He said as soon as they knew the date of the hearings he would book two rooms at the Ava Hotel for three nights.

He then ensured that the Villa was locked and secure and drove back to the Faro precinct to record and lodge the evidence bags.

67

Celebrations for the SWAT Team

The Faro police station was pleasantly quiet with an eerie silence now Martins was not shouting out his sarcastic comments at all and sundry officers who walked past his door.

Feliciano strolled into Giovanni's office feeling more comfortable than he had in years with a relaxed smile on his face. He was up to his neck in paperwork, writing copious pages of his report on the four sting operations.

'Hi ya Giovanni what are you up to at this early hour.'

'I'm just finishing my report on our operations and this is the part of the job I hate the most, paperwork bores me to tears, I would much rather be out catching criminals. The thing I don't understand is now that Martins is banged up, to whom do I send the report?'

'Well as I understand the situation, as I am acting deputy in his absence I guess you send it to me, I'll add my comments and then pass it onto the Justice Minister in Lisbon. Anyway that's all very mind-numbing routine stuff. What I came in to talk to you about is a 'Recognising success and Learning from failure' session with all of the lads involved in the stings. If you don't have any problems with that, I suggest that we all meet tomorrow at Lady Susan's restaurant at 20.00 hours. I will spend five minutes on the wash up meeting and I'll then treat them all to a slap up dinner to thank them for their efforts.'

'I don't think you could keep any of them away with an offer like that! I'll get in touch with them all and fix it up immediately.'

'Do make sure you ask the walking wounded to come as well, that is if you can prize them away from those pretty nurses in the hospital. Balaclavas need not be worn!'

'No problems there, as I understand it they are well on the way to recovery and raring to get back to their jobs, much to the relief of the nurses!'

The restaurant was full to bursting and the cacophony of noise was almost deafening. All the guys were talking at the same time about their sting experiences and trying to outdo each other with their stories. Susan was fussing around, plying them with their preferred drinks. She was enjoying the moment having a dozen young men all brimming with testosterone and giving her far too much attention as she was the only woman in the place. Robert the chef was a bit sour faced at the interest his wife was getting but pretended he didn't notice or care.

A few moments later Feliciano and Giovanni arrived through the plate glass doors to cheers from the team as they all started to sing 'For they are jolly good fellows.' etc. etc.

Feliciano tried to quieten them down but to no effect so they both sat down and waited for the singing to naturally end. When Feliciano thought he might get heard he stood up and said.

'Ok team settle down, settle down, and let's have a bit of hush. It really is a pleasure and privilege for me to see you all together tonight after you all completed such a professional and skilled operation in arresting the members of the drugs cartel and busting open a bunch of corrupt police and politicians. You all put yourselves in danger but selflessly completed the job with great flair and panache.

Some of you had a free ride in a helicopter. Others entered the ancient hallowed halls of Sao Bento Mansion, the office of the Prime Minister. The more unfortunate of you had to contend with armed thugs on a luxury yacht and lastly with me, almost got eaten by a savage Rottweiler. So well done and thank all of you.'

'Now before we all have too much to drink, one of the most important aspects of leadership after a task is done is to evaluate what we did well, not so well and would you suggest any changes if we did a similar mission again?'

There was a hush as they all looked at each other, shrugging their shoulders and trying to think of anything. Nothing was forthcoming until the two officers still in bandages stood up and said.

'It would be nice next time if we didn't get shot but the nurses in the hospital were a treat!'

That led to howls of laughter and joshing all-round the team and when the hilarity died down Feliciano stood again and said with a laugh.

'Well thanks for your thoughts guys and I'll make sure you're all equipped with suits of armour next time. So if there's nothing more, the evening is yours. Now select anything on the menu and the drinks list and it's all on me. Again many thanks for your support.'

After the applause died down there was a brief silence as they chose their fare, then they were off again drinking and talking nineteen to the dozen. Feliciano felt warm inside, fortunate and honoured to have worked with such a highly motivated, professional group of individuals. He hoped they would have a wonderful evening and was sure there would be many sore heads and upset stomachs in the morning.

68

Prime Ministers Trial

'Do you think that Ivor Gonagetim has whacked Martins yet, I think he should have done by now, it must be weeks since we gave him the fifty per cent?'

Sn Coelho was thinking aloud rather than asking for an answer as he lay on his hard prison mattress. Sr Rabbit dressed in his Muschi prison overalls with orange and white horizontal stripes, was lying on his equally hard mattress on his steel framed bed, hands behind his head with his legs crossed feeling that his world as he knew it was disappearing fast.

'You accountants really don't live in the real world do you, here we are banged up facing a long prison sentence and all you can think about is money. It matters not if that scroat has done the deed or not. If we don't get out of here then he won't get his other fifty per cent anyway. It's more important that the expensive smart arse lawyer we've employed to get us out of here pulls off a miracle rather than you worrying about your dosh! Tomorrow at the trial we'll know whether we'll be free or stuck here for the rest of our lives.'

'As Prime Minister, if you hadn't got into bed with that evil Dutchman and took bribes to keep your mouth shut about his narcotics, we probably wouldn't be in this stinking hole.'

'Oh shut up moaning you little turd. If you'd kept the money safe and undercover in Switzerland we'd possibly still be living the good life.'

'Don't keep call me LITTLE you big mouthed arsehole!'

Smothered with a pall of despair in their damp prison cell which smelled of urine, with very little sunlight coming through the tiny barred window, they continued to bicker well into the night: each one blaming the other for their misfortune. They would have been better employed concentrating on honing their excuses to defend themselves at the trial that was looming tomorrow.

James Richmond wanted to get back to Australia as quickly as possible to see his beloved Jenny. But he had been subpoenaed to attend the court as a vital witness to the conversation he had with Van Glytch and to give evidence that the tape recording was genuine.

The Chief Executive Eduardo Soares, of the motorway company 'Paramount Highways' who paid bribes to the Prime Minister, had also been subpoenaed to attend. He was very willing to spill the beans and try for a more lenient sentence.

As the trial was a high profile event because of the prosecution of the Prime Minister, the courtroom in Lisbon was packed to suffocation especially by the 'Gentlemen of the Press' who were all looking for a scoop.

The courtroom was a dismal and dowdy room with few windows, giving an impression of darkness and gloom. All the furniture and seating were made of battered old mahogany and the soft furnishings had seen better days. The jury seating looked more like pews from a church covered with green baize over thin foam filled squabs, which did little for the comfort of the bums of the jurors. The excuse for the lack of re-furbishing was that with

Portugal's impending entry into the Common Market, the whole building would be demolished and a new one built to modern standards and style.

The evidence against the pair was overwhelming with James's convincing performance in the witness box as he gave clear and honest answers to the cross examination of both prosecution and defence lawyers. The tape recording which was played in full backed his version perfectly. Eduardo Soares, trying to save his own neck, gave all the information asked of him and this completely dammed the pair. The accused could not give any convincing excuses for their corrupt actions nor could the defence lawyer make a credible case.

The jury was out for only an hour and they found them guilty on all counts. The Judge sentenced them to thirty years each in prison.

When they heard the severity of the sentence Sr Coelho collapsed in a faint in the witness box and as he dropped to the floor, Sr Rabbit shouted at him.

'Get up you snivelling little reptile, where's your dignity, your showing us both up in front of the whole Portuguese press.'

As he eventually passed out onto the witness box floor he cried out.

'STOP CALLING ME LITTLE!'

All the funds in the Swiss account were recovered together with their apartment in Paris which was sold. The many millions of Escudos salvaged were ring-fenced and used to repair the Jerry Built motorways.

Soares was sentenced to ten years with a parole review after seven years. The company went into liquidation and another Spanish firm was appointed to renovate the motorways.

The judge praised James for his brave actions in everything he did to expose the culprits, even at the risk to his own life. The press had a field day with the papers running the story for weeks after the trial which certainly improved their circulation figures. The President was praised again and again in the press for dealing so quickly and effectively with a corrupt Prime Minister and the rouge Finance guy.

The pair were taken down to the holding cells still complaining that it was the others fault and that they would appeal against the length of their sentence, especially as Soares was only given ten years.

69

The Trial of the Irish Twins

Folk country dancing evenings were a regular event at the Ava Hotel and these took place in the cellar beneath the ground floor every Thursday evening in the tourist season. There were some twenty dancers and musicians in the group, all dressed in traditional garb. The girls wore pretty flared skirts covered in flowery prints, multi coloured blouses, legs covered in white frilly stockings with black flat shoes. The boys in black trousers high heeled black boots, black waist coats over white shirts and black wide brimmed sombrero hats. The musicians played accordions, the traditional Portuguese Mandolin and guitars, plus a triangle which beat out the rhythm of the tunes.

Feliciano, Caroline and Shak arrived just in time to have a light dinner then enjoy the dancing until it was time to retire. The finale of the troupe ended with the group in a boy/girl circle whirling around at speed, the boys gripping the girl's waist and lifting them off the floor. Then they tried to involve the audience in the circle and then did the same again. This part of the dance led to the screams and embarrassment of the guests. Caroline having seen the exhibition before kept well out of the way in case she was whisked off her feet. The evening finished with a rousing, noisy, Portuguese song in which everybody joined.

Prior to the dancing when they were having their evening meal in the hotel restaurant, Shak was in a somewhat sombre mood. Caroline always sensitive to atmosphere, asked what was wrong and he just shrugged his shoulders, said the day had been tiring and he was ready for a good night's sleep. She knew him better than that and instinctively understood there was something seriously wrong but now wasn't the time or place to discuss the issue.

After the dancing the three then decided to take to their beds. Caroline and Feliciano had a double room on the third floor and Shak the same on the second.

The pair closed the bedroom door quietly and both embraced in a long loving hug. What happened next to a young couple so much in love has nothing to do with anybody!

Shak walked slowly to his room, closed the door and leaned gently against it for a few minutes breathing heavily. He stumbled onto the bed, lay on his back and started to review his life situation. He had lost his wife who he loved passionately, Jenny he had lost to Australia and James Richmond and now he knew that finally he had lost the only other love of his life to Feliciano. It was too late for tears as they had been shed in buckets when Feliciano came onto the scene. There was a large gaping painful hole in his heart and he couldn't see any point to his future life. Everything he held dear was disappearing so fast it left him breathless. To say that he was suicidal could have been an overstatement but he was not far from that situation. His sadness overwhelmed him as he slept fully clothed and had a nasty restless night with nightmares of a large black hole into which he was falling.

The next day at breakfast Caroline watched Shaks face very carefully and could see there was no change in his brown study, in fact she thought it had deteriorated. He hardly said a word all though the repast. Feliciano felt uneasy and embarrassed by the silence. She knew that before they went to the Tribunal she must catch him on his own and get to the bottom of the problem.

They decided to walk to the prosecutions of the Twins, Van Glytch and Martins, as it was only a short half hour stroll. The weather was warm and fine showing a light blue sky with a weak sun but no clouds, being September there was a cool nip in the air.

They turned left out of the hotel, past the bus station and immediately on the left was the weekly Gypsy Market. The dozens of stalls were covered by gaily printed canvasses to keep out any heat or rain and they sold anything from scarfs to garden tools. The top sellers were fake named handbags and white embroidered tablecloths. There was always loud beat music playing and pirated tape cassettes could be bought cheaply. The goods were mostly sold by women attendants, the husbands being in the beer tents! Often there were babies being breast fed whist the mothers were selling the goods. As they passed, Feliciano looked briefly to his left to the hundreds of shoppers and tourists and thought he saw the Gipsy King standing head and shoulders above the crowd with a pretty girl on his arm but in a trice he disappeared into the throng.

Foxy was walking out of the court with Kat, along the tall ceilinged mock Gothic corridors which link the various courtrooms and she had a broad grin on her face having finished the trial of the Irish twins which was an extraordinary success.

The jury had been selected to try the twins and was retained for the later prosecutions of Van Glytch and Martins. They were the normal mix of Portuguese males and females plus some Black Portuguese Angolans with them all aged between twenty five and seventy. They were good solid citizens and selected for their experience of life in Portugal and independence of thought.

Foxy and Kat were pleased that they had their prior session with the Eagle as he had taken into account their views and that had shortened the legal process. Once the prosecution and defence lawyers had finished their cross examinations, Judge Da Silva summed up for the jury to help them make their final decision. He concluded.

'These men have tried to make a living from sailing around the world on 'Mary the Virgin' with very little experience of world navigation, seamanship or trading. They are vagrants of the seas and have been extremely stupid and naive in their dealings. However they are not drug dealers and the narcotics they found in Vilamoura on the sea bed came from a haul which had been dumped under the 'White Ecstasy.' The owner of which, from a recent police investigation, had been proved to be importing various drugs. But they are guilty of harvesting Red Coral and trying to land in Portugal with incorrect or missing immigration papers. I now leave you to retire and make your decision.'

The jury was out for only half an hour and the foreman said that the unanimous decision was that they were only guilty on the Red Coral and immigration paper issues.

The Eagle committed the men to six months in prison. The twins were delighted with the decision as they were not done for the drugs issue. As they were being taken down the steep steps to the holding cells beneath the court, they were slapping each other on the backs with joy, which is a bit difficult to do wearing handcuffs. They clearly didn't know the conditions they would face in Portuguese prisons!

Foxy was walking towards the exit of the Court complex when she saw three people walking towards her. As they got closer the man with the long blond hair ran towards her and shouted out.

'FAY, FAY, FAY, it's my lovely wife Fay - I knew I would find you some day. It's Fay!'

She screamed out loudly just one word.

'SHAK!!!!'

Caroline and Feliciano were also running towards her and as all three reached her, her brain felt like it would explode. Her amnesia, the large block of interrelated lost memories, began to reboot themselves as the neural connections and receptors joined together and years of memories came flooding back into her consciousness. The pain was so great she collapsed into a heap onto the black tiled floor. She dropped her legal papers and her handbag, the contents spilling out all around her.

Shak was the first to reach her and cradled her head in his arms with tears of joy and concern streaming down his face. Luckily she was breathing steadily in her unconscious state. Feliciano took charge of the situation; he gave his phone to Kat and bade her call an ambulance. Then he raced into the court to tell the Eagle what had happened and he immediately adjourned all of her prosecutions until Foxy was back to full health. Shack was talking to Fay about the fact he knew he would find her one day even though she could not hear him in her comatose state. Caroline was picking up the contents of the handbag. Lipstick, make up, biro and a pencil, wallet with money inside together with credit cards, business cards, handkerchief and to her amazement and surprise a small plastic bag inside of which was a very faded thin cardboard packet of Blue Cornflower seeds!

70

Fay's Recovery

The ambulance arrived and took Fay and with Shak in attendance to Faro hospital where she was immediately taken to the accident and emergency wards with a red wrist band attached, saying 'Top Priority.'

Caroline and Feliciano took a taxi back to the Ava Hotel after dropping Kat at her home. Feliciano went straight to the reception desk and in a gallant gesture asked the receptionist to change Shak's room to the Honeymoon Suite and that when Fay and Shak arrived, there should be a bottle of Champagne on ice and smoked salmon sandwiches delivered to their room. Any extra cost incurred to be entered on his room account. Caroline also asked for three large bunches of flowers to be arranged around the suite, the cost also on Feliciano's account!

Shak had been sitting next to Fay's unconscious body until she awoke six hours later. She was drowsy and confused but did recognise Shak and was able to chat with him. As soon as she came round the doctor appeared to take blood pressure, temperature etc. and he decided that she should be kept in the hospital for observation for forty eight hours. Shak stayed by her bedside for all of this time without food or refreshment.

When she had fully recovered and was able to talk easily, in addition to the thousands of questions they wanted to ask each other, Shak was intrigued by one fact and asked.

'My love why did you carry the packet of Blue Cornflower seeds around with you for all these years?'

'I really don't know. The only memory I had after I left you at home was that I went out to buy the seeds, after that everything went black and I couldn't remember anything. I found myself in Portugal getting a position in Ilda & Ilda's Law Practice and the only memory I had of my last life was the packet of seeds. Every time I touched them I thought my memory would come back but it never did until I saw you at the Law Court.'

Fay signed the hospital release form at 18.00 hours and they took a taxi to the Ava Hotel. Shak asked for his key at the reception desk and the receptionist said that his room had been changed to the Honeymoon Suite on the top floor. She asked if there would be any more luggage for the porter to take up to the room. Shak said there was not. She looked at Fay with a half-smile on her face and thought 'Oh yes I've heard this one before a thousand times.' Fay blushed from the neck up as Shak asked.

'Who changed the room and should I pay now for the upgrade or wait until we check out?'

'No extra charges at all sir, everything has been arranged and paid for. No need to ask any more questions.'

Shak was intrigued then guessed it would have been Caroline, the generous one.

They took the lift to the top floor and found the Honeymoon Suite which had a large notice on the door saying 'Honeymoon Suite' which they thought could be embarrassing! They entered the room and were amazed at the size and plushness of the accommodation with an enormous terrace and French windows overlooking the Marina. They flopped exhausted onto the large soft settee and hugged and kissed for some minutes without saying a word as these would be unnecessary. Fay looked around the room and noticed the flowers, the champagne and the sandwiches and said.

'Oh Shak what a lovely surprise, you were always so thoughtful. Thank you.'

'Nothing to do with me my sweet but I can guess who did it for us!'

As they opened the bottle and devoured the sandwiches, having not anything to eat, they were both starving. Caroline crept stealthily along the corridor and hung a 'Do not Disturb' notice on the door handle and disappeared silently back to her room.

They sat on the edge of the bed, the first time in so many years. They both had tears of relief and joy in their eyes and they hugged each other so tight they were breathless. Fay exclaimed with a shy grin.

'I have many widowed girlfriends who tell me it's like riding a bike, you never forget!'

Shak looked equally shy and embarrassed and said quietly.

'It may well be but if that's the case I think I may need stabilisers for quite a while.'

After a very satisfying night they met Caroline and Feliciano at breakfast, Fay still looking a tad embarrassed and blushing and Shak looking tired. They all ordered smoked salmon with scrambled egg, plus another bottle of Champagne to celebrate her return to the family. Shak formally introduced Feliciano to Fay and they all talked nineteen to the dozen trying to fill in so many gaps in all their histories.

71

Van Glytch's Trial

With Fay fully recovered, the Eagle convened the trail of Van Glytch and had the jury return to the court.

As with the trial of the Prime Minister in Lisbon, the Faro court was full to its capacity, as there was much media attention. Again the press were in evidence as this prosecution was linked closely to Sr Rabbits conviction and his connection to the narcotics scam. There was an excited hubbub all over the room as everyone settled down to hear the trial.

Foxy was now raring to go and was making the last minute preparations to her prosecution case as the clerk of the court said loudly.

'All rise.'

As Judge Da Silva strode from his chambers with much ceremony and sat on his podium, he said to the assembly in an overly pompous voice.

'This is the trial against Mr Hans van Glytch who is accused of bribery and narcotics dealing. I remind the gentlemen of the press that they may make notes of the proceedings and as I notice many of you carrying cameras, as you well know photography is not allowed in this court. Clerk of the court please proceed.'

The clerk called Van Glytch to the witness box. As Hans climbed up the steep stairs from the holding cell in his striped prison uniform, he was puffing and panting.

Sweat was dripping from his face onto his ridiculous moustache, then onto his chin and his heart was pounding like a steam hammer. His face was white as a sheet and he was not looking forward to this one little bit. He stood in the polished teak witness box which was surrounded around the top with black wrought iron spikes and due to his diminutive stature could only just see over the top. The clerk held out a bible and spoke the standard oath.

'Do you Mr van Glytch promise to tell the truth, the whole truth and nothing but the truth so help you God?'

Hans said that he did but had no intention of telling the truth as he had some very plausible lies which he had rehearsed to help his case.

The Eagle could see that Hans was awkward standing in the dock not quite able to see over the top, so asked if he would be more comfortable if he sat on the chair adjacent to the clerk of the court. Hans replied with his breath coming in short bursts,

'Thank you my Lord that is very kind of you.'

As he moved away from the dock to step down the short flight of treads, he felt massive pains in his chest and additional pains down his left arm, as he suffered a colossal fatal heart attack! He fell down the steps and laid spread eagled across the chair and the floor.

There was uproar in the court as pandemonium broke out. The press were all over the room like a rash taking photos of Hans on the floor. A medic was bending over the body taking his pulse and shaking his head. The Eagle was shouting silence in court and calling for the police to arrest the reporters for contempt, who by now had fled the room faster than greyhounds. The jurors were looking amazed and bemused. The public leapt from the gallery and were walking and running all over the room trying to help or leaving the court. The Judge continued to shout for order and silence to no avail. He kept banging his gavel so hard that the head broke off the handle and fell onto the floor. People started laughing, until in the end the Eagle declared the trial at an end, left his podium and stormed back into his chambers in high dudgeon.

Foxy just sat in her seat watching the scene unfold with mixed emotions of frustration and disappointment that she had spent a lot of time preparing for the case. She was pleased that she had the rest of the day off to spend it with Shak. She was shaking with laughter watching the people kicking the gavel head around the floor. She was also upset to see her good friend the Eagle totally out of control for the first time in his life.

Dana who had come to see her boss convicted for his nasty drugs deeds was delighted to see the back of the old chap even though she quite liked him and overjoyed that she was now the new owner of the Hotel Paradise.

An ambulance was called and the medics took Hans to Faro Hospital where he was pronounced D.O.A, dead on arrival. Well, thought Foxy that saved the outrageous cost of a trial and the annual expenditure of keeping a jail bird in prison for a lifetime. She thought it was a win-win for everybody all round.

72

James Leaves for Australia

There were many travel bags arranged around the sofa in the concourse of Hotel Paradise where James was seated waiting for his taxi to take him to Faro Airport. Dana glided up and sat close to him putting her hand on his knee.

'You probably know by now James that I am the new owner of the hotel. While I was under the control of Hans I didn't have any choice but to do what I did to you but that is all over now and if I caused you any embarrassment or grief I can only apologise. Also I knew at the back of my mind that you weren't Gay, although the way you minced out of the hotel that day you could have fooled anybody!'

'Well Dana I accept your apology, that's water under the bridge as far as I'm concerned and it's all forgotten. I have already made the decision that we will hold our conference here next year as the facilities are excellent and I am sure you would look after us all exceptionally well. Of course I would expect a massive discount on your published rates!'

Dana gave him a big hug, kissed him lightly on the cheek, said that she would discount the rate by twenty five per cent and they shook hands to seal the deal.

As James stood up to check whether the taxi had arrived, Feliciano strolled through the massive plate glass doors, walked over to the two of them and shook James by the hand gave him a friendly man hug and said.

'So you're off now back to Australia James, I wish you bon voyage and a safe journey. I guess Jenny will be happy that you are on your way especially as you had to extend your time here. Please excuse me as I have to talk to Dana about arranging an event for our impending marriage.'

'I'm so glad you're are both tying the knot, congratulations and if at any time you fancy a visit down under, Jenny and I would be delighted for you to be our guests.'

The taxi driver was loading James's luggage into the boot as they bade their last farewells. Dana led Feliciano to her office to discuss the arrangements. She sat down in Hans's old desk and felt very important in her new role as owner.

'Dana we are having a modest wedding at the Buddhist Temple up in the hills and what we need from you is a sumptuous champagne dinner for four people at the best table you have in the Michelin restaurant. Now what do you think that will cost?'

'Well firstly Feliciano I would like to congratulate you on you impending wedding. Secondly I hear that you have become something of a folk hero as you cracked the narcotics ring. Thirdly as a mark of everyone's appreciation, as you have been so brave and helpful in the problems we have had with Hans and his drug situation; your wedding breakfast will be free and on the house. I will also personally serve you at table. Who will be the four guests?'

'There will be Caroline's dad Shak, her mum Fay, Caroline and myself. I expect you've heard on the grapevine about Fay's disappearance and her memory recovering after some thirty years?'

She said she had, as nothing much gets left out of the Algarve grapevine so when he saw Fay next to give her Dana's best wishes.

Feliciano was overwhelmed at her generosity, thanked her profusely and shook her hand. But he did say with great modesty that the four stings were carried out by the Giovanni's SWAT teams and he only had a small part to play in its organisation. He then left the hotel to make the arrangements at the Buddhist Temple in the hills.

73

Martins Trial

Martins sat in his cold soulless holding cell beneath the courthouse awaiting his trial. He was thinking about the luxury life he had in Travessa Do Pastor and now he was reduced to wearing his striped itchy prison overalls. He had broken out into a cold sweat and due to the prison food which he found inedible; he had lost a considerable amount of weight. He also thought about some of the criminals he had caught and then without a thought from him they were confined in the same miserable conditions as he was now.

The court was once again packed with interested parties. The jury hoping that on this occasion they would be allowed to do their job and not as in the case of Hans van Glytch, when they were dismissed without a thought.

'All rise!'

The Eagle strode into the room with his head held high looking much more confident than he was when he last left the court! He settled into his podium, sat on his high backed chair showing the green leather backrest, with the Portugal crest in the middle and shuffled his papers as the crowd noisily took their seats. He said in a sombre tone.

'I hope that we will have a much more civilised and orderly session today than we did at our last debacle!'

Then he smiled and held up a new gavel for the crowd to see.

'This is my new one and hopefully it's much stronger than the last, which many of you used as a football!'

A titter ran round the court as some looked embarrassed and others, thinking about the previous circus started to laugh all over again. 'Silence in Court' he boomed and banged the gavel hard on its block. With a chuckle he said.

'Well this one seems to be working well at present! Now seriously, we are here today at this trial to determine whether Mr Martins is guilty or innocent of the charge of bribery, corruption, blackmail and murder in the first degree. In this case I am breaking precedent and procedure as he has elected to present his own defence. So we will hear the prosecution's evidence first, then he will offer his own arguments. Bring in the prisoner.'

Martins looked weary and defeated as he walked into the dock as the clerk stated the oath holding the bible which he selected from the many leather bound Law books on his desk.

'Mr Martins, do you promise to tell the truth, the whole truth and nothing but the truth so help you God?'

'No I do not.'

The Eagle went red round the gills and gruffly said.

'Mr Martins, if you do not swear the oath, I will hold you in contempt of court and any sentence imposed for this offence will be added to sentences you receive today. Do you now understand and swear?'

'Yes I do understand my Lord but I cannot swear as you have asked, as I don't believe in God or the Bible. But I do promise to tell the truth the whole truth and nothing but the truth!'

The Eagle was clearly irritated and huffed and puffed a bit but told the clerk to record his words for the register.

Then he asked Foxy to present her evidence. She had spent days preparing her case and believed her findings were watertight.

Martins stood to attention, his sweating handcuffed hands holding onto the black wrought iron spikes surrounding the top of the dock, his unflinching ghostly pale face staring into the space in front of him. Foxy started her prosecution.

'My Lord I would like to start by showing a key, exhibit number one which was found in Mr Martins safe. Mr Martin please tell the court for what the key was used.'

'Yes, it is the key to the safe deposit box which is held in Sr Rabbits secret bank in Switzerland.'

'What was it doing in the safe in your house?'

'I blackmailed Sr Rabbit to give me a copy key so I could have access to the millions of Escudos in the safe which he took as bribes for the motorway scam.'

'Thank you Mr Martins. Could we now see exhibit number two, which is a pair of leather Timberland boots? Are these boots yours and if they are, when did you last wear them?'

'Yes they are mine and I wore them the last time I went to the RGZ mine in Oporto.'

'Thank you Mr Martins. Can we now see exhibit number three? Here is a plastic bag full of teeth and ten blackened finger tips. How did you come by them, what did you keep them for and what were they doing in in your safe?'

'I cut them out of Jos'e Barros's body so that he couldn't be recognised if the body was found and I kept them as souvenirs.'

'Thank you Mr Martins. Can we see exhibit number four, a kitchen knife with an eight inch blade? Is it yours, if so where did you get it from and for what was it used?'

'Yes it is mine, I bought it from a hardware shop and I used it to stab Jos'e Barros.'

'Thank you Mr Martins. Did you kill Jos'e Barros with the knife and if so what did you do with the body?'

'Yes I did kill him and I threw the body into the Slime Pit.'

'Why did you kill this unfortunate person?'

'Because he was blocking my promotion to Chief Inspector of Police for the whole of Portugal and I wanted this job so that I could make a fortune from bribery, blackmail and corruption.'

'My Lord, I rest my case and don't have any more questions.'

Foxy had been very succinct in her questioning and she didn't leave Martins any room to wriggle out of the answers. There was a deathly hush in the room with the press writing furiously on their note pads. The jury was open mouthed and couldn't understand why Martins had just admitted that he had murdered Barros.

The Eagle said to Martins that he now had the opportunity to present his defence. He had delivered the answers to Foxy's questions with a clear almost robotic voice. He remained upright in the dock with his head throbbing which he held high and puffing his chest out said.

'I swore that I would tell the truth, the whole truth and nothing but the truth, which I have just done. I don't have any defence other than I have been blackmailed by a high ranking politician from a Middle Eastern country who threatened to expose me if I didn't pay him millions of Escudos for him to keep quiet. I cannot and will not name him as to do so would cause political chaos in that country which could lead to civil war and thousands of civilians being killed, other than that I am guilty on all counts.'

The court erupted into utter bedlam and pandemonium broke out again with the people in the public gallery shouting abuse at Martins and asking when he would be executed.

The Eagle having suffered the debacle of the Hans trial had doubled the police guards around the gallery to ensure they didn't spill over into the court area as they did before. He banged three times with his Gavel on the block shouting 'Silence in Court'. This time the head stayed on the shaft and the court fell silent.

'Mr Martins, by your own admission you are guilty of a most ghastly and heinous crime. Whoever you claim has been blackmailing you has no bearing on this trial so the jury will not take this into account. Anything you have done regarding the narcotics issue pales into insignificance compared with the gruesome murder of Jos'e Barros. You are a callous and cold blooded killer, not having any thought for the victim, his wife or his children. You have not shown any remorse for your crime and have thought only of yourself and your selfish desires. I have no alternative but to sentence you to death. You will be moved from here to Faro Prison and from there you will be taken to a place of execution where you will be hanged from the neck until you are dead. So help you God. Take him down.'

Martin was marched slowly down the steps with his head bowed, flanked by two armed guards who escorted him back to his cell.

There was a stony silence as the Eagle banged his gavel and closed the proceedings. He walked slowly to his chambers with a heavy heart, even though he despised the act of murder, it gave him no pleasure to take another person's life.

The court emptied unhurriedly and quietly with the Jury disappointed that for a second time they had been summoned and not allowed to be party to the final decision.

Foxy waited in her seat until the room had emptied and sat in quiet contemplation for a few minutes, as she wearily tidied her documents and removed her black court gown. She was pleased that she had performed a perfect prosecution but had a sad heart that she had been party to condemning a man to death which did not give her any pleasure. She also shed a tear for her fine friend Jos'e and thought about the good times they shared together when convicting criminals. She left the Court House complex with her mind buzzing with the day's events and walked back to the hotel to share her experience with Shack.

74

Loose Ends

Sr Rabbit and Sn Coelho appealed against the severity of their thirty year sentence but after three new Judges considered the case, the original decision was up-held. They will die in prison.

Jos'e Barros was cremated and the only mourners were Caroline and Feliciano. They asked his wife to attend but she declined.

The Gipsy King shacked up with Floralegs Pinto and they disappeared into the wilds of Spain.

Ivor Gonagetim never had any intention of killing the two policemen but kept the fifty per cent; spent it on a new van and travelled back to Eastern Europe.

The Irish twins had their sentence reduced for good behaviour and returned to Waterford, spending the rest of their lives as Traders and Tinkers. They decided that travelling the world in their boat was not such a good idea but still liked sailing so they embarked on a tour of the UK coastline ending up berthed in the river Thames near the Houses of Parliament.

They had many artefacts and souvenirs of their travels and took them to Sotheby's in Belgravia to be valued. Then possibly to be auctioned and to their amazement the two figurines of 'Anubis' and 'Isis' turned out to be originals from the Valley of the Kings in Luxor and raised millions of pounds at auction! They were now millionaires. The first thing they did was to set up an anonymous Trust Fund for Kats husband John, to pay for his medical care and expenses until he passed on. Perhaps they weren't so stupid after all.

Jose's wife developed a passionate love affair with Giovanni and they planned to get married and raise a family of their own.

Hans's yacht was auctioned, the Red Coral was sold to a Middle Eastern jewellery dealer and the proceeds were used to help recovering drug addicts.

Dana legally inherited Hotel Paradise and became one of the most effective leaders any hotel in the area had ever seen. She had built her teams into cohesive groups and her managers had enormous respect for her ability to train and develop them all in every aspect of their jobs. Under her leadership the hotel made huge profits and she won the nineteen seventy eight Algarve Hoteliers Association Award for the best hotel in the Algarve.

She had a niggling doubt in her mind that someday the authorities will realise that the hotel was built and funded by narcotics money and she may lose it all. But that may be a story for another time.

Jenny and James delivered a stunning conference in the hotel, also in nineteen seventy eight and made significant profits for their company as well as creating millions of Australian dollars which flowed into the State Superannuation funds. They set up and paid for a clinic in Wagga-Wagga for Aboriginals suffering from drug and alcohol abuse, which Jenny visited and managed weekly.

Bruiser the dog was taken to the vet's surgery and was never seen again. But if there is a dog heaven, then he would be barking, snapping, snarling and biting the Angels.

Travessa do Pastor was put up for auction but because of the high price there were not many takers. Fay and Shak made a reasonable offer and bought it at a knock down price. They then decided to retire and sold both their businesses to pay the bill.

Kat Hart received a letter from Woodman's Solicitors in Belgravia, informing her that one of their clients had anonymously set up a Trust Fund which would pay for John's medical care until he died. She had helped so many people in her life that she had no idea who it was but was eternally grateful for the gift.

75

The Wedding

Moinho do Malhao is one of the highest points in the Loul'e region and houses the only Buddhist temple in the Algarve. Humkara Dzong is part of the Ogyen Kuzang Choling school of Tibetan Buddhism and it is mainly practised in France and Portugal. Ringu Tuku Rinpoche is the professor of Buddhism, who would marry Caroline and Fernando in a civil ceremony.

The building complex wasn't the typical Buddhist Temple one would expect to see in Tibet, Thailand or the Far East, where there would be many spires and towers fashioned in gold and black with ornate carvings all over the roofs. This was a much more plain and modest structure consisting of a few small square whitewashed houses with flat roofs. Only the temple itself boasted the more elegant gold encrusted tower atop the main entrance door. The whole area was surrounded by a whitewashed six foot concrete perimeter wall.

Caroline's wish for the wedding was that it should be a quiet affair with minimum attendees, those being Fay, Shak and Feliciano's parents.

Caroline looked sensational as a bride. She wore a cream fitted two piece suit with the skirt just below the knee, dark silver shoes with a two inch heel which showed off her shapely ankles. This then brought her up to Feliciano's height. Her hair was piled to the back of her head, was held in place with a black clasp and she wore

Fay's single row of pearls with the matching earrings. She carried a small posy of strong scented white lilies, whose perfume was competing with her Chanel Number 5. Her face was radiant and filled with peace and joyfulness.

Fay looked equally magnificent in a similar cut suit in dark navy with her hair hanging long down to her shoulders tipping up at the ends. There was a single diamond broach on her right lapel. On her left lapel was a small single lily. As she appeared some twenty years younger than her real age, both she and Caroline looked more like sisters than mother and daughter. She was overjoyed that she had found such a lovely, peaceful and charming young man to marry. He was a gentle man and a perfect gentleman.

Shak and Feliciano wore matching dark grey suits with white shirts and ties to match Caroline's shoes. Shak had even had his hair cut, well just a little bit!

Feliciano's parents wore traditional peasant dress similar to the dancers in the Ava Hotel. They could not speak or understand any English so were confused and perplexed for most of the marriage service. They were also upset that their son was being married into a Buddhist way of life and not their chosen Catholic religion.

The weather was brilliantly sunny, warm and due to the high altitude there was cool breeze blowing around the Temple which rustled the dozens of prayer flags. At the same time nudged the hundreds of miniature brass flower Temple bells hanging in the trees and they tinkled with a beautiful gentle sound which added to the peaceful romantic atmosphere. The ceremony took place in the open air just outside of the doors to the Temple which was flanked by two twelve feet high gold Buddha statues, arms folded, eyes closed with a slight smile on their faces.

The priest (called Bhikkhuni) whose name was Ringu Tuku Rinpoche was dressed in the traditional Saffron Robe

344

flowing down to the ankles and wearing nothing else but leather sandals. His hair was shaven, showing a tanned head and he had a peaceful benign smile on his face. He called the gathering together and asked who was giving the bride away. Shak who was holding Caroline's hand as tight as he could didn't want to let go. With a lump in his throat and a tear running down his cheek croaked.

'I am the bride's father and it is me.'

The happy couple stood together as the ceremony proceeded. When it was concluded and as they went to sign the register, Fay read a quotation on Marriage from Khalil Gibran's book 'The Prophet' in a clear but trembling voice laced with emotion.

Then Almitra said, what of Marriage Master and he answered saying;

You were born together and together you shall be forevermore. You shall be together when the white wings of death scatter your days.

Aye, you shall be together even in the silent memory of God but let there be spaces in your togetherness and let the winds of the heavens dance between you.

Love one another but make not a bond of love; let it rather be a moving sea between the shores of your souls.

Fill each other's cup but drink not only from one cup. Give one another of your bread but eat not from the same loaf.

Sing and dance together and be joyous but let each one of you be alone. Even as the strings of the lute are alone they quiver with the same music.

> *Give your hearts but not into each other's keeping, for only the hand of Life can contain your hearts. Stand together but not too near together. For the pillars of the temple stand apart and the oak trees and the cypress grow not in each other's shadow.*

When the ceremony was finished they all shook hands with the priest and Feliciano gave him a huge donation for the Temple. They all piled into their hired chauffeured minibus and travelled down from the hills to drop Feliciano's parents at their Casa. They didn't see much point in having them come to the evening meal as they felt uncomfortable not being able to speak or understand English.

They arrived at the Hotel Paradise around seven thirty, just in time for dinner. Dana met them in the foyer and Feliciano introduced everyone to her. She ushered them to the bar where she ordered champagne for them. Dana, as a special treat for the occasion had booked Lank Marvell and the Followers to play in the restaurant.

When they had finished their drinks and were well relaxed, Dana escorted them to the table in the Pod where James had his first meal with Hans. It was the best table in the house. Feliciano considered it strange as they walked through the restaurant doors and with his policeman's acute sense of anything out of the ordinary, he though he saw two black suited bodyguards with communicators in their ears, eating at a table near the door. They were well disguised as diners but that didn't fool him. He put it to the back of his mind as they were being seated. The band was playing quiet soft background music which soon put Feliciano's mind at ease.

Dana had really pushed the boat out with the quality of the meal, the wine was the best from the cellar and the food

346

was extraordinary and memorable, it was not something they would forget for many years.

After they had devoured the main course, Dana glided silently up to their table and quietly whispered in Feliciano's ear.

'Feliciano, there is a gentlemen in reception who wants to speak to you urgently, do you want to see him here or in the foyer.'

'Who is he and what does he want Dana, I'm not sure I want to see anyone while we are celebrating our marriage.'

'He didn't say who he was or what he wanted but he looks very well-heeled and respectable and he insists that it is an urgent matter.'

'Very well Dana show him in but I'll have to make our meeting short.'

She was right; he was respectable, well dressed and well-heeled as was clear to see as he walked through the restaurant with a large brown foolscap envelope under his arm.

'I am sorry to interrupt your celebrations Mr Neves. My name is George House and I run the estate agents business in Santa Barbara. One of my German clients, Hedda Valbruch, who prior to her death asked me to pass this package on to you the day you got married to Caroline.'

There was an expectant silence around the table as Feliciano opened the envelope. Inside were the title deeds to Hedda and Rolys house Casa Crao, with a note scribbled in shaky handwriting. *'I know you said that you couldn't accept my offer of the house but I am not a woman who takes no for an answer, so here it is, lock stock and barrel. I really do hope you both will be very happy in your new home.* Signed Hedda Valbruch.

There was a shocked silence from everyone as Caroline and Feliciano recovered from the enormity of the news. Then they all clapped as Feliciano went red with embarrassment. Caroline's face was full of joy and excitement as she said.

'What a wonderful gesture to make Feliciano, I think you were right to refuse whilst she was ill but as this was her last dying wish I think we should we should accept her kindness.'

Feliciano still embarrassed but impressed with Caroline's graciousness smiled as he said.

'Well at least it's a much better home than my current bed sit!'

Everyone made congratulatory comments and slapped him on the back. Caroline was thrilled with the news and gave him a big kiss.

Feliciano then asked Dana to bring the finest champagne for the wedding toast. When she returned she brought a bottle of Vintage Dom Perignon. She said that the two gentlemen seated with their backs to their table had seen the joy and celebration of their wedding table and had sent it over with their compliments.

As the champagne cork popped the two diners seated with their wife's, turned around to offer a toast and Feliciano recognised them as the President and the Justice Minister, his uncle! Clearly that was the reason for the two body guards seated at the table by the door.

A toast was made to the happy couple and to Fay and Shacks reconciliation. The Justice Minister then walked purposefully over to the wedding table and said in a quiet voice so that the rest of the diners couldn't hear.

'I would like to propose another toast to Feliciano on his promotion to Chief Inspector of Police for the whole of Portugal, replacing Fernando Martins.'

Feliciano didn't know about the promotion and being of a shy nature found the situation uncomfortable and embarrassing as the toast was offered in public but naturally he was delighted. What he didn't know was that the Minister had told Dana about the promotion and she had secretly told the other small collection of diners. They all stood up and toasted the wedding table and burst into clapping and appreciation that they had a new Chief Inspector.

Dana nodded to the band who then struck up Cliff Richards hit 'Congratulations'. She escorted the four who were now glowing with pride, happiness and ecstasy to the dance floor where they led the dancing. They were then followed by the Ministers, their wife's and the rest of the diners. They all danced the night away to Sixties and Seventies music until the small hours. What a wonderful end to a fantastic celebratory day of reconciliation, joy, love and marriage.

76

Martins Demise

Fernando Martins lay on his uncomfortable prison bed on death row staring at the filthy ceiling, musing about how he found himself in this situation. He wondered what had happened to his brain which turned him into a revolting, sickening psychopathic killer, blackmailer and drug dealer. Perhaps the cancer had moved to his head or was it a brain tumour? Perhaps he might have had an easier, less criminal existence if he had stayed in Spain and not got hooked up with the Portuguese Ministers?

He didn't have any feelings of remorse or regret. His whole body was at rest and his heartbeat regular. He was perspiring more than normal and his hands were clammy. Also he didn't have any fear of death as he had lived an unusual life with many highs and not many lows. Born as a peasant, he understood the trials and tribulations of people of the lower classes and disliked the upper crusts. This all changed when he turned into an evil killer.

He also couldn't understand that having meticulously planned what he believed to be the perfect murder; the body was discovered floating in the Slime Pit. What he didn't realise, was that in his haste to sink the body into the slimy depths, he had used the weight belts he liberated from Paddy and Micks boat. Being the cheapskates they were, the belts they had bought from the auction had a link missing which they had tied together with thick black string and the acid in the Pit had rotted the rope! The bloated body then rose to the surface.

Perhaps he would have been better off staying as he was, having been one of the most famous and powerful men in the world. The President of Egypt,

Abdul Gamel Nasser!!

Perhaps he should have stopped paying the extortionate blackmail money to his old military friend, General Hussein Sirri Amer who was now his sworn enemy and had him assassinated!

He was suddenly aroused from his day dreaming as he heard the keys jangle in the heavy steel door of the cell which opened with a loud creak. He turned his head to see the tall lanky Priest standing there dressed all in black with a Bible in his hand. The blood drained from his face leaving it looking like a ghostly transparent white mask.

He once again scratched the unhealed scar on his stomach and thought that the cancer or the brain tumour would have killed him before the hangman's noose!

THE END

BRIAN EVANS